Living Ghost

Living Ghost

A GOING GHOSTLY NOVEL
BOOK ONE

by

GINNA MORAN

ISBN 978-1-942073-98-7 (soft cover)
ISBN 978-1-942073-17-8 (epub ebooks)

This is a work of fiction. All of the characters, organizations, and events portrayed in this novel are either products of the author's imagination or are used fictitiously.

Cover design by Silver Starlight Designs
Cover images copyright 123RF

For Inquiries Contact:
Sunny Palms Press
9663 Santa Monica Blvd Suite 1158
Beverly Hills, CA 90210, USA
www.sunnypalmspress.com
www.GinnaMoran.com

This book is definitely NOT dedicated to the one who broke up with me during lunch my senior year of high school in front of all our friends. However, this book IS dedicated to anyone who has ever experienced The Worst Breakup Ever. I hope you find the one person who sees your soul for how beautiful it is. <3

1

❧Worst Breakup Ever❧

CALLIE

"IT'S OVER."

My heart sinks into my stomach as I stare into Brendan's glassy eyes. He clenches his teeth, his boxy jaw twitching. I can't believe those two little words came from his mouth. My hands tremble in front of me, and I shift at the table in the middle of the crowded cafeteria.

I suck in a breath, the edges of my vision darkening, and then I find my voice. "I don't understand. You told me you loved me last week." It takes everything in me not to burst into tears.

It's hard to ignore the heavy gaze from the table over—the

one full of Brendan's friends. They probably all knew before I did. Now, they're waiting for me to break. The whispers sound louder than the pounding in my head, yet I don't understand a word they're saying. I need to get out of here.

Brendan grabs my hand and squeezes it. "Graduation is in a few months, and I've decided I don't want to be with anyone when I head to college in the fall. It's better for you, too."

I gape at him. "So...you never loved me." I'm having trouble processing this. All I want to do is get up and leave, but I can't find the strength to pull my hand away. It doesn't help that Brendan's blue eyes practically hypnotize me with their aqua color. This might be the last time I ever get to hold his hand—it will be. Like he said, it's over.

He drops my hand, and it knocks against the table. "Don't act like this is such a big deal," he says, crossing his arms.

I haven't acted like anything. I'm too numb to think. "Excuse me?"

Glancing over his shoulder, he stares at his smiling friends for a second before turning back to me with a goofy grin—one I want to slap off his face. "Really, Callie. I don't want you to over think this like everything else."

The numbness clinging to me morphs into anger, and I straighten my shoulders. "It's better than not thinking at all, and don't try to say this is better for me. I can't even remember when you did something for me."

The smile melts off Brendan's face, and he leans across the table. "Well, if you weren't so damn boring."

"I'm sorry I don't like the parties you go to." I stand up,

wishing I could disappear. Mixed emotions swirl through me like a raging tornado. It's like Brendan flipped a switch in his personality and changed overnight. It sucks that even though he's treating me this way, I still can't help the feelings I have for him. I just want to turn off my stupid emotions.

He twists his lips up and looks from my head to my chest. "It's not just at parties."

The laughter grows louder, but I refuse to look at his friends. I'm sure they can hear everything we're saying. I'm sure the whole cafeteria can. Tears burn my eyes, and blinking them away just makes it worse, because they spill onto my cheeks. Heat slithers up my neck in waves. I cover my face with my hands, my legs too weak to get me out of here. *Universe, if you can hear me, now's the time to make me disappear.*

My ears pop.

I watch as my body falls away from me, crashing to the tile floor. The world stops around me, and I gawk between Brendan, who doesn't move at the table, to my body sprawled out for all to see, blood oozing from my head.

If I could feel my heart, it'd be racing a million beats a second. Drawing my eyes away from my body on the floor, I look at my translucent form. I snap my fingers, hearing the click of skin rubbing skin, but no one looks in my direction.

"Am I dead?" My voice sounds normal, yet no one glances at me.

A scream rips through the air. "Oh, my God! Oh, God, Callie!" Lily rushes the twenty feet from the door to where my body rests and brushes away the dark hair veiling my face with her shaking fingers. "Help! Someone get help."

Her high-pitched wail kicks the cafeteria into chaos. People run around, mostly just my classmates fighting to get a better view, and then a teacher orders everyone to clear out.

I step forward, weightlessly, suspended an inch from the ground. Kneeling next to my best friend, I wave my hand over Lily's bleached blond hair that makes her tawny skin appear darker. My ethereal fingers dip into her blue sweater, surprising me, and I jerk my hand back. She pulls my lifeless body onto her lap, swinging her arm out when Mr. Augustine tries to stop her. Her tears spill onto my colorless forehead.

"I swear I'll never forgive you if you don't wake up, Callie." Lily blinks her round, espresso-brown eyes.

"I don't know if I can." As much as I want to stay by my best friend's side, seeing her crying over me sends a whirl of panic and grief through my spirit. This can't be happening. I can't be dead.

Within minutes, the double doors swing open, and paramedics rush into the cafeteria. Students gather outside the door, watching the show. I turn away as Mr. Augustine holds Lily back, and they move my body to a stretcher. I can't watch this anymore.

"I'm not leaving her!" Lily screams.

I bound from the cafeteria and into the quad, Lily's voice fading away behind me. Dozens of voices trickle into my mind as I rush through my classmates, picking up on their thoughts in my ghostly form. I shake the voices away, glad that most aren't actually thinking about me.

Stopping, I peer around. "Hello? What am I supposed to do now?" I expect someone, maybe my grandma, to show up and welcome me into the afterlife. But no one comes with my calls. I'm trapped in some sort of dimension that prevents me from rejoining the living.

My tears, like glittering droplets, hit the ground and fade away. "Please, help me. Is anyone here?"

Nothing changes.

I don't know what to do, so I turn toward the exit and leave.

MASON

"Mason, duck!"

I drop to my knees, glass shattering over my head. Lunging forward, I smash into a guy with a mouthful of sharp teeth. He narrows his red eyes, clenches his jaw, and we collide with the concrete.

I grip a handful of his T-shirt in my fingers. "Resist me again, and you'll regret it."

The guy sneers. "The Creature Council will hear about this."

I lift him up by his shirt and slam him back down into the pavement. "It's a good thing that's where we're headed then."

A scream rips through the air, and I jerk my head to look behind me. My partner, Kat Suarez, stands with her back to the brick wall with her knife drawn. A guy and a woman, both with glittering green auras, corner her.

Hands grab my wrists, tugging my attention back to my captive. He knees me in the gut, sending me reeling. I suck in a breath as I twist back and fall on my side. *Shit. Get it together.*

The guy's nails transform into daggers, threatening to impale me. Foam drips from his mouth, drizzling down his chin before soaking into his shirt. Kat yells again, except this time I don't look at her. I have my own skin to worry about, and she's capable of taking care of herself.

The guy approaches, holding his fingers together to turn his nails into a long point, and he aims them at me. "Let's forget about this whole thing. If you do, I won't kill you."

I touch the hilt of the knife at my side. It'd be so easy to rip it free and kill this creature. After reading the list of offenses against humans and creatures alike, given to me by my boss, I'm tempted to fall into my old ways. There was once a time I'd have killed this guy without question, but I'm trying to do better. Be a better person. And accepting a job offer and joining an elite team of people in charge of policing the supernatural world under the authority of the Creature Council, the governing force of creatures and supernaturally gifted humans, has done just that. I gladly serve a purpose in the supernatural world only brave or reckless humans deal with, which I've been called both.

Luckily for this guy, my first protocol entails me capturing disobedient creatures for assessment by the council. If I can't capture a creature, then I'm supposed to track them. The only time killing is allowed is if my life is in danger. Since this guy wants to negotiate, it'd be against Creature Council law to take care of him on my own.

They're more useful alive. They're more useful alive. I chant the words silently to myself. "You know I can't let you go. The council sent an order for your arrest." I prop up on an elbow and look past him at Kat still holding her ground.

The guy turns to follow my gaze before meeting my eyes. "Look, the council is mistaken. Whatever they think I did, it wasn't me. I haven't done anything wrong."

I sigh. Every creature I bring in claims innocence, even with human or creature blood staining their clothing and hands. "You can plead your case to them."

He shifts on his feet. "Please, man. I swear. I'll do anything. There something you want? I can get it. Anything." He turns toward the people blocking Kat against the wall. "I'll also call my associates off."

It goes against my instincts to bargain with a wanted creature, but I'm outnumbered. The last thing I need is bloodshed. I've experienced enough death over my seventeen years of life to last me for eternity.

"Do it," I say. I don't like the way the other two creatures wait for the word to attack Kat.

The guy clears his throat. "Kill her."

My vision shadows as I jump to my feet. The world flies around me, and I abandon the guy to run toward Kat. I narrow my vision, concentrating on the creatures' auras, and the world slows down—at least it does to me. I'm not only highly skilled in combat after a lifetime of training—I've also been genetically altered into the perfect soldier to fight against the rising threat the council faces from their own kind.

Adrenaline pumps through my veins the longer I study my targets. A gut-feeling, like a sixth sense, draws me toward the woman. Bending my knees slightly, I catapult at the woman next to Kat. She attempts to hop out of the way, but her reflexes are nothing compared to mine. I'm faster and stronger, and she doesn't have time to fight before I bind her arms behind her back and toss her at the wall.

The woman's wail cuts through the air, clawing at my eardrums. If I didn't know better, I'd suspect she was a banshee with how powerful her lungs are, but banshees are on the lower level of the danger chart I've put together over the years. They warn when death is near, nothing more. Kind of a crappy situation for them.

Kat leaps on the man with auburn hair and green eyes. He blinks out of existence, and I swear under my breath. It takes a second, but I spot his aura flash into view a few feet away. As an elf, he has the ability to evade people with magic by not allowing humans to focus on him, but luckily for me, I've met elves before. I know if I concentrate hard enough, I can spot their auras even if I can't see their physical forms.

I hold my knife up. "Touch my partner and you'll have a knife in your back. This is your only warning."

The green aura of the elf shifts, and then it flees into the street and out of the alley. I spin to check for the other creature, but the guy is gone. I lost the chance to capture him.

Disappointment washes over me as I meet Kat's gray eyes. She tugs the woman, another elf, to her feet, and holds her up by the back of her shirt.

"Don't look so scared," Kat tells the woman. "You get to meet the council. I'm sure if you cooperate, they might let you go with minimal mind manipulation and a new life."

The woman glares but doesn't open her mouth. She won't talk unless she's forced to do so. Her loyalty lies with whoever she's working for. I've seen it a dozen times. On the other hand, I've also seen creatures care more about themselves and give up the information we need to better police the creature world.

I pull my cell phone from my pocket and punch in one of the few numbers I've memorized because I can't keep it saved.

It rings once. "Hey, Mase. I'm surprised you've called. Thought you were too good for me since joining the Creature Council."

"Never too good. Just been busy." I haven't spoken to Evie Thompson in months. We were friends in what feels like another life, before I decided to put my skills to use and signed up to be a soldier with the council.

"So? What's up?" she asks.

I frown at Kat, who watches me while holding onto the elf. "I was hoping you could help me."

A puff of air echoes through the line. "And I thought you were going to ask to hang out. I should've known. You know I've given up that life and don't like to track creatures anymore. It's dangerous." Though she hates it, Evie's been gifted with the ability to track creatures with a simple touch, sort of like psychometry. All she has to do is touch something a creature has had contact with to glimpse the world through a creature's eyes to see where they are. The Creature Council has tried to get her to join our team, but she prefers a normal life outside the creature world, which I can't blame her for. But that's a world I've never known.

Being raised by a woman devoted to saving humanity any way she can had impacted the way I look at things. I could never sit back and pretend everything in the world is normal, that I'm not gifted to see things a normal human can't. I prefer harsh reality over Evie's love of her rainbow-tinted glasses.

"Evie, please, wait. I know I suck at being a friend, but I'm begging you to hear me out. I need you." I press the phone against my ear, waiting to see if she hangs up. It wouldn't be the first time.

She doesn't answer for a long moment, and then says, "Fine, where do you want to meet?"

I rattle off the address of a coffee shop a block down the street before hanging up. I take a breath and turn to Kat. "Can you handle transporting the elf alone or should I call someone?"

Kat rolls her eyes. "Do you think I'm incapable?"

I raise my hands. "Definitely not." I pull the keys from my pocket and toss them to her.

Kat hooks them to her belt before removing a syringe from her pocket to jab into the woman's neck.

The woman screams. "You can't do this to me! I'm not some sort of animal."

Kat hoists the woman onto her shoulder, ignoring her kicking legs.

I wave. "See you later."

The woman burns daggers at me with her eyes. "Macario will hunt you down and kill you!"

I shrug. I've heard worse threats. They just roll off my

shoulders now. "Thanks for the name."

Kat throws her into the back of the car, slamming the door to cut off her screams. I peer around the alley a moment longer, and then I turn on my heels and head toward the coffee shop to hopefully get a lead from Evie.

I need to catch a break.

2

ᕗStrangest Thingᕐ

CALLIE

I HAVE TO admit, being without a body is kind of awesome. I'm not chained to the earth by gravity, and I figured out that if I try hard enough, I can jump ten feet at a time, almost as if I can propel myself while floating.

Standing on a freeway overpass, I watch as the sun sets behind the city in the distance. The windows sparkle in the sunlight, glittering off each other in a fiery light show. Who needs the stars when concrete and glass can be so beautiful?

Without having a clue of where to go or what I should do, I've spent the last few hours strolling around the quiet world, hoping someone would eventually show up to guide me. The last thing I want is to remain aimless, watching the world move on while I remain trapped. A break up today was bad enough. But this? I must've messed up pretty badly in another life.

If I could feel pain, I'm sure my stomach would be in knots. I've thought about going to my house to check on my family, but I'm afraid of what I'll find. I've never felt so helpless and out of control before. I'm afraid to see all the pain I've unintentionally caused. Like, seriously? Who dies from embarrassment? I never thought it was possible. I feel like I should've been warned.

Cars zoom by on the freeway below. I step to the edge of the overpass, past the barrier, and tilt my chin to my chest to peer down. Fear slithers in my mind out of habit, but I push it away before I jump.

Confusion leaves me frozen in place. Without the sensation of falling or landing, I wasn't even sure if I made it down. A car races toward me, and I flinch as it passes through me. The faint sound of a radio rings in my ears, but it only lasts a split second. At least I still have some of my senses.

Another car zooms my way. This time, I bend my knees and jump as high as I can. I fly over the car and land just in time to jump again over a truck in a game of leap frog. I laugh, losing my concentration when I hop over another car and catch a couple being a little too intimate on the road. A moment later, a bus full of kids rumbles through me. Chattering voices circle me, and I jump again, propelling myself toward the glittering city.

It's amazing, jumping and floating weightlessly. It feels as if

I'd float away on the breeze if the wind picked up. I could go anywhere, see everything. Maybe that's why no one has come to find me. They're all too busy exploring the things they had missed in life.

Sadness tickles my mind. I still can't believe it. I almost don't want to.

Pushing the thought away as the city grows closer, I find myself standing in the middle of a road jammed with rush hour traffic. A red Porsche rolls into me and rock music blares through the stereo. A woman applies lipstick in the visor mirror, clearly not paying attention to the road. I lean forward, sticking my head through the seat to look out the windshield, and her thoughts erupt in my ears.

"Stupid traffic is making me late. All I need is another lecture from Hank about leaving on time. God, he's annoying. Maybe I just won't show. Teach him to criticize me." The woman continues her rant as I pull away. Listening to a stranger's thoughts is a lot more boring than what I had expected. I was hoping she'd spill some crazy secret.

I stroll from the car and glide to the sidewalk. If I try hard enough, I can step on the ground, but it's so freeing to move without making an effort.

As I pass a busy coffee shop, the smell of hazelnut and sugar wafts through the air. My mouth waters, or at least I imagine it does, and I wish I could have one more iced coffee with caramel. I'd have eaten a better breakfast had I known it was my last meal. Mom's plain corn cereal, since Dad still hadn't gone shopping, is nothing to brag about. I didn't even get to eat lunch because of stupid Brendan and the Worst Breakup Ever.

"He's still in town. On fifth street. I don't sense the other man with him. If we leave now, we can probably catch him." A girl with dark, chin length hair and a flawless, golden brown complexion presses her hands against the wall of the coffee shop.

If I weren't standing so close, I doubt I would've heard her. A boy, with equally dark brown hair, cut short and styled with product, stands a few feet from her. He looks young, but his scruffy cheeks make him look older. It's hard to tell from where I'm standing.

I glide a foot closer and listen.

The boy leans into the girl. I expect him to kiss her, but instead he says, "Not we, Evie. Just me. You don't even have a weapon."

I step back in surprise, fear slithering over me. I consider running away, but then I remember I'm a ghost and no one can hurt someone who is already dead.

The girl, Evie, tugs at the boy's hoodie, revealing a belt with what looks like a knife, some sort of gun, and a few other things I don't recognize. "Give me one of yours, Mason. You asked me to come all this way, and I want to help. What if the goblin leaves before you get there? I'm not going to come back to help you again."

"Whoa," I say out loud. I have no idea what she's even referring to, but it's the strangest thing I've ever heard someone talk seriously about. I cover my mouth like they can hear me, but they're too focused on whatever they're doing.

The boy, Mason, rubs his chin. "I'll take the chance. The council would be furious if I got you involved without running it by them. You're a civilian. I could get in trouble for even calling you."

Evie huffs and rolls her eyes. "Fine." She turns in my direction, keeping her eyes trained on the ground. "Next time, how about you call to hang out? I don't want to only talk to you when you need something."

Mason touches Evie's shoulder. "How about this weekend? I haven't seen my brother in a while. We could all hang out."

Evie looks over her shoulder. "Sounds good. Call me when you find the goblin. I hate knowing he's out there."

Evie strolls away, rubbing her fingers along every surface she passes. It's a weird gesture to witness, but no one seems to notice. I take a few steps to follow her, and a strange sensation rushes over me, like I'm being watched.

I stop in my tracks and look behind me.

Mason stands absolutely still, staring right at me. I look behind me to see if it's something else, but there's nothing there. He's definitely glaring at me. His hand touches his belt, and I don't know whether to laugh or cry. I'm a ghost. I'm dead. I have nothing to be afraid of, but I can't stop the fear from consuming me.

Mason steps forward, a darkness in his eyes that stings my soul. Something about him leaves me on the verge of panic—because I think he can see me—and whatever he sees in me scares me.

He clears his throat, holding his hand out like he wants me

to stay back without actually saying the words out loud.

But he has nothing to worry about. I want to be nowhere near him.

I turn on my heels and bound away, jumping at least fifteen feet at a time. I need to get away from him. Because the way he holds me in his gaze makes my world feel utterly wrong. Like something about me is wrong, and I'm his enemy. If I stayed for any longer in his presence, I'm not even sure death could protect me.

MASON

I can't believe my eyes.

I drop my hand away from my weaponry belt as what I'm pretty sure is a wraith, a spirit who hasn't moved on into the afterlife, flies away. Its soft pink aura shifted and moved from only feet away, watching me and Evie. I for sure thought it was going to possess me at any moment, because I've never seen a wraith that didn't already inhabit some poor human's body. They survive by possessing humans, and the only reason I can see them is because the ability had been manipulated into my DNA. It's the only way a human like me can really stand a chance against creatures. Unfortunately, even if I can see the wraith, I can't kill something that's already dead as much as I want to, but that doesn't mean I won't try to track it to stop it from hurting an innocent person. It's my job.

I dash across the street in the direction the wraith disappeared in. It crosses through the wall of a building, and I groan. I'll get nowhere going after it. Not only is it too risky when wraiths are known for possessing bodies, because I have a pretty awesome one, but it'll be safer to notify the council of the sight-ing instead and have them investigate. Plus, I have more im-portant things to do.

I head in the direction of Fifth Street. It's getting darker than I'd like, but at least I can hide in the cover of the shadows along the buildings. The empty street hums with city noise from the surrounding area. The stench of garbage from the alley assaults my nose, and I pull my shirt up over my face.

Cutting between buildings to the alley, I lurk close to the wall and weave around the dumpsters near the exits of a few restaurants. I pause in the shadow of a small awning and listen. Footsteps echo off the cement block wall, and I hold my breath to not make any noise. I'm not looking for a fight—that's risky to do without back up. All I want is to sneak up if I can and sedate the goblin if it's him. That way I can take him back to the council for interrogation.

A scream rips through the air.

I hesitate. I can't get a good view of where the voice came from, but I know it's not far.

"Please, you can have my purse. Just don't hurt me." The silhouette of a woman cuts through the pale light of a bare bulb above the back door to Phontastic, a Vietnamese cuisine restau-rant, and another figure emerges beside her, blending the two together.

"Get your hands off m—" The woman's voice abruptly stops.

Moving closer, I slide next to another dumpster and catch sight of the goblin, Macario, standing over the body of a brunette woman in a trench coat. Her hair veils her face, obscuring my view to see if she's still breathing.

Anger burns through me at the sight. Sliding my tranquilizer gun from my weaponry belt, I hold it up and point. I pull the trigger, aiming at Macario's neck. He jerks his gaze to me and ducks, the dart grazing his thinning hair.

I shoot again.

Macario uses the woman as a shield, and the dart sinks into her clavicle. I swear under my breath. I'm out of darts because my stupid ass accidentally left them in the car with Kat. I didn't even think about it. I'm usually a pretty good shot, but I didn't anticipate the goblin's quick reflexes. I've never encountered one before and only knew what he was because Evie told me. She's like a creature encyclopedia. One of the smartest people I know.

I reach for my taser. It's tempting to grab my knife, but protocol is pretty clear even if I don't agree with it all the time. This creature is clearly breaking Creature Law, and he's already proven he's not coming with me easily.

"Your little elf friend gave up your name, Macario. The longer you put off coming in, the worse it is for you. The council isn't forgiving of resistance, especially since I've caught you in the act of causing harm." With my free hand, I pull out my phone and snap a picture.

Macario jumps back in surprise.

I quickly send it to Kat in case the goblin goes after my phone. It wouldn't be the first time some savage monster tried to destroy evidence against them. This is my third cell in a month.

"What do you think you're doing? You're putting us all at risk!" Macario charges forward, exactly like I expect him to. I jerk out of the way and press my taser to the back of his neck. He screams as electricity rushes through him, setting his skin aglow. *That's strange...*

The taser isn't enough to knock him out. He snarls, revealing a mouth full of razor-sharp teeth. His eyes reflect green like a cat's, and he charges me.

I hit my back on the corner of a dumpster, the metal jabbing hard between my shoulder blades. Pain radiates down my spine, and it's enough to slow me down. The goblin snatches the front of my shirt and drags me forward.

I stumble, wrapping my hands around his neck to steady myself, and he snaps his teeth. The clicking sound resonates in my ears, and I pull a hand free and punch him in the jaw. He reels back and then uses the wall to propel himself forward again.

The world slows, and I spin on my heels, concentrating on gathering my strength. It only takes me a second to get into fight mode. I focus on Macario's glittering aura. The world melts away as I consider all of his next moves. His aura leans left before his body does, and I jab my arm out and connect with his solar plexus before he can move. I don't have a cool power like Evie, but my body was programmed to fight. I'm stronger and faster than a normal human, but it only keeps the playing field even when it comes to monsters like this guy.

As the shock of my hit catches up with the goblin, I swing

my arm again and punch him in the throat. He gasps, unable to breath, and I kick him in the stomach, knocking him into the wall. He slides to the ground, his head lolling as he slumps over.

"I didn't want to fight you," I mutter, clipping the taser back on my belt before unlatching a pair of elfin spelled handcuffs. I squat down, grab the goblin's hand, and flick a cuff on his wrist. He doesn't move, and I study his closed eyes. His aura shines brightly, so I know I didn't hurt him too badly, but even if I did, he deserved it.

His other hand remains lodged behind his back. The only way to restrain him is to shift him forward. Gripping his shoulder in my hand, I study him a moment longer. Some creatures play hurt to get you to let your guard down. Those ones are the worst. It comes in second on my list of things I hate about this job. The number one reason is that when the fighting is over, I have to drag creatures through the city without being seen, and if I am, I have to call someone to clean up my mess. I get paid decently enough, and it beats most other jobs. But damn it; why couldn't this stupid goblin just cooperate to make my life easier?

I pull myself from my thoughts and yank Macario forward to finish restraining him. Before I have time to react, he jerks his hand up and latches onto me. His talon-like nails slash over my shoulder and down my arm, flaying my skin through my shirt.

I yell out and fall back to move out of the way as Macario launches at me. The spelled handcuffs won't work if they're not both in place, and my stinging arm makes it hard to focus. I blink the haze from my eyes, trying to slide my knife from my belt, but the goblin lands on my stomach. *Ah! Shit! No!*

I jerk my elbow up, forcing distance between the goblin's snapping teeth and my face, but my strength weakens. He's going to rip my face off, and I can't stop him.

I'm outmatched.

3

ꙮMurderers and Monstersꙮ

CALLIE

"NO!" I SCREAM.

Propelling forward, I land inside the frightening creature who transformed from a man minutes ago. An inky evilness wraps around my soul, but I don't pull away. Instead, I listen to the raging thoughts coursing through this monster.

"*The Creature Council will regret ever sending this kid after me. I always knew they were idiots.*"

"Let him go!" I yell.

Mason's eyes roll back in his head. I don't know why I let my curiosity overpower my fear, but I couldn't resist following him. What if I can figure out how to communicate with him, and he can answer my questions? He sends fear through me, but I'm more afraid of not knowing what to do. I'll never know if this monster murders him.

"*What the?*" The man shakes his head, and I jump out of him. I can't believe the monstrous man heard me.

I hover over Mason as the man straddles him. Mason comes back to his senses and his eyes focus on me before they shift to the man, and then the man wails. Mason shoves him back, the handle of a knife protruding from the man's chest.

Guts spray through me, the man exploding before my eyes. I cover my face out of habit, though nothing touches me. The walls of the alley drip with innards, a grotesque sight that would've made me gag in my body. Mason coughs and spits while wiping red goo from his eyes. He props up on an elbow and peers around.

He glares in my direction. "Why did you help me?"

I freeze and look over my shoulder to make sure he's actually talking to me. "You really can see me." I inch closer.

Mason flinches and holds his hands up. "You have five seconds to get out of here before I call the council. They don't take kindly to your kind hanging around."

"My kind? What are you talking about?" I ask, floating even closer, close enough to catch flecks of gold in his brown eyes. Even covered in monster guts, I can't help thinking how handsome he is. But that's beside the point. He can see me. "I need help. I don't know what's going on, and you're the first person who c—"

"I said get out of here or you'll regret it!"

I hop back at his yell, realizing that he might be able to see me, but he can't hear anything I'm saying.

"Go! If you leave now you might have a chance of getting away. Because if I find you here again, it's going to go differently." His voice deepens with his threat, sending me gliding backward. I thought the monster was scary, but something dark lies within Mason's eyes, and I can't stop the panic from washing over me.

I turn on my heels and dash away. It was a mistake to follow him or to intervene. He's no better than the monster I saved him from. I wish I had never left my body in the first place. Maybe I needed to be near it to figure out what happens next. This death stuff should come with a handbook or something.

I glance over my shoulder, expecting to see Mason following me, but he picks up the woman he rescued and slings her over his good shoulder. His face scrunches in pain as he hobbles away.

Leaving him, I head to the freeway to follow it home to find my body...and hopefully some answers that don't involve murderers and monsters.

MASON

I heave a breath, searching the alley once more for the wraith. I'll never admit it to anyone, but I haven't been this scared facing a creature in a while, and I'm not talking about the goblin.

When another creature intervenes like that, it's not always to save the human. Some creatures are highly competitive with prey, especially one who fights back like I do, and that's what I was expecting. It did follow me all the way here after the coffee shop.

But, something was different—weird—because it didn't possess me. It was almost like it wanted to help by distracting the goblin. Either way, wraiths are on my list of top scariest creatures since so few people can see them. I hate knowing I had no choice but to demand it leave me alone, because I wasn't prepared to handle something so dangerous. Now, it's somewhere out there, probably making its next move on some helpless victim. Glad it wasn't me.

Pushing through the pain in my arm, I slump the woman the goblin tried to kidnap against the wall of the building near the street. I'm in too much agony to carry her to the closest safe house, but I can't leave her here. I pluck the tranquilizer dart I accidentally hit her with from her chest and tuck it in my pocket to hide the evidence. I notice an elf talisman around her wrist and consider removing it, but it's probably best if she doesn't see me.

I slide down next to her and tug my cell phone out of my pocket. The sound of ringing cuts through the eerily quiet air through my speaker. I sigh when I hear a click and say, "I need a pickup and an escort to the hospital. I've been injured." The words spill out before Dmitri Petrov, my boss and the protector of the Creature Council, can even spit out a greeting.

"Creature or human?" Dmitri asks.

"Human. You can send a cleanup crew to get the creature if you want." I wipe my dirty face on my sleeve.

Dmitri doesn't answer right away. "I got your location. A team will be out in ten."

I squeeze my eyes shut, pushing the pain away. "I think I only have five."

"Hold tight."

The line cuts off, leaving me in silence. I inspect the woman, making sure she's still breathing, and then I force myself to my feet and head to the street so I can be seen. Dark haze nudges the edges of my vision. The streetlamp light dances as dizziness swirls through my mind.

Pull yourself together. I've faced a lot of deadly creatures, and I expected to fail at some point, because a guy can only be so lucky, but this is crap. Death by a stupid goblin scratch is the sorriest way for me to go, like a shark getting killed by a guppy.

I drop to the curb, my legs refusing to support me any longer. The excruciating pain in my arm won't let me ignore my wounds. Rolling up my sleeves, I inspect the bloody skin where the goblin's nails ripped through me. Four deep gashes tear down my arm, the skin hanging slightly around the edges. My stomach heaves at the sight. If it wasn't my own arm, it wouldn't even faze me. All I know is if I don't do something soon, I might lose the damn thing, and I'm pretty attached to it.

Grinding my teeth to force the stinging away, I tug my shirt over my head the best I can and press the dirty fabric on my wounds to staunch the bleeding. My heavy eyelids obscure my vision, and the beams of headlights wash over me.

I lean back and lie on the ground.

"Mason? God, man, what happened?" I'm surprised Dmitri sent my brother. It's been a few weeks since I've seen him. He doesn't usually get involved in council affairs.

I open my mouth to answer, but it's like someone glued my mouth shut. I blink through the blinding light, trying to clear my vision, but it's useless.

"Mason? Don't go to sleep. What did this?"

I try my best to answer Hunter's question, but I can't.

A flash of white glides up next to him, and I draw my gaze to Nadia Petrov, Hunter's girlfriend and Dmitri's daughter. She kneels next to me, lightly touching her cold fingers around the outside of my wound. "Oh, no, Hunter. These are goblin scratches. Their claws are venomous. We need to hurry."

The world shifts as Hunter hooks his hands under my armpits. He drags me to the car, and Nadia helps him lift me onto the backseat. A groan escapes my mouth, blinding pain threatening to knock me out.

"My dad said there was a human. I'll stay and look around. Just get Mason to the hospital. Now." Nadia's voice cuts through the darkness.

A door slams. "Hang on, Mase. If you die, I swear you'll get the sorriest inscription on your grave ever."

If I could laugh, I would. Instead, I hold onto my consciousness the best I can.

CALLIE

I stand in front of my two-story, stone-fronted house. My parents' cars aren't in the driveway, so I know they're not home. Sticking my head straight through the living room window, I peek at my grandpa flicking through channels on the TV without stopping on anything in particular. Just pounding the button over and over again like something besides what to watch is on his mind.

I'm not sure what I was expecting. I guess my body wouldn't be here, but I have no idea where it is. It's not like I can ask my grandpa, either. His furry brows hang low over his eyes, yet he's not as upset as I thought he would be.

"Poppy!" My little brother, Max, rushes into the room. "Where's Callie? She said she'd help with my project."

My grandpa sets down the remote. "How about I help you, kiddo?" He doesn't answer my brother's question, and it unnerves me. I'm glad he didn't, though. I'm not sure I could handle seeing my brother's reaction to finding out I'm not coming home at all. He's too young to have to experience that. I imagine my heart being heavy with the thought.

The doorbell rings, startling me. I turn and see Lily standing under the porch light. If I didn't know any better, I'd have thought she was a ghost like me with her silence. Gliding to her side, I run my translucent hand through hers. Mascara smudges under her eyes, and she blinks away tears.

When my grandpa opens the door, she crosses her arms and sniffles. "No one is answering their phones, and I've been waiting all day for answers. Have you heard anything, Pops?"

My grandpa twists his lips to the side. "I'm gonna be honest with you, Lils. It doesn't look so good right now. But Callie's stro—" He chokes up, swiping his hand across his eyes.

Lily covers her mouth, muffling a sob. She sucks in a shuddering breath and says, "I need to see her."

My grandpa nods. "She's at University Medical Center in room 2B. Not sure they'll let you in, though. It's intensive care and family only."

"I am family," she says, shifting on her feet.

My grandpa's words hit me hard. I'm not dead. If I were dead, I wouldn't be in the hospital. I guess it's why no one from the afterlife showed up to tell me what's going on—if that even happens at all.

Lily hugs my grandpa and heads toward her old Camry parked at the curb. I follow behind her and step into her car before she opens her door. I imagine what the hard, worn seats with the pokey springs feel like and how often Lily would drive me to school even though I have my own car that I hate to drive. It was always much more fun to ride with her and occasionally ditch with her, too.

She starts the engine, and the world shifts as she puts her car in gear. It takes me a moment to realize I'm sitting in the front seat. The memory must've tethered me down, because now I'm hitching a ride with her to the hospital.

To fill the silence, she turns on her stereo, and one of our favorite boy bands blares through the speakers. More tears spill on Lily's cheeks, and she swipes them away. She speeds around the corner to the main street. I brace myself even though nothing can happen to me at the moment.

I lean over and stick my head into Lily's. "Calm down. I don't want you getting into a wreck."

She swerves before straightening the wheel just as quickly.

"Callie?" Lily's voice echoes over the music.

I don't respond. She heard me.

I'm afraid she's going to either think she's going crazy or think I'm dead and haunting her, which I'll definitely do if I don't make it. That was always an ongoing joke between us. We promised to hang around for the other, but that wasn't supposed to be until we were like eighty. *Don't talk like that.*

She turns the stereo up and shakes the thoughts from her head. Slowing down to the speed limit, she drives more cautiously the rest of the way. I lean back in the seat and watch as the hospital rises into view.

The six-story, cinderblock building looms near the local university. Lily parks in the lot near the Emergency Room, and she doesn't hesitate before she gets out.

She skips going through the ER and strolls down a path that winds through a garden and over a bridge with a pond under it. We pass a fountain sculpture with trickling water that sends tranquility vibes through the air. When we reach a side entrance, she enters as a woman exits, skipping the front desk with a note that says to visit the ER to check in after hours.

Lily struts down the open corridor, like she knows exactly where she's going, and calls for the elevator. I don't follow her on it. I'm not sure if I could concentrate enough to let it carry me. It seems easier to move over stable floor. The car ride was one thing, but I'm not even sure I could do that again. It was the strangest sensation, like I was being pulled to the hospital instead of sitting solidly on the seat.

I follow the signs to the stairs and enter the cool stairwell.

The tile gleams under me, shining off the fluorescent lighting. I bound up, taking the stairs a flight at a time. I can't get over how cool this is. It's like the ground is a trampoline. I wonder if it'll be hard to adjust when I get my body back—if that's even possible.

I exit the stairwell to the second floor and head to the nurse's station. Lily is nowhere to be found, and I stare at the whiteboard behind the nurse at the desk.

I spot the name C. White in 2B, and I know I have the right place. Strolling to the right, I turn and spot my door. My dad leans against the wall, his cell phone glued to his ear, and I glide up to him and listen as he whispers into the line.

"They're still running tests. The doctors can't find a reason why she's in a coma. Brendan swears she passed out before she hit her head, so it might be caused by something unrelated." He taps his head to the wall and listens for a moment before saying, "I don't know. They won't give me a straight answer."

I can't listen anymore. Gliding through the half opened door, I find Lily sitting next to my bed, holding my hand. My mom's not here, and I wonder where she is. I'm glad they didn't leave me alone.

"Please, Callie, don't leave me. We're supposed to go to college together, remember? I can't imagine having to live with anyone other than you. You're my perfect roommate." She leans forward and brushes my hair from my face. Machines beep and whirl, and an IV drips fluids into my hand.

Voices murmur in from the hallway. Lily turns and watches the door, listening as intently as I am.

"Why can't you figure out what's wrong with my daughter?" Dad asks.

"We're doing the best we can. All the tests have come back normal so far apart from the MRIs," a masculine voice speaks in a hushed tone.

"So nothing has changed on the scans?"

Silence.

I turn back to Lily. She shakes my shoulders, like I'll somehow be jolted awake.

The doctor and my dad move away from the door, both whispering so I can no longer hear them. Dread seeps into my soul, and I consider leaving again, but I can't bring myself to abandon my best friend as she talks to me. I regret leaving her side at all. I don't know how anyone can move on when they leave behind so many broken pieces. *Shut up. You're not going to die.*

I move to the bed and run my hand over my hair. A sucking sensation crawls over me as my body tries to absorb my soul, and I step through the bed until I'm standing within my comatose form. My soul buzzes with life, and heat seeps up my stomach and to my heart.

Whoa.

When my translucent hand meets with my physical hand, it's like something grabs hold of me, refusing to let me go. As I move my fingers, I watch my physical fingers twitch. I hook my thumb over Lily's hand where she touches me, and she freezes and looks down.

"Callie? Callie, can you hear me? It's Lily. Move your hand

if you can hear me." Lily's eyes widen with hope.

I twitch my fingers again.

"Oh, my God!" Lily grips my hand.

I study my connected hand for a moment and then dip my other hand into my body until it connects with my physical form. I can feel my fingers but nothing else. It takes me a minute of concentration, but I find myself sitting up on the bed instead of in it, and sensation returns to my feet and legs.

I wiggle my toes.

"I need a doctor!" Lily screams. She punches the call button above my head. A voice buzzes through the line, and Lily cuts her off by saying, "She's moving! She's moving!"

I peer around the room one last time, afraid of the pain I might feel once I reconnect completely. I also think about the humiliation of today's events and the Worst Breakup Ever. It'd be so easy to leave and head back to the city and enjoy my new-found freedom.

"Come on, Callie. Wake up." Lily's voice changes my mind. I can't avoid returning forever unless I'm ready to give everything up, which I'm not.

I lean back, my ears popping, and heat rushes over me before darkness consumes me.

4

ᚙ Miracle Girl ᚙ

MASON

"DAMN IT!"

Dr. Harvey pours a black concoction over the deep gashes in my arm. The room spins, fiery pain rushing from my fingers to my feet. Swinging my arm out, I knock Dr. Harvey away. As he collides with the door, Hunter rushes to me and grips my arm in a position I can't move it in.

"Stop fighting, bro. You're not helping any," he says.

No shit. Whatever Dr. Harvey pours on my arm hurts like hell. Staying still while he drenches my wounds in acid-like liquid is impossible. I might prefer losing my arm.

"I'd like to see you sit still while having acid clean your wounds," I snap.

Dr. Harvey steps closer without missing a beat. He's used to working with people who fight back. I tense, grinding my teeth, severely hating his presence, though I normally like the guy.

Dr. Harvey straightens his white coat. "The worst is over, Mason. You can relax. After I bandage you, I'd like to keep you here for monitoring, though."

I grimace. "How long?" Being stuck in the hospital is equivalent to getting locked away. I'd rather return to the compound to take part in the investigation and interrogation of Macario's companion. We're still missing his henchman, too.

"Overnight."

"But—"

Hunter pinches my arm, cutting me off. "The world will wait. You're no use hurt, anyway."

I punch my fist at Hunter, but he twists out of the way. "I'm not staying locked up in this room. I'm fine."

Dr. Harvey scribbles on his clipboard. "Explore all you want, just don't leave the building. If you do, I'll suggest you take time off from work for a week for disregarding my medical advice. The council takes good health seriously, and you're in a state that poses a risk not only to yourself but everyone around you. An injury puts a target on your back."

Seriously? He's threatening to put me on leave for a week for wanting to do my job? Like that'll go over well.

I glower, knowing that Dr. Harvey's bluffing, but I won't

call him out on it. It's better to agree and let him go on his merry way before he decides to call the council. If he does that, I'm sure I'll never hear the end of it from my mom. She's in charge of my division of the council alongside Dmitri, and she definitely doesn't play favorites because I'm her son. I like it that way, though.

"Deal."

I look away as Dr. Harvey dresses my wounds. Hunter sits in the corner of the room, texting on his phone, probably with Nadia. When Dr. Harvey finishes, he hands me a shirt with the hospital logo on it and helps me pull it over my head.

"All done. The nurse will bring your next dose of pain medication and change your bandage. Call me if you need anything, Mason." Dr. Harvey glances at Hunter. "Give me a ride to the compound?"

Hunter's gaze shifts from Dr. Harvey to me. "Will you be okay?"

He's not asking to see if I'll survive. He's asking to see if I can stay out of trouble without his help. It's not like I can do a lot with an injured arm while dressed in scrubs without my weaponry belt that was left in Hunter's car. I raise an eyebrow. "Just go. Tell Mom I'm fine and try to keep her off my back, will you? I don't need any visitors. They can talk to me tomorrow when I'm released."

He laughs. "I'll stop by to pick you up in the morning."

Before following Dr. Harvey out, Hunter pats my good shoulder and reminds me to stay out of trouble. You'd think he was years older than me, but he's only a year and a half. Life within the creature world does that to a person. With a mother like ours, who even knows how we managed to have a childhood.

Sitting on the edge of the bed, I turn on the TV and flip through the channels before shutting it off. This sucks. I'm bored and annoyed, and would prefer to be anywhere but here.

Noise hums into my room as commotion breaks out in the hallway just in time to provide me with some much needed entertainment. I have never been one to sit back and relax.

I shuffle across the cool tiles and push my cracked open door wider. An unfamiliar doctor zooms by, heading around the corner. I step from the room and follow in his direction.

Voices sound from the second door on the right. A girl with shoulder length, dyed blond hair with side swept bangs leans her back on the wall. Her aura flares yellow, matching her hoodie, and she draws her deep brown eyes to mine.

She glances from my face to my arm, and then frowns. "What?"

I shrug. "Heard commotion. Was bored."

The girl narrows her eyes. "My best friend just woke up after being brain dead."

My forehead creases. I've only known one person to have woken up from being brain dead, which was my brother, and that's because Hunter's soul had been taken from his body by a sin-eater our mom was after. The experience drew him into the supernatural world, and it's where he met Nadia, but that's another nightmarish story altogether.

Nothing about what she says seems normal. People don't

just lose all brain function and miraculously return without some sort of supernatural involvement. I have to meet this miracle girl, but I can't exactly barge into the room for questioning. Not only would that send the Creature Council into a fit, it would probably result with me in human jail. The council has a lot of influence and could pull some strings to save me in the human world, but they might let me rot for doing something so crazy.

"That's unbelievable," I say, responding a little too late. I sound as insincere as I feel.

The girl shrugs, probably lost in her thoughts because of this supposed miracle. "Callie is a fighter. I knew she'd pull through."

Callie. I tuck the name in the back of my mind. Shifting on my socked feet, I try to peer into the room, but the girl blocks my way.

I cross my arms. "Was it some sort of accident?" I try not to come off as interrogating, but talking to Miracle Girl's best friend might be the closest I get to her.

"She passed out and hit her head at school. They didn't think she'd wake up." The girl leans closer. "I blame her boy— ex-boyfriend. I always had a bad feeling about that guy. Can you believe he just stood there and watched her bleed? Makes me sick. They're not even going to expel him. Called it an accident."

A million thoughts rush through my mind. The way she blames another guy makes me think it's creature related. It wouldn't be the first time a creature attacked a fellow classmate.

Now, I know I have to figure out how to talk to Callie. It's my job. Most things turn out to be nothing, but I can't pretend everything is normal. The girl woke up from being brain dead after all. Dr. Harvey told me I couldn't leave, but he didn't say I couldn't do some work.

"Did you see it happen? Did he touch her?" I meet the girl's eyes as the questions fly from my mouth.

"Why do you wanna know?" she asks with a frown crossing her face.

I shrug. "I've heard about some weird things. It always fascinated me."

She peeks over her shoulder. "Well, I can't help you there. I only saw Callie after the fact, and even then, Mr. Augustine wouldn't even let me ride in the ambulance with her. She hasn't said much since she woke up, either."

The teacher's name sounds vaguely familiar. I'm not sure where I've heard it, but I know I've heard it before. It's possible the guy has the same last name as someone else, but I doubt it. I feel my pocket for my phone and sigh when I realize it's not on me.

"Lily?" A woman with dark hair peers into the hallway. "Callie wants to see you now."

The girl, Lily, looks at me. "See you later." She doesn't pause to ask my name, and she doesn't look back as she struts into the room to her best friend.

The woman offers a small smile. I nod to her before I head in the direction of my room. The only thing I can do now is make a few phone calls and wait until I can sneak into Callie's room. I need to get to the bottom of this.

CALLIE

The crowd of people poking and prodding me finally disperses. They're forcing me to stay until a few different therapists and specialists agree I'm fine. Apparently, I'm some sort of miracle or scientific anomaly or something, because when I left my body, my brain showed no activity. Without a soul, my body would've eventually died. I'm glad I returned when I did.

"Callie!" Lily's high pitched voice cuts through the somber hospital air. "You have no idea how scared I was. You can't ever do that crap again."

I hit the button to raise my bed up higher. "It wasn't on purpose. Brendan broke up with me, and I was so embarrassed I willed myself to disappear..." The doctors would never believe me if I told them the truth, but I know Lily probably wouldn't think I was crazy. "And then something really strange happened."

Lily leans forward. "That jerk literally almost made you die from embarrassment."

I nod, knowing that her words sound hilarious, but I can't find the will to laugh. "Actually, that wasn't the strangest part. I didn't pass out. I kind of popped out of my body."

Lily tilts her head to the side and studies my face. "You what?"

"I thought I was a ghost. I watched you hold me until the paramedics came, and then I couldn't stand it, so I left. It's been a really weird day." I fiddle with the corner of the white blanket, not meeting Lily's eyes in case she doesn't believe me. It sounds so ridiculous recounting what happened out loud.

She touches the back of her hand to my forehead. "You sure you weren't dreaming? I heard people in comas dream. Or maybe you just heard the whole thing and your mind filled in the rest."

She does think I'm crazy.

I meet her bold, brown eyes. "I swear on our friendship I saw you go to my house and talk to my grandpa. I sat with you in the car on the way here."

She waves her hands in front of her watery eyes. "I thought I was going crazy." Using her thumb, she combs her blond bangs from her face. "Man, Callie, this is so freaky. Did you tell the doctors? Maybe you did die, and my pleas brought you back."

I highly doubt it. I can't believe dying would leave me alone in the world like that. I expected a lot more or nothing at all. "Possibly. I won't know unless I try to leave my body again."

"What? No way! You're crazy."

"Maybe I am. But I want to try." I'd rather do it here and now rather than wait until after they release me...just in case.

She rubs her hands together while staring at her fingers. "Don't do it without me around. I need to make sure you're okay."

"How late can you stay?"

"My mom's out of town. I can stay however late I want."

MASON

The cool night air fills my lungs as I suck in a long breath. I lurk in the shadows outside of the streetlamp light on the corner of Palomar and North Way. It's past midnight, and the quietest part of the night in the suburban neighborhood surrounding the hospital.

Headlights illuminate the street in front of me, and a red Corolla pulls to the curb. Nadia rolls down the front window, and I wave at Alyssa Callaghan in the driver's seat before climbing in the back next to Evie. Dr. Harvey was crazy to think I'd remain in the hospital. Death by boredom would scrawl across my death certificate if I stayed much longer without properly being able to investigate Miracle Girl.

I strap on the seatbelt as Alyssa pulls from the curb. Being around a seer takes a lot to get used to, but she's glued to Nadia as much as Hunter is. Knowing she can predict the future based on the decisions a person makes always leaves me uneasy. Not because she can tell me about my future, but because she rarely tells anyone about her visions. It's obvious to those who know her when she has them. It's like they take her away from the present completely—leaving her with eerie, green glassy eyes.

Alyssa glances at me in the rearview mirror, a smile playing on her lips, and then she turns her gaze back to the road. If she wasn't a seer, I'd think she was a mind reader.

"See something good, Alyssa?" I ask.

She laughs from the driver's seat. "Not happening, Mase. I don't want to mess up your future."

I lean back in the seat. "At least I have one, right?"

Evie slaps my arm, drawing my attention away from Alyssa and her secret visions.

I wince and then scowl at Evie while scooting closer to the door. "Hey, watch it."

"That's for almost dying. I knew I should've gone with you," Evie says. Anger edges her usually sweet voice as she threatens to pummel me again with her raised hand.

Creatures, I can handle. The wrath of Evie? Not so much.

Nadia turns in the seat to look at us. "And then you might've been hurt, too."

I rub my hand over my face. "Can we forget I made some mistakes today?"

Evie scoffs. "Today?"

I sigh. "Who's Mr. Augustine?" I spit out my question before anything more can be said. I couldn't get the name out of my head since Lily mentioned it. I could've asked on the phone, but I'm not quite ready to let the council know, and I was afraid to risk asking it at the hospital where someone could overhear. If anyone knows anything, it would be one of these three.

Alyssa swerves her car a lane over and pulls into the empty lot of a strip mall. She shuts off the engine and turns in her seat so three pairs of eyes stare at me. I knew they were the right people to call. Alyssa might see glimpses of the future, but I have gut-instinct.

"So, you know him?" The weight of their stares makes me shift in the seat.

Nadia tucks her pale, almost white, hair behind her ear. "He's a family friend of mine. Why do you ask?"

"He's a teacher?" I lean my elbow on my knee so I don't

fidget.

Nadia shakes her head. "No, but he's a librarian at Northern Bell High School."

"That's all I needed to know. Can you take me back to the hospital now before someone realizes I left?" I blink a few times and wait for Alyssa to start the car. She doesn't. Of course they won't just drop this so easily.

Evie flicks my knee. "You can't ask us about Mr. Augustine without an explanation. Where did you hear his name? What are you planning?"

I swing open the door and step from the car. "I'll walk." I'm not in the mood to give an explanation. Miracle Girl could be just that—a miracle. If the council—or anyone for that matter—suspects anything, her life could be changed forever. That's why I need to investigate.

Nadia jumps out after me. "Mason, wait. You're acting really weird. Please, let us help. I don't want you to do anything stupid."

I turn my back on her. "Don't worry, Nadia." I peer over my shoulder. "And please, don't tell anyone, all right?"

"Alyssa, what's he planning?" Evie's voice rings through the darkness.

"I don't know. He hasn't made any decisions," Alyssa says.

"It's nothing to do with the creature world," I call, walking backward to watch my friends glance at each other.

Alyssa laughs, the soft sound echoing through the air. "He's right. It's about a girl."

"A girl?" Evie asks.

If only they knew. It's so much more.

5

⟶Living Ghost⟵

CALLIE

"IS IT WORKING?" Lily's voice breaks my concentration.

"Shhh!" I squeeze my eyes shut. *You can do this. Just let go. You want to be free. You want to leave your body. Come on, Callie!*

Nothing happens. It's the tenth time I've tried—always unsuccessfully.

Maybe Lily was right. Maybe I was dreaming the whole thing. Stupid Brendan, making me pass out and hit my head. It was embarrassing enough. Now, I have to go back to school soon and face him. Face everyone. I really don't want to. I'd give anything to skip it.

My thoughts wander as I remember the events of today—yesterday? It's past midnight now. Anger burns under the surface of my skin. I should call Brendan and yell at him. He should feel guilty for how he ended things. The nerve he had to break up with me in front of his stupid friends. *Ugh!* I thought I still loved him, but the more I think about me the more I—

My ears pop.

"Callie? Did it work?"

I sigh. "No, I don't think so. I can't do it."

"Callie?"

I open my eyes and sit up. It takes me a moment, but I realize it worked. I almost don't believe it. Smiling, I float from the bed and stand next to Lily. I run my hand through her face and stick my tongue out at her. She just stares at my body, her brows knitting together, and then she shakes me.

I lean forward until my head is in hers. *"Please, be okay. Please, be okay."*

"I'm okay, Lily. It worked. It wasn't a dream. I can really leave my body." My voice echoes through her head, and she jumps to her feet and looks around.

"This is so freaky, Callie." Lily glances around once more before sitting back down.

I laugh and lean forward into her head again. "And fun."

A light tap sounds on the door, and I rush back to the bed. I focus on attaching my soul back to my body. The last thing I need is for a nurse to think I'm in a coma again. They'll never let me leave, if that's what they think.

My fingers attach first and then my legs. I glance toward

the open door, and if I could feel my heart, it would be racing. Haloed in the light of the hall stands Mason with his hands clenched into fists at his sides. Even though his face is shadowed, I'd recognize him anywhere. I'll never forget the boy who could see my soul.

And he sees it now. Instead of looking at my body or Lily, he stares at me as I lie half in and out of my body.

"Get out," Lily whispers. "She's sleeping."

Mason doesn't move. He doesn't take his gaze off my spirit, either. "You sure she's okay?"

"Yes. Now, leave. I don't know why you're so interested in Callie. It's kind of weird to be honest. I don't want to have to call the nurse." Lily stands up and blocks his view of me.

I lean back into my body and concentrate on attaching myself completely. Lily's words swim through my mind. Mason's been here before. He spoke to Lily. It must've been when the doctors were examining me. But how did he find me?

Fear washes through me as I settle into darkness before my eyelids flash red, and I know I'm back completely. I jerk upright, gasping as I do, and then I cover my face with my hands. I take another deep breath and find the nerve to open my eyes. Going from my ghostly form to my solid form leaves me disoriented as the weight of my body presses down on me.

I certainly don't want to face the boy whose world revolves around things I can't even explain. When I relax the best I can to remove my hands from my face, Mason's already gone.

Relief rushes over me. "Who was that guy?"

Lily places her hands on her hips. "Some weirdo from

down the hall. I wouldn't worry about him, though. He's only curious. I talked to him earlier and told him what a miracle you were."

I rake my teeth over my bottom lip. How can I tell Lily it's more than that? She's already worried enough about me. If she knew what I knew about Mason, she'd kick herself for making the mistake of talking to him. A part of me also doesn't want to tell her I saw Mason kill a man—or something like a man. It's all too strange for me to process.

"I'm not a miracle," I say.

Lily rolls her eyes. "I know that now. You're more like a freaky living ghost girl."

I flick her arm, a wide smile crossing my face. While going ghostly freaks me out, it's also exhilarating. I can't wait to try it again. Just not here. I'd rather do it when no one knows. As long as I don't stay away from my body for too long, I'll be fine. I think. I can see so many things and go places I wouldn't normally be able to.

Another knock sounds on the door, and my heart drops into my stomach when it swings open. I'm about to throw my pillow if it's Mason again, but my parents shuffle in instead. Maybe he won't come back and will leave me alone for good.

Something about him scares me to death, but I can't get him off my mind. For one, he's cuter than he should be, considering he's a monster slayer. And two? I have this deep-seated need to know how he can see me. Why he can see me. Maybe I need to face him to shake these feelings. Maybe, just maybe, he'd know what was happening...

My mom crosses the room and kisses my forehead. "How are you feeling, baby?"

"Dealing with an annoying headache," I answer, shimmying down on my pillow.

My dad helps me recline the bed. "Need anything before I go? Mom's going to stay here with you."

I shake my head and turn to my mom. "You don't have to stay here. You both look exhausted, and I feel fine. It's late and I'm going to go to sleep."

My mom wrings her hands together. "I don't know."

The truth is, I want to be alone. Her worry stresses me out. I can only take so much babying. "Mom, it's only a few hours. I'm in good hands."

She peers at my dad, and he shrugs. Lily remains quiet, glancing between the three of us. I'm tempted to ask if it would make her feel better if Lily stayed instead, but I doubt that would go over well. Alone it is.

"Fine, but I'm coming back first thing in the morning," Mom says.

I stretch my arms over my head. "With breakfast."

My dad chuckles. "I guess you really are feeling better."

Lily leans forward and taps my hand. "She really is."

My parents each kiss me before strolling toward the door. They glance at Lily. "You should get going, Lily. It's past midnight and you have school tomorrow."

I was hoping they'd forget she was standing by me, and by the frown on Lily's face, she had the same thought I did. "Ugh, don't remind me." She gives me a quick hug and whispers, "I'll ditch last period and come early."

My parents wait for her, and together they leave me alone in the quiet room. I contemplate trying to leave my body again but decide not to. Tossing and turning for a few minutes, I can't force the unbidden image of the boy who can see my soul from my mind. So instead of waiting for his next move—one I'm not even sure will ever come—I plan mine instead. I fling my legs over the bed and stand. Lily mentioned Mason was staying down the hall. I need to find him and confront him on my terms. Maybe then I can forget that seeing him tonight ever happened.

MASON

I pace my room. I can't believe what I saw, and I don't know what to do. I should call the council immediately and tell them I saw a wraith in the city, and that same wraith just happens to possess the body of a girl down the hall. I know it was the wraith I saw earlier. The light pink aura was unmistakable. It tried to possess the goblin before I killed him.

The only thing stopping me is that a wraith's aura is usually the same glittering type like other creatures in the world. A creature's aura shines brighter than humans, making them more easily identifiable.

I couldn't see the sparkle of the wraith and nothing looked out of the ordinary. When it attached to Callie's body, it remained the same with no other auras fighting through. I can't imagine telling the council and then having them kidnap her because of my suspicions. I don't have any real proof. Ruining some poor girl's life because of a thought would make me an asshole, but I also want to save her if she's in trouble.

"Mason?"

I jerk to look at the door. Dr. Harvey peers in with a clip-board tucked under his arm. I didn't even hear him knock, and I don't know how long he's been standing there. Hopefully not long.

"How's your bandage?" His gaze flicks to my arm.

I hold it up, grimacing at the brown stain oozing through the dressing. I've been so lost in my thoughts that I didn't even notice how gross it was getting. "I guess it needs changing."

"Didn't the nurse come by?"

I hold my face expressionless. If I admit I wasn't here, he'll notify the council. "Yeah, but it just started oozing." Seems believable enough.

Dr. Harvey's aura changes from blue to red even though his face is as expressionless as mine is. He's about to either say something that'll force me to lie more, or he will flat out tell me he knows I'm lying. "I checked the log. You were marked MIA for over an hour. Larry saw you leave. Where did you go?" Ah hell. I didn't even stand a chance.

I drop my gaze to the floor. "Out. I needed some fresh air."

"I told you to stay here."

"Well, I'm sorry. I won't leave again."

Dr. Harvey pinches the bridge of his nose. "I know you won't, because if you do, you'll be required to take an additional week of leave on top of the one that starts tomorrow."

What the? He looks serious. "Oh, come on! It was an hour."

"And staying here was an order!" Dr. Harvey has never raised his voice at me, and I shut my mouth instead of arguing. "You're very important to our team, and it would be devastating to lose you. I think a break will be good for you, anyway. You were lucky you didn't succumb to the goblin's venom."

Yelling at him won't make a difference. For some strange reason, he thinks that leaving for an hour could've killed me when I'm on the front line of danger every day. Maybe because it wasn't required. "Sorry, Dr. Harvey. I wasn't thinking." I don't need the good doctor pissed at me. A week off doesn't mean I have to hide in my apartment, anyway.

His face smoothes as he calms down. "Thank you. Now, if you'll sit down, I want to change your bandage before your wounds get infected."

CALLIE

I hover in the hallway outside Mason's door. His name wasn't on the log on the whiteboard at the nurse's station, but his room was easy enough to find since it's the only one not listed. I lean over and peek into the room. My stomach twists as I see a doctor unwind a bandage on his arm, revealing the most horrifying gashes from his shoulder to his elbow. A translucent black sheen shines over the nasty wounds, and I consider running away.

"Damn, that hurts," Mason mutters. I grimace as he grimaces. I can't even imagine how that feels. It's so disgusting.

The doctor pats a damp cloth down his arm. "The goblin got you good. I need to put more ointment on."

Mason pales. "Really?"

Instead of answering, the doctor rolls a metal table closer to them and sets Mason's arm down. He twists open the lid of a glass bottle with black liquid inside and pours it over the wound. Smoke drifts from Mason's arm. The scent of burning flesh wafts in my direction, nearly causing me to gag, but I can't turn away.

Mason's eyebrows pinch together, sweat breaking out on his forehead. He yells out when the doctor continues to pour the black liquid. Seeing him in such pain hurts my heart more than it should. Seeing anyone in pain is bad, but something about seeing Mason so vulnerable makes it worse. He was intimidating, tough, and now...not so much. His vulnerability messes with my emotions.

Something splatters on the floor, and the world shifts, leaving me lightheaded. My stomach twists and turns, and if I don't look away, I'm going to throw up on the floor. I suck in a breath and force my legs to move. I stroll in front of the door and pause.

Mason's dark eyes flash open, and he meets my gaze. He winces through the pain, the muscles on his jaw twitching as he grinds his teeth but doesn't take his eyes from mine. His hard gaze feels like he's glaring right through me to my soul.

I offer a pity smile and lift my hand to wave like that'll somehow help. I don't even know what I was thinking or how stupid I probably look. I drop my hand to my side. He grimaces and closes his eyes, clearly in agonizing pain. I can't force myself to stay any longer.

He doesn't want me standing here, observing his moment

of weakness. And if the doctor looks up and sees me, I'd have to explain myself. What would I say? That I came to talk to Mason and heard what he said about being attacked by a goblin? That I saw the attack with my own eyes? No, I'd surely be in trouble. I don't know what I'm even dealing with.

Without a second glance, I head back to my room and close the door. Leaning my back on the cold wood, I slide to the floor and pull my knees to my chest. It was a terrible idea to think I could face Mason again.

I just hope the doctors decide to release me in the morning. I need to get out of here. There's enough weirdness going on in my life. I'm afraid Mason would just add more.

MASON

Dr. Harvey winds a clean bandage over my arm, and the pain finally subsides. When I open my eyes, Callie is gone. She couldn't have possibly found herself outside my door by coincidence, but it was hard to tell through my pain and her ill expression. She looked worse than I felt, and I bet she wished she didn't witness Dr. Harvey cleaning my wound.

In the few moments I was able to study her aura, I still couldn't see signs of something off. No glitter, no second soul, nothing. But I can't think of an explanation for seeing her aura leave and return to her body. Maybe she died and revived herself. But twice? She wasn't fully connected when Lily shooed me away.

The only way I'm going to get answers is if I confront her again, but if she's dangerous, now isn't the time or place to do it. It's too risky. She could've been at my door for nefarious reasons, and I was fortunate enough to not be alone. No matter what, I'll get this figured out. I know how to find her outside of this hospital.

"All done." Dr. Harvey throws the old bandages in the medical waste bin, drawing my attention away from my thoughts of Callie. "Now, why don't you rest and let your body heal. You'll feel a lot better in a couple hours."

I lie back on the hospital bed. "Thanks, Dr. Harvey. I guess I'll see you around."

"Call me if you need anything, Mason. I don't want another phone call that has me driving back here in the middle of the night, understand? Take it easy. Do something fun over the week. You can't always live to work. You're technically not even an adult and have the rest of your life for that."

Like my age has anything to do with it. I've been training to kill for years. "It's not work if you enjoy doing it."

He chuckles and shakes his head before walking to the door. When he opens it, he waves once and then leaves me to think in silence.

The pink aura possessing Callie lingers in my mind. If I could study her some more—talk to her, see how she lives her life, I might understand what's going on. If I can submerse myself in her world...

An idea hits me. I know exactly what I'm going to do about Callie. I just hope I'm successful.

6

~Stalker~

CALLIE

I SIT IN my car in front of Northern Bell High School. It's been two days since the Worst Breakup Ever, and I had to beg my parents to let me come back. They'd have kept me out forever if they could've, but I know I'm fine. The doctors agreed with me for the most part, except now I have to go back for more tests in a few weeks since my episode has left them stumped.

A tap on my window startles me. Lily hovers outside my car, her bottom lip pouting. Her dark eyes smile despite her fake frown, and she tugs on my locked door.

"Last chance to go home," she says through the glass. "I don't mind. I'll just come with you."

I hit the unlock button without unbuckling my seatbelt. Her offer to ditch with me is a lot more appealing than facing all the questions or ignoring all the looks of pity. Lily opens the door and leans in, unbuckling my seatbelt for me. She'll drag me from the car if I don't force myself to move.

Sunlight blinds me as I stare at the blue sky above the red-brick building like I can somehow float away, body and all.

Lily nudges me forward. "It's going to be fine. I swear. No one has even talked about you."

"That's because everyone knows we're best friends. I doubt they'd talk about me in front of you." I trail next to her on the way to the stairs leading up to the entrance.

Her smile melts away because she knows I'm right. If I were someone else, I'd probably talk about me, too. It's boring enough that any sort of drama will keep people talking for weeks. I wonder how many people know I was supposedly brain dead. Hopefully not many. My parents were worried about word getting out, and people coming to interrupt our lives, looking for their own miracle. It freaked me out a little, too. Not because what happened to me seemed impossible, but because I don't want anyone to discover my secret.

I open the door and enter the cool corridor. Students wander about, some digging through their lockers and others chatting in the hall. I head to my locker and fling it open. Catching my reflection in the hanging mirror, I peer at my dark hair as it hangs slightly in my face. My blue eyes shine with the worry I can't shake. I thought I could do this, but I'm not sure I can. Nerves bunch in my stomach, and I imagine myself jumping from my body again. The thought of doing it here freaks me out more than anything.

"Callie?" Lily pinches my shoulder. "Psst! Callie. Brendan is heading this way. Want me to intervene?"

My heart races as I clutch the metal door of my locker for support. "No, it's okay. Maybe he won't say anything."

"He's getting closer. I can stop him."

Leave me alone. Please, just keep going. I don't want to talk to you. Please, just g—

"Callie, you're here." Brendan's voice sends a shiver down my back in a terrible way.

All the love I thought I felt for him vanished the moment I had popped from my body. I can't stop the anger rushing through me. How dare he approach me after the embarrassment he put me through? If I didn't think I'd draw so much attention, I'd push him away.

I dig my nails into my palms instead. "Well, yeah. I go here," I say, answering his comment with heavy sarcasm in my voice.

He clasps my shoulder, trying to spin me around, and I jerk away. His breath blows my hair as he steps closer. "I know. It's just, you know?"

"What?" My voice comes out stronger than I expect it to.

"You passed out. Are you okay?" He rubs strands of my dark hair between his fingers.

Spinning around to face him, I use the heel of my hand to

get him to step back. "I'm great!" I press my palm into his chest, forcing him back even more. He has no right to invade my space anymore, and I don't know how to make it any clearer.

He shifts on his feet. "Well, I'm glad you're okay."

I don't know what comes over me, but I can't stop the words from spilling out. "Are you? I bet you were so relieved you didn't have to deal with me anymore."

"Don't be like that. I care about you, Callie." He sounds sincere, and I almost let my guard down, but then the cruel words he said to me replay in my mind. His sudden nicety doesn't change things.

Lily stands silently next to me. If she didn't poke me to get my attention, I'd have forgotten she was here. Jerking her head, she motions for me to walk away, but I can't. I'm frozen in place. If Brendan had the nerve to come up to me in the hall, then he gets what he deserves. Maybe next time he'll learn about common decency and break up with his next girlfriend in private. I'd have taken a stupid text over being humiliated.

Ignoring Lily, I press my lips together and jab my finger into his chest. "You care about me? You *care*? You're so full of crap, Brendan. If you cared, you wouldn't have broken up with me in front of everyone in the cafeteria. All you care about is yourself."

His ears redden. "I was hoping you wouldn't make a scene."

I throw my hands up. "A scene! What's wrong with you?"

"What's wrong with me? Nothing is wrong with me. You

should look at your—"

Brendan shuts his mouth as a shadow falls over me. His sky blue eyes peer over my shoulder, and before I have a chance to turn, a familiar voice says, "Don't say another word if you know what's good for you."

Mason moves forward from his position in front of my abandoned locker and steps between me and the boy I'd like to slap. Crossing my arms over my chest, I let Mason intervene. He's a good few inches taller than Brendan and intimidating as hell with his scuffed up black boots, muscular arms, and dark eyes that seem to see things—darker things—that no one else can see.

Brendan raises his hands. "I don't want any trouble, man. I'm just having a conversation with my girlfriend."

Lily scoffs, speaking up for the first time. She lifts an eyebrow at me before grinning at Mason. "Ex-girlfriend, you mean."

"It looks like she doesn't want to talk to you," Mason says. "Why don't you leave, and I'll forget about this." Forget about this? What is going on?

Mason sounds exactly how he sounded when he threatened me in the city after he killed that monster man thing. The surprise of him showing up at my school leaves me speechless and does nothing for my sudden anxiety.

I thought after he caught me outside his hospital room that he'd corner me there for sure while I was still admitted, but he never came. I assumed he was gone from my life for good. And until now, I wasn't sure how I felt about it. I refuse to believe this is coincidental. He's definitely following me. He might look my age, but he was working a job no high school student would possibly have. I wonder how he even found me. *Calm down. You're in public. Nothing bad will happen here. Take a breath.*

Without saying another word or arguing, Brendan turns on his heels and rushes away. Brendan must have the same feeling I have—Mason isn't someone to mess with—because Brendan isn't usually one to back down or fear anyone. No one at school would ever pick a fight with him.

I'm thankful for his fear, though. I don't know how much longer I could've taken Brendan before I body jumped to get away. I never thought I'd be the type to run, but it's pretty clear that I'd flee in a bad situation instead of fight.

"Hospital guy, what are you doing here?" Lily breaks the moment of silence. I still haven't formed the courage to look him in the eyes. "Stalking is against the law, you know."

Mason laughs, and every dark thought I had about him fades to the back of my mind. A smile lights up his face, the intensity from his stare nowhere to be found. And I wish he would never stop smiling again, because it looks amazing on him. "I go here. I'm new."

I hold my face expressionless as I finally force myself to stop staring at his straight teeth and pouty lips to meet his brown eyes. Lily doesn't know I stalked him myself in the hospital. "How's your arm?"

Smirking while flashing his cute dimples again, he says, "You saw that?"

He knows I saw it. Why doesn't he admit it in front of Lily? "How'd it happen?" I ask instead of answering his question.

He shifts his gaze to Lily for a split second before leaning down to whisper, "I think you know."

A wave of ice washes over me, freezing me inside and out. Goosebumps prickle over my skin, and the edges of my vision shadow. Fear twists knots in my stomach.

Reaching out, he steadies me as I wobble on my feet. His touch sends a wave of conflicting emotions over me—fear, intrigue, attraction—it's overpowering my thoughts. What is wrong with me? I have no business experiencing any of these feelings.

He studies my reaction, his stare never wavering. I can't even find the will to shrug away from him.

Blinking through the oncoming haze, I lick my lips and say, "I have to go. I don't want to be late."

Without saying another word, I pull away from Mason, grab my books, slam my locker shut, and jog away.

MASON

"Callie, wait!" Lily grimaces but doesn't chase after her friend. She turns to me. "What was that about? You're crazy for talking to Brendan like that, you know."

I turn my gaze to watch Callie leave. "Why?"

"He's punches people for less with his crazy temper, and for some reason, Principal Higgins won't expel him."

I shrug my shoulders, knowing all too well why he's allowed to stay here. "He won't bother me. I know his type."

Northern Bell High School caters to both humans and creatures. I'm sure if the principal wasn't a creature herself—a shifter like Brendan—he'd have been long gone.

"Well, aren't you Mr. Confident." Lily pushes her bangs out of her face. "Just so you know, that doesn't work on Callie. It might not seem like it, but Brendan was amazing at playing the nice guy to Callie. I warned her, but she hates people telling her how to feel about someone."

I thought I was being nice. I was trying to get a dude Callie clearly didn't want in her face out of the way. "I, um—" I pause. Did I want it to work on Callie, like Lily's suggesting? Maybe.

Lily flicks my healing arm, and I jerk back. She covers her mouth with her hand and touches my arm again. "Oh, my God. I'm so sorry. I forgot."

I roll my shoulder. "I'm fine."

The bell rings, sending the bustling crowd of students toward their classrooms. Lily picks her bag up off the floor and hooks it on her arm. "You know where you're going?"

I shake my head and dig my schedule out of my pocket. It was easy enough to enroll here. My enchantress friend, who has the ability to influence the decisions of others, owed me a favor and enrolled me with a fake transcript.

Lily takes it from me. "Perfect! You have English with me." Her smile widens. "And guess who else? Callie."

"Cool."

"Cool? I saw the way you looked at her. Not to mention the way you stood up for her. You're interested." She smirks, nearly giggling with her assumption.

I'm definitely interested in Callie, but not for the reasons Lily assumes. I want to get down to the bottom of what I saw. "She is a miracle girl after all."

Lily snorts and then covers her mouth with her hand. She blushes. "Come on. I don't want to be late."

Trailing behind Lily, I let her lead the way. It's been a long time since I've hung around someone who doesn't know about the creature world that I'm a tiny bit worried I might say something incredibly strange. I have to stay guarded, watch what I say, and do my best to keep her out of it.

Humans are better off living in ignorance. It's too risky unless they've trained to protect themselves like my brother. It's why I haven't cornered Callie yet. If she doesn't know, I want to protect her innocence. The creature life is an adjustment for even those who know of the creature world. Hell, I'm still adjusting.

Having a mother whose life's work involved studying creatures and their danger to the human world instilled a fear of creatures into me since I was a kid. It's all I knew most of my life, and I thought all creatures were bad and out to get humanity until the Creature Council offered to truly train and guide me in the supernatural world. Sometimes, it's still hard to process that all creatures aren't bad and not all humans are good. It leaves me suspicious of everyone. I can't help it. But suspicion is what makes me a better agent for the council. I want to make the world a safer place for everyone.

The bell rings before we get into English with Mrs. Padilla, and the moment we enter, all eyes fall on us. I peer around the room, watching some creature students frown or shift their eyes. I'm well-known in the community and not exactly for the best reasons. People distrust that the council chose me, a former enemy, to work for them to assure humans and creatures are safe.

I search the room and spot Callie sitting in the front row, keeping her eyes trained on the cover of her copy of Dante's Inferno. She doesn't return my gaze.

"Ms. Millan, you're late," Mrs. Padilla says.

Lily drops her bag at the desk next to Callie. "Sorry, I was showing—" She pauses. I didn't tell her my name.

I hand my schedule to Mrs. Padilla. "Mason Sullivan."

Lily smirks. "I was showing Mason around."

A few students mumble but then quiet down when Mrs. Padilla glares in their direction. "I'll excuse the tardy today, you two, but don't let it happen again." She turns her green eyes to me. I concentrate on her aura, seeing she's human, and then focus on turning off my ability. It's like someone threw up a rainbow haze around the room, and gets nauseating if I keep it up for too long.

Mrs. Padilla points at the empty desk on the other side of Callie. "Take a seat next to Ms. White. You can fetch your books from the library in the basement later, but for now, share with Callie."

Callie sighs and tosses me her copy of Dante's Inferno. "I've already been through enough hell this week, so help yourself."

I flip through the pages, trying not to laugh at her sarcasm.

"Thanks."

She doesn't respond, and I turn my gaze to Mrs. Padilla. I zone out through her lecture, not really caring about anything, since I've already established a career. Passing a few classes at Northern Bell isn't on my list of priorities. I don't think I'll be here longer than a week anyway, especially if the council discovers I've enrolled.

At the end of class, Mrs. Padilla hands out an assignment. "Finish reading the Inferno this weekend. On Monday, you'll start your final projects for the book. With a partner, I want you to pick a passage from one of the nine circles and present a visual interpretation to the class. You have free range of the project. Be creative. Have fun. I'll choose partners today if you'd like to get started early." Using her index and middle finger, she points at pairs of students. "Jamie and Eric, you'll be partners. Mason and Callie, you'll be partners. Lily and Abigail, you'll be partners."

I tune out Mrs. Padilla. Callie pales, looking faint, and I frown. I lean over and whisper, "You okay?"

She draws her gaze to mine. "Yeah, it's just—" The bell rings, cutting her off. She packs up her books without finishing.

I follow her out, staying on her heels, and tap her arm before she can run away from me again. "Do you want to meet after school to do the project?"

She shakes her head. "Can't."

I press my lips together. "Tomorrow?"

"I'm busy then, too."

I adjust my backpack. "Well, how about we talk about it

on the way to your next class? Where are you heading?"

She doesn't say anything for a moment. Her blue eyes narrow. "The library." She turns on her heels and looks over her shoulder. "Let me guess, you're heading that way, too."

I laugh, because she's right. I made sure to have the secretary enroll me in as many of Callie's classes as she could, which was three, and being a library aide happened to be one of them. I won't be showing up for the rest.

She stumbles, dropping her books, and falls into me. Steadying her on her feet, I concentrate on her aura, watching it dance around her, like it's trying to escape before it returns to normal. When she finds her footing, she lets go of my arm and pushes her dark hair from her face.

I bend down and pick up her books, tucking them under my arm. "You look faint. Do you need to go to the nurse?"

She tries to snatch her books away, but I shift so she can't grab them. She drops her hands in defeat. "I'm fine. Still recovering from my head injury." She strolls ahead of me and turns to look over her shoulder. "I thought you wanted to talk about the project."

I jog to catch up. "Yeah, but there's more."

She sighs. "No. Whatever it is, just drop it. I want you to leave me alone."

"Why are you so afraid? I know you know me."

She stops in her tracks and leans to whisper in my ear. "Because you're a murderer, and I don't trust you."

I shiver as her warm breath tickles my ear. I don't know what to say. Her accusations are true, but she doesn't know that

I don't kill without reason. The goblin would've killed me. I was only doing it to keep people safe.

One look in her blue eyes tells me she won't understand, and she won't listen to anything I say. Not yet at least. In this moment, I know she doesn't know anything about the creature world. I'm not sure for how long, though. The urge to tell her consumes me, but she doesn't give me a chance to say anything. She snatches her books and dashes toward the front of the school. She exits, the door unlocked for the seniors without a first period, and I don't move to follow her.

I'm afraid I did enough damage, and she'll never trust me.

I wouldn't if I were her.

But damn it, I hope she comes around. Something about Callie's aura draws me to her—actually, everything draws me to her. Her feistiness, her no-nonsense attitude, her suspicion even—all those things make me want to follow her out those doors to corner her. To tell her everything.

But I can't.

If I want her to trust me, I have to give her a reason to. And right now, I don't have one.

7

⁓Dangerous⁓

CALLIE

I LIE ON my bed in the dark. I've been hiding in here since the moment I got home after I left school early. I don't want to face the world. Mason showing up at Northern Bell got under my skin. I almost jumped out of my body right in the hall for everyone to see just to get away from him and everything his intense stare was doing to me.

My cell phone rings, and Lily's picture flashes on the screen. Holding the phone to my ear, I say, "Sorry I abandoned you."

"You better be. If it weren't for Mason, I'd have had to eat alone. We've been cast out from our usual table because of stupid Brendan." Lily breathes into the phone.

I shift on my side. "You don't want to sit with Brendan anyway."

"That's what Mason said."

I puff air through my lips. "Of course he did." My words line with anger.

"Whoa, Callie. What's your problem with Mason?"

I sit up on my bed. I wasn't going to tell Lily about seeing Mason on my trip to the city when I thought I was dead, but she'll badger me until I do. I wonder if she'll believe me. I'm not sure I would if I were her.

"Mason isn't who he says he is. I've met him—well, saw him before. When I was, you know, a ghost." I press the phone harder to my ear to see if I can hear a reaction.

Lily whistles through the line. "You're not joking, are you? Some coincidence that he happened to be at the same hospital as you and now he goes to our school. Maybe it was destiny you've met—I could get on board with this. Nicer than Brendan. And he's definitely hot. You know he likes you, right?"

Her words spill out faster than I can keep up. My cheeks heat. "What? No, he doesn't. And I doubt all this was a coincidence. I'm pretty sure he's stalking me because he thinks I'm a monster or something. He saw my soul. I know he did. He's not...normal." I contemplate my next words for a second. "I watched him kill a man who morphed into some crazy monster. He's like a hunter or something. He's dangerous."

The sound of breaking glass echoes through the line, and

Lily swears under her breath. She doesn't respond for a moment. I hear her breathe into the phone, and then she says, "Do you know how crazy you sound?"

"I know what I saw."

"But—"

"I don't expect you to believe me, but it's true," I say, cutting her off.

"I do believe you but wow. Monsters? Doesn't that kind of make him a good guy? If not, he's a damn good-looking bad guy."

"Unless he thinks I'm a monster, then what?"

"Oh, crap. I didn't think about that." A door slams, and the line goes quiet for a second. "I'll kill him if he even tries to hurt you."

I laugh. "Thanks, I feel so much safer with you around."

"Hey, I took kickboxing over the summer," Lily says. "I can do some damage."

I fall back to my bed and look up at my dark ceiling. "I don't doubt it. Just be careful around him, all right? And don't tell him anything else about me, blabber mouth."

"I won't. I promise."

I glance at the clock. It's after one in the morning. "Hey, I have to go. I'll call you tomorrow, okay?"

"Why do you have to go?"

I sigh. "I want to try to body jump again."

Lily sighs. "I know I can't talk you out of it, so be careful."

"I will. I'll text you when I'm back."

MASON

Music hums through the walls of the VIP room at The Haven. Hunter sits across from me, drinking some non-alcoholic elf concoction in a crystal goblet, and I try not to smirk every time he takes a sip. The club isn't exactly my style, but it's not like I can get in anywhere else. Hunter worked security here before he started college, and people usually don't hassle me. Plus, VIP access rocks.

He raises an eyebrow. "I didn't choose the glass."

I sip my soda from the can. "I know."

"Then stop smirking."

"It's a good look."

He throws a fry at me. "It's a good drink."

The door swings open, the hum of music turning into a pulsating beat, and I catch a look at Nadia, Alyssa, and Evie dancing in the middle of the dance floor. Working for the council has its perks, and being able to hang in the VIP lounge at The Haven is one of them. It helps that the owner, Cian, is a family friend of Nadia's.

A group of enchantresses waltzes in and sits in the corner away from us. Hunter lifts his hand to wave, and the sisters smile before focusing on each other. The door closes, cutting off the sound, and I mess with the end of the gauze on my arm.

Hunter leans forward. "How's vacation?"

"You mean my mandatory leave of absence? It's fine. Haven't done much." I lean back in the chair, rocking two of its legs off the floor.

"Hard to believe, Mase. I know you better than that."

I sip my soda and tap the can on the table. "I'm not doing

any unauthorized dangerous field work if that's what you're implying." Okay, maybe sort of unauthorized. But dangerous? High school is as torturous as desk duty.

"But you're still in the field." He doesn't have to ask.

"It's not what you think. I have some things I need to figure out. The council doesn't need to know yet, either. I don't even know if it's worth my investigation." I rub my scruffy chin. If my mom didn't complain about my facial hair and the dangers of growing a beard when it comes to combat fighting, I'd probably never shave.

Hunter tips his head forward. "You're not going to tell me anything else, are you? You know I can keep a secret, Mason, and I'm willing to help you."

I nod. "Thanks but no thanks, man. You're a civilian and it's a delicate situation. The fewer people who know, the better. If things change, you'll be the first one I'll call."

The door swings open again before Hunter can say anymore. "Come dance with us!" Nadia motions to Hunter with her fingers, her voice rising over the music.

His eyes shift from concern to something else—love, maybe—and he stands. I follow behind him even though dancing isn't my favorite thing, but I'll do anything to get my brother off my back. If he pressures me enough, I'm sure I'll break and tell him about Callie.

When we step from the lounge, rainbow lights flash in my eyes, blending and moving with dozens of glittering auras. As a creature hangout, The Haven is basically a Member's Only club. The only ways humans can get in are with a creature escort, are on the guest list, or if they work for the council. It's safer this way. Many creatures are wary of humans, and this is a place for those in the know. Creatures aren't forced to hide who they are here.

Evie and Alyssa dance together. Hunter joins Nadia, sliding his hands around her waist. She tips her head to the ceiling and laughs, and I move and sit on a barstool near the bar. I peer over the crowd, drifting my gaze from one creature to the next. A shadow falls over me, and I twist to look at a familiar face.

Brendan plops down in the seat next to me. "You shouldn't be here."

I snort. Who does this guy think he is? I twist in my seat to look at him. His boxy jaw twitches as he clenches his teeth. His brows furrow, and he stares at the bar instead of looking at me. Typical for a guy who wants to test the limits while having a good dose of fear for approaching me.

"I know Cian. If he's cool with me being here, then I'm pretty sure I'm welcome here." I point over my shoulder at Nadia. "See that girl, the nightmare inflictor? She's the daughter of Dmitri Petrov, and she's dating my brother. Want me to introduce you to her? She's always looking for volunteers."

Nadia and Dmitri are one of the most feared creatures in the creature community, and it takes a brave person to volunteer to let them invade their sleep. Hunter once told me Nadia used to hate how she survived by giving people nightmares, but I guess that's changed. She's always seemed so confident to me, even teasing me, asking me to volunteer. She's joking, I think, but I can't tell for sure. I've always laughed it off.

Brendan stiffens. "Volunteers have to be eighteen."

I smirk. "For Dmitri, yes. Nadia's flexible." I wave when she looks at me, like she knows I'm talking about her. She offers a bright smile and motions for me to come over, but I shake my head. "Want to talk to her or are you afraid?"

Brendan smacks the counter. "I don't have to prove anything. I just wanted to warn you that people are talking about you."

"Yeah, I'm sure that's it." I stand up. "I think you're mad about me intervening with Callie. You know it's against council law to harass a human or persist with unwanted attention."

He growls. "Shut up."

I raise an eyebrow. "Make me." My own words make me cringe. This conversation sounds like one I've had with my brother when we fought as kids. And I know exactly what's coming.

I concentrate on Brendan's next move, the world slowing. He launches from the chair, his bones cracking as he morphs into a stronger, larger version of himself, and he raises his fist. I twist out of the way, faster than he could ever move. He punches a pixie behind me, sending the boyish creature flying into the air.

I tense, preparing for the chaos about to break loose.

CALLIE

The city hums with life. I propel down the street, hopping in and out of cars as they drive down the busy Friday night road. It doesn't take me long to enter the heart of the city, where people scurry about, walking home or looking for something fun to do.

A woman in a gold sequin dress and nude stilettos hangs on the arm of a guy with enough muscles to be a body builder and the face of a movie star. They stroll down the sidewalk, whispering to each other, and I can't help but follow them.

The woman, with her black hair tied in a top knot, has the prettiest blue eyes I've ever seen. She's absolutely gorgeous. I wonder where the couple is heading. It has to be somewhere entertaining in outfits as glamorous as those.

I glide behind them until I'm close enough to eavesdrop on their conversation.

"Dinner was amazing, Anthony. It's been a while since I've been out," the woman says.

I jump ahead of them and walk backwards so I can watch their faces. The woman's blue eyes shine like glass, like she's lost in a memory, and then she blinks a few times. Her gaze turns to Anthony and she smiles.

"I'm glad you agreed, Liv. I thought you could use some fun." Anthony drapes his arm over her shoulders. "Want to go dancing at The Haven? It's still early."

She nods. "Sure, I haven't been there since—" Her words cut off. "It sounds like fun."

I stop on the pavement and let Liv walk into me. I stay with her as her thoughts drift through my mind. A warm sensation crawls over my soul, but it's not bad. Liv feels different than any person I've been in so far. It's strange and exhilarating. I wonder what it'd be like to be her.

"*Don't mess this up, Liv,*" she says to herself. "*Camden*

would want you to move on with your life. You can't be a shut in forever."

I hop from her mind as a flash of grief bats at me. I frown, feeling bad for invading her private thoughts about someone she clearly loved and lost. Strolling next to the couple, I follow them as they turn into an alley leading to an apartment building.

I linger behind them. This doesn't look like a place for people to go dancing, but the couple saunters into the parking structure, waves to a security guard, and then they head to a set of stairs instead of the elevator.

Liv's stilettos tap on the concrete stairs as they climb up. Fear threatens to stop me from following, but my curiosity gets the best of me. This isn't some normal, public club. This place is different. A simple lobby leads to a door. I'm afraid to see what's on the other side. What if it's horrifying? Or really embarrassing?

I steel myself and rush ahead of the couple and straight through the lobby into an empty hallway with a chair sitting near a touch screen computer set into the wall in front of another door. I don't bother to look at the computer, since it's not like I can snoop. I can't touch the screen. Whoever attends to the door is absent. Not like they could stop me anyway.

Nerves make me hesitate at the door. "You can do this. Just peek in. If it's weird, you can leave."

I lean forward and stick my head through the door. Music blasts around me. Bright, colorful lights twirl over a dance floor, and black booths line the room. I step all the way into the small club and spin through a crowd of people near the door.

The air tingles with life and exhilaration, the exact feelings you want to get from heading somewhere fun on a Friday night. I can't stop the smile from spreading across my face, knowing how awesome it is that I'm here in some random private club I'd have never found with my body.

A cute guy with tattooed sleeves and buzzed hair dances next to me. Sweat drips from his temples onto his leather jacket, and he keeps perfect rhythm with an upbeat song. The saying, *Dance like no one's watching*, couldn't be any more appropriate. Without the fear of embarrassment, I feel so free.

"You're a great dancer," I say to the guy. Lily would crack up if she knew I was pretending to have a conversation with Mr. Hottie, because he definitely can't hear me.

Spinning away, I dance from person to person and laugh as I wander in and out of their thoughts.

"*Damn it. Not now, Brendan.*" The foreign thought trickles into my mind and catches me off guard. The familiar name grabs hold of my bliss and snuffs it out. The last name I want to hear is that of my stupid ex. I doubt it's him, though. He'd never get into a club like this.

A tall, well-built man with red hair pulled into a ponytail rushes away from me, taking his thoughts with him, and heads toward the back of the club near the bar.

Gliding closer to the bar, I notice a crowd. It parts as the towering man nudges people out of the way. I use the break in people to step closer without meandering through anyone else's personal thoughts.

I freeze in my tracks. *What the heck is going on?* I can't believe what I'm seeing.

Mason, wearing the same clothes he wore when I last saw him, watches as Brendan stumbles past him. Surprise forces me to step back. I take in the situation, a million questions rushing through my mind. This is the last place I expected to see either of them. Why on earth is Brendan in a club he's clearly too young to be in? Why is Mason? And how do they even know each other?

I hate feeling like I'm missing some vital information surrounding my own life. Neither of these boys should be fighting each other.

Confusion and anger roll through me. What has my life turned into? I don't even know what's happening anymore. And after seeing these two boys—one I loathe and one I'm confused about—I'm not sure I want to find out.

MASON

The pixie, a small guy with midnight black hair and an eyebrow piercing, raises his hand and blows a handful of pixie dust at Brendan, freezing him in place before he can try to attack me again. Another shifter pushes through the crowd, and the pixie jumps a few feet into the air, taking flight again. He blows more pixie dust, and the other shifter freezes, unable to move.

The blaring music pulses through the room. Another two shifters dance through the crowd in our direction, trying to come to their friends' rescues. Most creatures tend to band together with their own kind in times of trouble. It's how they've survived so long. And shifters, they're at the top of the human world because of their ability to change into anything they want to be. Most change between human forms, but there are the ones who'll morph into animals.

I raise my hands up, palms out, and yell, "Back off! This was all a misunderstanding." I point at the pixie. "Chill, dude, and stop dusting people."

"Last I knew, you weren't a council member." The shifter with long, red hair pulled into a ponytail strides closer. He's a good few inches taller than me with muscles that make my arms look like twigs in comparison. But it's all for show. I doubt the guy has ever worked out in his life.

I tense, waiting for him to make a move. "No, but I act on behalf of the council."

The guy drops his arms. "Have that little glitter bomber release my son and brother."

I peer up at the pixie. "Please?"

He does what I ask without arguing and disappears into the crowd. The shifter nods his head just as Cian, the club owner, pushes through the crowd. The troll crosses his arms over his chest and glances between me and the shifters. His blue-framed glasses match the blue of his dress shirt, and he turns to me.

"Is there trouble, Mase?" He ignores the shifters.

The red-haired shifter shakes his head.

I press my lips together for a second. "Not anymore. Thanks for checking. You know how it is sometimes."

Cian turns to the shifters. "You get one warning. Next time you're out. I know your kid is young, Brock, but I can't have him attacking people in here. Especially humans."

"He won't do it again, Cian." The guy turns to Brendan. "Right, son?"

Brendan narrows his eyes at me but nods instead of arguing. I hold my face as expressionless as possible. A cool hand touches my shoulder, and I spin to look at Evie, with the rest of my friends, ready to back me up. Hunter jerks his head toward the VIP door, and I nod.

"I'll just go to VIP until things settle down. Sorry for the disruption, Cian."

He waves me away, and I follow my brother, Nadia, Evie, and Alyssa through the dance floor and back to the safest part of The Haven—at least the safest part for me.

Evie pokes my hurt shoulder, and I wince. "Alyssa's going to take me home. You know how uneasy I get when things heat up around here."

I frown. "Sorry. I'll see you around."

Evie and Alyssa hug all three of us, and then Nadia opens the door to the VIP lounge. I watch Evie and Alyssa weave through the crowd. A flash of pink light catches my attention on the dance floor, and I blink a few times, thinking my eyes are tricking me.

I'd recognize Callie's aura anywhere, or at least what I thought was Callie's aura. But if she were human, she'd never end up at this place. And now I'm mad at myself for being hopeful that everything was okay with Callie.

Seeing that pink life essence here confirms my suspicions that I'm dealing with a wraith—maybe one Callie has no idea is sneaking into her life. There is no other explanation for it. It's strange that the wraith doesn't stay in Callie, though. I thought the only time they left a body was if the body died or it was ripped free by a soul manipulator.

"Mason? You coming?"

I turn to Hunter as he waits in the lounge. "Yeah, sorry."

Even though everything in me says to keep my eyes on the pale pink spirit drifting about, untethered to a body, I force my legs to take me into the quiet of the lounge. I know what I have to do now. I don't have time to build Callie's trust. I have to corner her and make her tell me what's going on. It's the only way to know for sure. I'll take her back to the council if I have to.

8

⮂Going Ghostly⮀

CALLIE

I SHIFT AND move to stop from entering the minds of the dancers around me. I have a lot to think about. Peering over my shoulder, I watch Brendan leave with a man who sounded like his dad. I'm not sure though. I've only ever met his mom.

When they leave the club, I turn my gaze toward the door near the bar where Mason was heading with a group of people. The intensity of his gaze locks me in place. His brows furrow as he studies my soul—it's the same expression I've seen on him the few times he caught sight of me out of my body—and then a second later, he turns and enters the back room.

Unable to shake the nervousness clutching onto me, I turn toward the front door and step forward into a blond woman wearing a halter dress and sparkling chandelier earrings. A guy with a faux hawk, wearing black jeans and a printed T-shirt, way underdressed compared to the woman, places his hands on her hips. They sway together for a moment, his piercing green eyes drinking in the woman as she pulls away and dips in front of him. He doesn't let her get far before he clutches her hands and spins her around. The woman thinks about how cute the guy is, but she also thinks he's a little young for her taste. She doesn't mind the attention, though. She rather enjoys it.

A strange feeling suddenly tugs at me as I stand within the woman. The sensation stings like a pinch to my very essence. I cry out and back away from the woman, but I can't move more than a foot away. Something invisible grabs hold of me, keeping me in place. Fear courses through me, and I stumble forward like someone hooks me on a fishing line and reels me back into the blonde.

The sudden movement forces me to face the guy as he inhales a few breaths through his mouth. His eyes close in satisfaction, not exactly what I'd expect from just dancing with a woman. It's creepy and unnerving, and I'm trapped watching him take another deep breath, like he's sucking the woman in. Only he's not.

He's sucking *me* in.

For the first time in my ethereal form, I feel pain. My soul burns like an invisible fire lights me ablaze. With every breath he takes, he steals my essence. If he doesn't stop, he might consume me completely. Then what would happen? *Oh, my God. No!*

I fly forward instead of resisting his pull and enter into the guy's head.

"She's so amazing. Just one more breath, then let her go. Don't slip up. The council will hunt you down for sure."

The pulling sensation continues, but still, I can't break free.

"You have to stop, Jax. Come on, you have to stop. No more." He's arguing with himself, unaware that he's not actually siphoning the woman's soul like he thinks, and he's having trouble stopping. If he can't control himself, I have to make him stop before something terrible happens to me.

"Let me go!" I scream. "I'm not your dinner! I swear, I'll hurt you if you take another breath."

The sucking sensation stops, and my ears pop. Stumbling out of the guy, I fall to the floor, and people dance through me. The soul sucker freezes, his fingers clenched at his side. He stares right at me like Mason. I scramble back, putting a few feet of distance between us. How is it even possible that he can see me? I wonder if Mason wants to devour my soul, too.

The guy abandons the woman on the dance floor and shuffles in my direction with an outstretched hand. He's ready to touch my soul if I let him, but I don't want him anywhere near me.

I propel back, launching myself away, and then the music stops. I let out a breath out of habit even though I don't need to breathe. Spinning, I peer around the quiet room with black booths and tables, and not much more. I'm no longer in the main section of the club. I must've flown through the wall.

A knock sounds on the door to the lounge, but no one in the room bothers to answer. I sense a pair of eyes on me and shiver when I meet Mason's dark brown eyes. His smile melts from his face, and he clenches his jaw when he spots me.

The knock on the door turns into a bang, but he doesn't draw his attention away like everyone else. It sounds like whoever is on the other side is desperate to kick it open, and I can only guess who it is.

A blond girl sitting across from Mason with her back facing me gets to her feet and glides across the room inhumanly fast. I blink a few times, unsure if I imagined it, and then she cracks the door open.

The soul sucker pushes the door completely open and knocks the girl off her feet. Commotion breaks out when the boy next to Mason jumps to his feet and races across the room toward the girl. Both the girl and boy, who I assume is her boyfriend, start yelling at the soul sucker, but he ignores them, entering the lounge.

But Mason doesn't move. He stares at me, mouth half opened, and I stare back until the soul sucker starts waving his hands. He dodges around the couple at the door and runs toward me, pointing his fingers in my direction.

I scream. I can't help it. Scrambling away as he closes the distance, I do the only thing I can think of. I race toward Mason and propel myself into his body. Even though I don't trust him, and I don't know who he really is, I've seen him in action.

I just hope he decides to save me.

MASON

I can't stop the wraith from entering me. The pale pink aura sinks through my skin, but shockingly, I feel nothing except for some foreign emotions—panic, anger—nothing I felt a second ago. I close my eyes, half expecting to lose complete control of my body, but nothing happens. I'm still in complete control, though I see the pale pink aura mingling with my own red one.

"*Mason?*" A familiar voice echoes through my mind. It's Callie. "*Please, you have to help me. That guy is trying to eat me.*"

I scrunch my brows, trying to figure out what's going on. I'm not imagining her, but I wasn't expecting to hear Callie's voice in my head. What I was expecting was a monster to possess me. Instead, I got a girl asking for my help with a shaky voice I can't just ignore.

I eye the incubus she claims is trying to eat her. "*What are you?*" Callie isn't a wraith. She'd have to be dead to be a wraith, and I've seen her very much alive.

The incubus lurks closer, causing another bout of panic from Callie. He's on the edge between deciding whether or not to attack me. "*I-I don't know what you mean. I'm not anything,*" Callie responds.

My eyes don't leave the incubus while he shifts on his feet. Hunter and Nadia stand behind him, waiting for me to decide the next move since his attention is on me and no one else. "*You don't have to be afraid. You can tell me.*"

"*I'm telling you the truth. This is new to me. I didn't know I could go ghostly until the other day. I thought I was dead, but it turned out I wasn't.*" Her voice rises in pitch. "*Now, please, he's coming closer! I don't want to die!"*

I raise my hand up. "Stay back," I say to the incubus. They're one of the few creatures who can see life forces like me. Part of an incubus' DNA was used to create the virus that made me the soldier I am.

The incubus stops. "You're not alone."

I touch my index finger to my mouth. Peering past him, I notice Hunter and Nadia dashing out the door and into the club, probably going to get Cian.

I rub my hand over the side of my neck. "I know. Now, get out of here before you get in trouble."

"I'm trying to help you. The council put out a warning about wraiths. It could possess you at any moment. Let me try to extract it." The incubus moves closer.

Stepping back, I hold up my hand again. "She's not what you think. She's alive."

The incubus' eyes widen. "Alive? You know her?"

"Yes." I keep my face expressionless. Callie's fear pulses through me, and I try my best to ignore it. It's getting harder and harder to separate her emotions from mine. I don't really know her, but now that I can feel her in my mind, I know one thing is sure—she's not evil.

"I didn't know there were any around. I've heard rumors about them but that's it. The council really does acquire the best people, don't they?" The incubus crosses his arms.

I try not to frown. "What are you talking about? You know about her kind?"

He raises his eyebrows. "If she is what I think she is, she's not a creature."

I kind of hate that I don't know what this guy knows. "She's not? Then what—"

He holds his hand up, cutting me off, and glances over his shoulder. "I'm guessing the council doesn't know about her."

I nod. "No one does, and I don't know if I want them to. What do you think she is?"

"What is he talking about, Mason? Should you even be talking to him?" I ignore Callie. I can't help it. I need the guy to keep talking.

"She's called a projector. She's basically a living ghost when she's without her body."

Of course a soul manipulator would know something about this, since we're dealing with Callie's escaped soul.

The door to the club swings open and music blasts in with Cian as Hunter and Nadia follow behind him. He storms closer, anger furrowing his brows, and I know Cian is seconds away from banning this incubus from ever coming to The Haven again.

I cut Cian off. "Everything is fine, Cian."

He points past me. "He's not on the list."

I walk backward in front of the troll. "I invited him."

He stops in his tracks. "You know him?"

"Yeah, everything's good. We were just leaving."

CALLIE

I stay safely in Mason's body. It's weird falling into step with him, like my soul is held in place with tape. Any sudden displaced movements will pop me out.

"You still here, Callie?" Mason thinks to me. This is one way to have a private conversation, I suppose.

"Not for long. Once we're out of here, I have to get home to my body. I don't want my parents to think I'm in a coma again." Worry sweeps through me. I'm not even sure how long I've been gone. I hope my body is okay.

"I think we need to talk. There's a lot about the world you don't know." Mason glances behind him to make sure the soul sucker is following us.

"You think? This soul sucker just tried to eat *me. If I didn't jump in his head and threaten him, he might have succeeded."*

"He's an incubus. If he really wanted to consume your life force, you would be gone already."

Dread settles in my core. Great. My threats weren't effective. I got lucky. I can't even imagine what would've happened to me if the soul sucker—Jax, as I recall—couldn't stop himself. What would've happened? Would I just not exist? The thought startles me. I need to get back to my body now. Leaving it at all was a huge mistake.

Mason steps into the stairwell.

"Bye, Mason."

"Callie, wait." His voice echoes against the concrete. "Don't go."

I propel myself down the stairs and through the door to the parking garage without stopping. As much as Mason wants me to stay or how much I want to figure out what's happening to me, I can't, not until I know my body is safe.

MASON

I don't feel any different when Callie jumps from my body and disappears through the door. The incubus strolls next to me when we exit into the parking garage. I don't have a lot of experience with his kind, but I know they're not ones to be messed with. Besides living on the life forces of others, they're parasitic in nature, making them hard to kill. If you kill an incubus, its rotting form secretes an irresistible smell that makes the killer want to consume the flesh. It then body jumps into its new host and continues on its merry way.

The council said it's not always the case, that most incubi don't kill to survive, and it's rare for them to be confronted and hurt. They'd have to seek it out. If I couldn't tell an incubus by its aura, I'd never know. Only those intent on harm are ever brought before the council.

"I'm parked over there." The incubus points at a white pickup truck under a light.

I crack my fingers, contemplating what to do now. "Can I catch a ride?" I came with Hunter, so it's not like I can tell the guy to follow me somewhere.

He hesitates before saying, "Yeah, sure."

"I swear I won't do anything funny. I'm an agent with the council. My job would be on the line if I do since I'm on mandatory leave." I regret saying the last line, but I want this dude to trust me. He should anyway, since I saved his ass from getting kicked out of the club.

He hits his key fob, and his alarm beeps off. "What for?"

Rolling up my sleeve, I show off the edge of my bandage. "Injured on the job." I get in the truck when he does and then say, "By a goblin trying to kidnap a human." I don't know why I say it. It's more of an afterthought, but I figured he'd ask.

"I don't know how or why you do what you do—"

"Mason." I offer my hand to him.

He shakes my hand. "Jax."

Jax starts the truck and reverses before navigating out of the parking garage. It's quiet for a minute, neither of us knowing exactly what to say. I'm not sure how much information I want to tell him about Callie. Her life might be in danger now. A ton of people would be interested in her ability if they were to find out—both good and bad people. That's just the way the world works.

After he turns out of the alleyway and onto the street, I peer out the windshield. "Will you tell me everything you know about projectors? I've never heard the term before."

He taps his fingers on the wheel. "I don't know much. I've heard of a succubus who was feeding on a life force of her lover. He suddenly jumped out of his body, but he didn't die. The succubus was distraught until he reconnected to his body and told her what he experienced. He described it as an out-of-body experience but soon mastered it."

I lean forward. "Where is he? Can I talk to him?"

He shakes his head. "He supposedly died."

Blood rushes from my face. "How?"

"Disappeared and never returned to his body. Without a soul, the body will eventually die without medical intervention."

If I knew where Callie lived, I'd ask Jax to drive me there

now. I have to warn her of the consequences. "You sure he died?"

Jax side glances me in his peripheral vision. "What else would he do without his body?"

I shrug. "You make a good point."

CALLIE

I stroll through my window and stand in the darkness of my room. My body rests on my bed, on top of the comforter, exactly where I left it. Hovering in front of my bed, I glance at my vanity mirror. It's strange not seeing my reflection. I wonder what it would be like to never see myself again.

My cell phone buzzes on my nightstand, and I glide into my bed and run my translucent fingers over my body. The sucking sensation pulls at my soul, and I lie down and let myself reconnect, starting with my hands, then my feet, legs, torso, and lastly my head.

I jerk upright and gasp.

My phone buzzes again, and I pick it up and scroll through five messages from Lily and one from Brendan.

I read Brendan's text first. *Stay away from Mason, please. He's dangerous.*

I stare at his words for a moment and then delete our train of text messages from the last few weeks.

I click on Lily's text message next. I reply with, *I'm back & OK.*

Lily responds the second after I hit send. *You sure?*

I snap a quick picture and send it. *Yeah. Tell U everything @school.*

U better. Mason called. Asked for UR #. Gave it. Sry.

Srsly?

Swore it was life or death.

I nearly drop my phone, trying to ask her what that means, but a text message from an unknown number pops up on my screen.

You make it home?

I know it's Mason without asking.

I consider ignoring the text, but I'm afraid he might call me, or worse, find out where I live. He did say he wanted to talk. I'm not sure I'm ready after today. I'm not sure I'll ever be.

I finally get the nerve to text him back. *Yeah. All good.*

Can I come over?

I frown and reply. *Definitely not.*

Please, don't project until we can talk.

I almost consider giving him my address so he can come over, but the soft hum from the living room TV warns me it's a terrible idea to invite a boy, especially Mason, over in the middle of the night.

K, I text back.

See you tomorrow.

With a sigh, I plug my phone into the charger without responding.

Today's events have left my head reeling, and I want nothing more than to relax and forget any of it happened. If I can't shut my mind off, I won't be able to sleep though I desperately want to. Maybe going ghostly means I don't have to sleep ever again since my body gets the rest without me.

But I really want to sleep.
It's the only escape I have now.

9

◦Fate◦

MASON

MR. AUGUSTINE POINTS at a stack of books. "Once you two put these away, you are free to relax." Sandy Augustine is a long time friend of Nadia's father, and the school librarian of Northern Bell. He's known about the creature world since he was a teenager but doesn't participate other than keeping an eye on all the students here.

It worked out for me, because he didn't know who I was, but he did say my last name was familiar. I won't put it past him figuring it out and telling Dmitri, but I'll deal with that when the time comes. I might even be able to convince him not to for Callie's sake.

"Sounds good, Mr. A," I say as I grab a stack of books.

Callie pulls a rolling cart over and helps me set them down before she organizes them into piles by section.

Mr. Augustine heads toward the wraparound counter in front of his office and leans on his elbows to read a book I can't see the title of.

I bump Callie's shoulder. "You haven't said one word to me today. Can we please talk?"

Focusing on organizing the stack without looking up at me, she says, "What if I don't want to?"

I grab a few books from the pile and set them aside. "You can't pretend nothing happened. What you can do, it's—"

"It's not a big deal," she says, cutting me off. "And I can pretend nothing happened if I want to. Maybe I won't ever body jump again. It's too dangerous, anyway."

I let out a breath. At least she recognizes the seriousness of the situation. "It's called projecting. You're a projector."

She grabs the pile of books I set aside and adds them to her organized stacks. "What does that even mean?"

I lean closer and whisper, "It means you're in a lot of danger if the wrong people find out."

Her back stiffens, and she curls her fingers around a book, turning them white at the knuckles. "How do I know you're not one of these wrong people, Mason?"

"I guess you don't. But, I'll be honest with you to hopefully gain your trust. You can ask me anything." I take a book and place it on the shelf.

She pushes the cart a few feet away. "Why were you following me? First the hospital and now my school. Are you even a senior?"

I roll my sleeve up to reveal my bandaged arm. "The hospital was a lucky coincidence for me. The man you saw me kill, well, he wasn't really a man. He nearly killed me with the venom in his talons. The people I work for have affiliations to that hospital. Finding Lily in the hallway outside your room helped me find your school. I was investigating you."

Her cheeks redden. "She told you where we went to school?"

"No, she mentioned Mr. Augustine. I just happen to have a friend who went here and knew him."

She puffs air through her lips and tosses a book back on the cart. "This is crazy, you know."

"You'll get used to it." The lie comes easy enough. No need to scare her just yet, but honestly, I grew up in this world. While things don't seem strange to me, I've never grown used to it. It makes me question everything.

From her pursed lips, it looks like she isn't buying it. "Do I even want to know why you were investigating me?"

I pick up the discarded book. "I wanted to help you. I thought you were being possessed and that your soul was a disgruntled ghost using your body."

"What?" She presses her fingers to her temples. "What have I gotten myself into?" She's not asking me. I've grown up in the world where monsters were real, so I forgot that it could be a lot to handle.

I reach out and touch her shoulder. She drops her hands and stares up at me, not flinching away from my touch. We gaze at each other in silence for a few moments, and then she blinks before turning back to our task.

I finish putting away the last few books. "Callie? You okay? I can help you figure things out if you want."

She draws her eyes back to mine. I could get distracted by their blue depths if I'm not careful. It's funny how different she seems to me now that I know for sure she's not a wraith. That she's a girl with a new ability, lost and confused, jumping directly into my world. Coincidence that she found me? Maybe. But I like to think it really was fate. My brother would laugh at me.

"What if I don't want to figure things out?" she asks, a pout puffing out her bottom lip. She runs her tongue across it, and I realize how intently I'm staring.

I twist my lips to the side. "Because if you don't, you'll leave yourself open to attacks, and you'll put your family—and Lily—in danger. You might not think projection is a big deal, but you can go anywhere, listen to anyone's thoughts, and basically go unnoticed by most. People kill for less."

Her bottom lip quivers. Damn do I want to touch it to make it stop. Tears shine in her eyes as my words sink in. She swipes her fingers under her eyes to stop them from falling, but it smears her makeup. The color leaves her face, and she tries to say something, but the words stay locked in her throat.

She teeters, her eyes rolling back into her head. Before she falls, I wrap my arms around her waist and pull her against me.

My fingers lock onto her sides, feeling the smoothness of her skin where my finger catches her shirt. I hold her up so she doesn't hit the ground, her feet dangling an inch from the floor. Looking over her shoulder, I cringe at the sight of her pale pink aura hovering in front of me.

Without warning—and I'm pretty sure without wanting to either—Callie projected from her body. In this moment, I know it's not going to be as easy for her to stop and never body jump again. From my knowledge, humans gifted with abilities can go forever without knowing until something triggers it. And then it controls them, reacting to something within them. If Alyssa, the only other naturally born gifted human can't control her visions, then I can't imagine Callie will so easily either. This simple fact is enough to get her killed.

CALLIE

No. No. No. This isn't happening. I did not just jump—project—from my body in the library. So many thoughts rush through my mind. I can't seem to focus on anything. It's all too much to take in. Why me? Why now? What did I do to deserve this?

Mason's words resonate with me. The fear he put in my head caused me to react the only way I knew how, which was to flee. I don't even know why this started happening. This is wrong on so many levels.

"Callie," Mason whispers. He clutches my body, his chin resting on my shoulder with my dark hair veiling his face. "You have to return before someone sees you. Please, it's going to be okay."

His eyes train on mine, and I reach out and run my translucent fingers across his cheek. I wonder how much of me he can see. I never thought to ask him about himself apart from how he found me. He talks about all these dangerous people—monsters—but what if he's one of them, too? I still haven't found out if he was a soul sucker like the guy from the club. But I doubt it. *Ugh! Pull it together.*

Leaning forward, I study Mason's worried eyes. He cradles me against him like he's afraid putting me down would leave my body in danger. The fear I carry of him lessens as he pleads for me to return to my body. "You can do it, Callie. Just reconnect."

The anxiety about projecting in public makes it harder to return. The pull I feel when I'm near my body is there, but it doesn't attach to me right away. After a few tries, ignoring the fear of someone spotting me in Mason's arms the best I can, I manage to reconnect my feet and legs.

"Almost there," Mason whispers.

The world shifts, and a heavy weight crushes my soul. My vision turns dark as I pull myself together. Warmth rushes through my veins, feeling the grip of Mason's hands on my waist, his breath tickling my ear from his head on my shoulder.

The scent of his lavender laundry soap engulfs me. I bury my face into the nape of his neck, trying to reel in my embarrassment. I'm mortified that I projected, and that Mason was nice enough to stop me from spilling to the floor, but his close proximity stirs something within me I've been trying so hard to ignore about Mason. I'm not terrified of him anymore, not even a little. All I can think about is how he's still hugging me and how safe I feel knowing he's right here.

I finally get the nerve to lean my head away. Mason's chocolaty eyes don't hold the same fierce intensity capable of burning my soul in this moment. Quite the opposite, actually. A huge smile crosses his face, like everything about this moment is hilarious, and I cringe, managing to pull myself away. His silence says absolutely nothing about what he's thinking, but he's the most relaxed I've seen him. And that smirk lighting his face looks hot on him, a million times better than the brooding glare constantly dominating his expression.

"Callie? Mason? What's going on?" Mr. Augustine's voice cuts the moment short.

I scramble away from Mason, putting more space between us. "Sorry, Mr. Augustine. I tripped."

His bushy eyebrows pinch together as he swipes a purple handkerchief over his gleaming, bald head. "You feeling okay?"

"Yeah, I'm great." My words sound forced, high-pitched, panicky even.

Mason gazes at me, a grin still tugging at the side of his mouth. "Yeah, great," he says, his eyes still not wavering, like he's looking through my skin to all my blood and guts, and even that still doesn't faze him.

And now, I realize I'm smiling back like an idiot. Who knew smiles were really contagious? All I know is if I don't force myself to look away, I'm never going to be able to stop my racing heart.

"Great," I repeat again, wishing I could get my mouth to

say something else before it turns into the last thing I say as I truly die of embarrassment. What is wrong with me? Mason's entire world screams danger, and here I am, covering my ears, ignoring my good sense that says to stop smiling back and inviting Mason into my life.

Mr. Augustine clasps his hands together. "Okay, then. Great."

Ugh. I strut past the two of them and head to the wraparound table where I keep my tote bag. Leaving is my best option if I ever want to escape my newfound greatness. Scooping up my belongings, I head toward the door. The bell rings seconds before I reach it, and when I stumble into the cold basement hallway, footsteps sound behind me.

"Callie, wait," Mason calls.

I freeze in my tracks. How is it possible that I want to run to and away from Mason at once? He's the answer and cause of my problems. His dark eyes and irresistible dimples do nothing to help the battle between my heart and mind.

Spinning around, I face him, accidentally planting my hands against his chest. "What's happening to me? I couldn't even control it." I was so close to being discovered by Mr. Augustine.

Mason reaches up and grabs my shaking hands in his, holding them between his palms like he knows I'm going to run away. "I'm sorry. I didn't mean to upset you. I should've been more cautious."

"You think? All I want to do is get out of here." I yank away and adjust my tote bag higher on my shoulder.

"Then let's go. I know a place you'll be safe."

"I—I don't know, Mason. I'm just—I'm freaking out. I barely know you, and what I do know is—"

He steps forward. "Let me show you who I am. I know we didn't exactly start on the best of terms, but it was a misunderstanding. If you only knew what I know, you'd get it. I want to help you if you let me."

I hesitate. Do I want to risk leaving with him? He does know so many things that I don't, but a part of me doesn't want to know anything, especially after what happened in the club. And how do I even know I can trust him? He followed me to my school. *He saved you from the soul sucker.* He said he was investigating me. *He thought you were being possessed.* Every question I have regarding him has an explanation, but do I want to trust him?

He holds out his hand. "I'll get you home when your parents expect you. I promise."

I run my fingers through my messy hair before I take his warm hand. "Fine, but I'm telling Lily where I'm going. I want the address and everything."

He smirks. "Deal."

MASON

Callie pulls her gray and pink sweater off and tosses it on my couch. I kick a pair of work boots under my coffee table and pick up a few empty glasses, moving them to my small open kitchen. I wasn't exactly prepared for guests, and I don't want Callie to think I'm a slob. I'm just never really home except to sleep.

Since the council prefers me to be near the city, they rent me an apartment on the other side of the river, so I'm near but not downtown. Only my mom has ever been here, but I try not to think about a girl being in my apartment as a big deal. Callie barely even trusts me. It'd take a lot more than a clean apartment to impress her anyway. Though I want to.

"You live alone?" Callie asks, peering around.

I scoop up a few discarded jackets and hide my weaponry belt under my computer desk. "Yeah."

"How old are you, anyway?" She sits down on my couch and rests her hands in her lap.

"I'll be eighteen in a few months." Sitting down next to her, I reach toward my small stereo on the side table and turn on music to drown out the silence.

"That surprises me." Her gaze flicks from my knees to my face as she tries to determine if I'm telling the truth.

"Me, too. It's easy to forget when you're in my line of work."

After staring into my eyes long enough to make me shift uneasily on the couch, she leans back, satisfied by my answer. "So, you know a lot about me, and that doesn't make me feel all that great."

I press my lips together, holding back my smile, because she swore she was feeling a little too great earlier in the library. I'm also surprised she doesn't immediately ask about what I do. Maybe she figures she knows from the little I've said.

She tilts her head in my direction, her dark hair cascading over her shoulder. "Now, I want to know more about you before we get into anything else. Are you a soul sucker like the guy from the club? Is that why you can see me? You *can* see my soul, right?"

My forehead creases. "Most definitely, and no I'm not an incubus. I'm human—well, I'm a genetically altered human. I volunteered to be part of an experiment to be a better soldier, and luckily for me, it worked. Things have changed a lot since then, though. I police the creature world instead of fight against it."

Callie lifts an eyebrow, scrunching her nose. "Why on earth would you volunteer to do something like that? Who would want to do that?"

People who want to make their moms proud and who want to do great things with their lives, that's who. I scratch the back of my head, trying not to take her question as an insult. "It was an offer I couldn't refuse," I say. "When you're aware of the truth about the world, it leaves you open to a lot of bad things. I needed to protect myself, and risking my life to be in the position I am now was totally worth it at the time." It's not the exact reason, but it's the reason I like to think about now.

I spent my life following orders and doing everything I could to make my mom proud. All that time, I had believed in her lies about the creature world being a place out to destroy humanity. But that's not what it really was. I was a dangerous soldier, willing to blindly do anything I was asked in the name of saving the human world, but as it turned out, my mom had been going about it all wrong. I've killed innocent creatures out of fear, something that'll haunt me for the rest of my life. I'm embarrassed about how little I did to discover the truth. That's changed, though. I'm not that person anymore. But how am I supposed to tell Callie all this? I'm ashamed of my past that led me to this point.

Callie remains silent as she thinks about what I've said. Finally, she says, "Do you think it's worth it now?"

Good question. Do I? Maybe not for the same reason. "Yes, because if I hadn't been altered, I'd have never seen you." *Smooth, Mase.* I can't help that it's true, but damn does it sound like a stupid pickup line. There's something about Callie, about seeing her soul. It's done something to me. She's already beautiful, but her soul? Incredible.

She doesn't laugh and call me out for being lame. Instead, her gaze lingers on me. I don't meet her mesmerizing sky blue eyes. She's waiting expectantly for me to continue, but I'm not sure what to say now. It's easy to tell her about our world, but she won't truly understand it unless I show her. But am I willing to risk putting an innocent person in danger?

She shifts on the couch and tucks her legs under her. "Thanks for letting me come here. My parents are already worried enough about me. I'm afraid to tell them, too. They wouldn't believe me."

Maybe it was the look on my face or the weight of my words, but thankfully Callie's decided to change the subject. I don't know how many more personal questions I could answer. Want to know how to spot an elf? I'm your guy. Want to know why I thought risking death for a special ability that makes me hated among creatures was a good idea? Go ask someone else.

"It's better if you don't tell anyone. This world isn't safe for humans who don't know how to handle themselves. While most creatures want to live a normal life amid humans, some don't feel the same. They think they're above them and use them."

Her mouth drops open as horror crosses her face. "I've already told Lily."

I sigh. "I can fix that."

"How?"

"I know someone who can manipulate her memories. It wouldn't hurt her, but it'd make sure she doesn't remember what you can do and what you told her."

"Are you kidding me? No. She's my best friend, and I'm not letting you do that to her."

"Even if letting her know puts her in danger?"

"She's not in danger yet, is she? I won't let you do it. By fixing it, I thought you meant doing something that would protect her, not mess with her head."

"It will protect her."

Annoyance furrows her brows as she pushes to her feet. I grab her hand, but she yanks it away and places her hands on her hips. The way she looks at me with narrowed eyes and a tight mouth, I can't help but shrink back. I've faced a lot of scary creatures, but never a girl who's standing up for her best friend.

I raise my hands up in defeat. In the end, it might not be up to me and Callie. No way I'm telling her that, though. "Fine, but maybe you should ask Lily first. It's her life, you know."

"And she's a part of *my* life."

Leaning back and crossing my arms, I stare at the ceiling. I can't argue with her. She's more stubborn than I am.

The sound of the doorbell jerks my attention from the unknown stain on my ceiling. I wasn't expecting anyone to stop by. It's the reason I brought Callie here.

Holding my index finger to my lips, I point to my bedroom door. Callie crosses the room without asking a single question like I expect, and she leaves my bedroom door open. I'd do the same thing if I was in her position.

I shuffle to the door and peer through the peephole. A hazel eye greets me as my mom stands on my small porch. Without opening the door, I watch her step back. Her brown hair, a little lighter than mine, blows in the spring breeze. She's not wearing her glasses.

I contemplate ignoring her. So what if my car's out front? I could be sleeping. Plus, she can't stand outside forever. I'm sure she has a body guard waiting in the car. While she's not on the Creature Council, she manages my division with my boss, Dmitri, and wouldn't dare risk going out alone. Enemies come with the job. We fight to keep creatures under control. The council is the governing body of the community across all the United States.

When she knocks again, I relent and crack open the door. "Hey, Mom. I'm surprised to see you here."

She peers past me into my apartment when I don't immediately let her in. "Is this a bad time? I wanted to check up on you."

Not wanting her to think I'm hiding something, I open the door all the way and invite her in. She peers around my small apartment, her eyes trailing over the clutter I don't bother to organize. I motion for her to sit down on the couch and then swear to myself when I spot Callie's sweater on the cushion.

Before I can hide it, my mom holds it up. She stares at it for a second and then lays it on the arm of the couch. Without taking her eyes off it, she eases onto the couch, crossing her legs at her ankles. I force myself to sit next to her even though I can see the hundred questions crowding her head. We've—well, I've—never kept many secrets, but I don't want to tell her about Callie. She'd go directly to the council.

"It's Nadia's," I say without thinking about it. My mom doesn't know that Nadia and Hunter have never been here, and it's better than telling her it's Kat's, my partner's, sweater since Kat would call me out on it. Kat's also probably pissed off at me for getting hurt. It's why I haven't heard from her. She is queen of the silent treatment.

My mom nods, accepting my response. "So, how are you feeling? Goblin venom does a number on its victims. You were lucky."

Peeling up part of the bandage, I show the healing wound to my mom. She'd ask to see it anyway since she's a doctor. "I'm fine. Bored. Dr. Harvey shouldn't have put me on leave. I have work to do." I don't care about being on leave anymore, but my mom expects me to complain. It's what I would've done if Callie hadn't distracted me.

She grimaces as she looks at my arm. "You have a capable

team. They can handle the work. I want you to rest."

I sigh. "I am resting."

"Good. Now for the reason I'm here." She pulls a notepad from her purse and flips a few pages. "Cian informed us of some trouble you experienced at The Haven. First some shifters and then an incubus. I wanted to let you know I'm having Nate and Mira follow up with them."

"That's not necessary," I say, afraid Mira and Nate might get Callie's name out of Brendan and realize I'm not investigating a creature family new to this area like I told Mira to get her to use her enchantress abilities to get me into Northern Bell. I shift on the couch and glance at my open bedroom door. Without having to see Callie, I know she's listening. I wish I would've shut the door myself. "It was a misunderstanding. I don't need you fighting my battles, either."

"I'm not fighting your battles. A shifter attacked you. Who's to say he wouldn't attack a normal human?"

"Brendan is just a kid. He didn't attack me because of who I was." I regret saying his name out loud.

Callie gasps from my room, drawing my mom's attention to my room. "Who's here, Mason?"

I knew this was coming. "No one."

"I'm not stupid, Mason. Whoever is in there, please come out." *Damn it.* My mom leans closer, anger edging her words as she whispers, "You're lucky I didn't say anything confidential."

Ignoring my mom's quip, I turn my gaze to Callie as she hovers in the doorway to my room, holding herself. She half smiles at my mom with worry lining her eyes, and then she meanders forward but keeps her distance between us.

Damn, this is awkward. I shouldn't have answered the door. Now, Callie has to face the craziness that is my mom.

"Hi, Mrs. Sullivan," Callie says. Addressing her as Mrs. instead of doctor is enough to let my mom know that I told Callie nothing about her. She turns to me without missing a beat. She looks ready to run out the door, and I don't blame her, though I really want her to stay. "I should get going, Mason. I have a ride meeting me down the street, so you don't have to take me."

With another small smile, she crosses the room to the door and exits. As much as I want to chase after her, I don't. I can't. Fortunately, my mom doesn't move to go after her either. She knows better than to do something absurd, but her hard gaze reminds me of all the times she's threatened to ground me or feed me to the river monsters when I was especially rebellious.

I stand up, ready to leave if she starts threatening me like a child. This is my apartment, and I can have whoever I want over. I don't tell her that, though. I'm not a glutton for punishment or arguing with the woman who still manages to control my life by controlling my job.

"Callie's just a friend."

"How do you know her? What is she? How much does she know about you and the council?" Question after question flies from my mom's mouth, and I take a second to figure out how to answer them the best I can to satisfy her curiosity.

Pulling my phone from my pocket, I look at the time even though I have nowhere to go. I bring my gaze back to my mom's. "I met her at The Haven. She's Brendan's ex-girlfriend." It's partially a lie, but I'm not telling her about how I technically met her soul during my fight with the goblin. Some things my mom doesn't need to know.

"Oh." My mom's eyes soften, and she forgets all her other questions. "I can see why Brendan would be angry with you."

I laugh. "She's only a friend, Mom."

"She's pretty." My mom grabs Callie's sweater and hands it to me. "She left this. You should go after her."

This is a side of my mom I've never seen before. She looks almost smug now that she thinks I might possibly like Callie.

Twisting the sweater between my fingers, I turn toward the door. This is my chance to get away without a million more questions, and I have to jump at the opportunity.

I kiss her cheek and head to the door. "Don't forget to lock up," I say, leaving her in my apartment as I race out the door to find Callie.

I'm sure finding out her ex-boyfriend isn't human has Callie's thoughts flying. I just hope she doesn't accidentally project from her body. That's the last thing she needs. It's the last thing I need.

10

∽The Whole Creature Experience∽

CALLIE

I RUSH DOWN the street, keeping my gaze glued to the ground. My cheeks freeze with tears in the cool, spring air. With every step, my heartbeat pounds faster and faster until it's beating so hard it might smash through my chest and onto the ground.

Mason's surprise at his mom showing up at the door couldn't have been more obvious—and for the first time ever, I think I glimpsed fear in his wide eyes. I thought for sure I was in trouble—not for being with Mason but for just existing. He never said he worked for his mom and for one reason or another, he doesn't think anyone should know about me. Now I'm freaking the hell out.

My cell phone rings, and I answer immediately. "You're taking forever. How close are you?"

Music hums through the line. "What's your cross street?" Lily asks.

"Marsopa Avenue. Hurry, I'm scared." I pick up my pace to the corner. If I didn't think running and screaming would draw attention, I'd be doing just that.

Leaning against an elm tree on the corner, I take in slow breaths to calm my nerves. I peer around the quiet neighborhood, expecting hideous monsters to come out at any second, but nothing happens. Not a single car drives past me.

"Almost there. Hang tight." The line clicks off, and I shove my phone into my pocket.

Shivering in the chilly air, I rub my hands over my arms. I turn my gaze from the road to the sidewalk and startle at the figure nearby. Mason strolls closer, only a few feet away. I never even heard him coming. I'd be a goner if there were monsters around.

He holds out my sweater. "You forgot this."

I force a smile while I slide it on, my teeth chattering from more than the cold. "Wasn't expecting to have to leave so quickly or else I would've kept it on."

He touches my arms, running his fingers up and down my sleeves as I still shiver. "Sorry about that. Everything is okay, though. You don't have to worry about my mom."

"You told her about me?"

He doesn't drop his hands, holding me a foot away. "No, but she doesn't suspect anything."

"What'll happen if she does?"

"She won't."

"Mason..." I can't stop the sinking feeling in my stomach from making me want to fold up and disappear. He doesn't have to say it, but I know I'd be in trouble if his mom were to find out. Maybe she'll have the same reaction as the soul sucker did. What if she sees me as a threat?

A horn beeps, drawing my attention to Lily's car as she drives closer. She pulls her Camry to the curb and unlocks the doors. I glance from her to Mason, and then I pull the door open and slide into the passenger's seat.

Without missing a beat, Mason hops into the backseat, surprising me. Lily shrugs and turns around in her seat.

She smirks. "What are you doing?"

"Making sure you two get home safely," he says.

I peek at Mason over my shoulder, trying my best to hide my smile. Now that I'm in the car and away from Mason's mom, I'm starting to relax. "Lily wasn't taking me home."

"I'm not?"

I smack her leg. "No, we're going to the city."

Mason's smile melts into a frown. "You can't be serious."

As Lily pulls from the curb, she laughs. "Oh, she's always serious. Lead the way, Callie."

"Actually, Mason, you lead the way. I want to go to that club if it's open," I say. "I think I'm freaking out because I feel like I don't know anything. And you owe me." I don't know where my sudden courage comes from, but I'm glad it's arrived to pull me from the dark recesses of uncertainty my mind has created. "If you're going to follow me around, I might as well take advantage of you."

He rubs his hand over his eyes, probably wishing that taking me deeper into this world he claims is so dangerous wasn't how I'd want to take advantage of him. "You want to take Lily there? Even after what almost happened to you? Are you insane? If you want to learn more, we can do it right from the car."

"The car? Where's the fun in that? I like Callie's idea and since I'm driving..."

I twist in the seat. "Hanging out in your room when your mom showed up scared me more. The club is like a kid's play place after experiencing that."

He laughs, his eyes lighting up with a smile that makes me smile. "She really is that bad, huh? I do kind of owe you for that."

"And for you know what," I say. Without having to mention Brendan's name, Mason gets what I'm insinuating. I'm not ready to tell Lily yet, but only because I don't even know what any of it means or what could happen if I do.

"What?" Lily asks.

He frowns, shaking his head. Ignoring her, he says, "I don't know if I can get you in."

I stare at him in the mirror, but he doesn't meet my gaze. "Don't lie. You're someone important with the creatures."

"What kind of creatures?" Lily asks, forcing herself into the conversation like this is something we talk about on a normal basis. She's always been great at going with the flow of things. Apart from being outgoing, she also loves experiencing new things. It helps that she's pretty fearless and even the scariest movies make her laugh.

I shrug. "Mason can fill us in."

MASON

This is the worst idea ever. I could refuse to take them to The Haven, but I know that even if I didn't, Callie would try to take Lily by herself. She's brave and crazy and stubborn—and that's what I've learned about her from the last few days—and knowing Cian, he wouldn't ask any questions if she dropped my name.

"Turn right into the alley. The entrance to the parking structure is past the dumpster." I stick my arm in between the seats and point. "Roll down your window for the security guard."

Lily slows to a stop and opens her window. "Hi there," she says to the security guard.

I roll down the back window as well, poking my head out. "Hey, Nigel. Put this car on the guest roster."

The security guard nods and writes Lily's license plate into his log. "Take spot 4A. It's the first one on level four."

Lily beams at me in the rearview mirror worsening the anxiety tightening my nerves. I'm not scared to take them in, but their excitement about this overwhelms me. Clearly, they don't understand the dangers of coming here. Sure, I can protect them now, but I can't always be around.

"Thank you, Nigel," Lily says to the security guard. Her

sweet voice puts a smile on his face, and he waves her forward.

The parking lot lacks life this time of day. It's why I didn't try harder to persuade Callie to change her mind, knowing she probably wouldn't anyway. Waiting until she wore me down with her smile would have put us into the night crowd. Most creatures work normal nine to five jobs and won't be showing up until after dinner time, and those evening goers get rowdier, more aggressive. As of now, I doubt anyone will be a threat that I can't handle.

Lily parks the car, but neither she nor Callie rushes to get out. They both swivel in their seats to look at me like I'm supposed to tell them what to do next. Callie bats her long lashes at me, and it's hard to resist her now that she's not constantly doubting me or giving me a hard time. She's also smiling more. A beautiful smile, one that I think—at least I hope—is just for me.

"Well, you going to show me a good time?" she asks, biting on her bottom lip with a grin. Now I can't stop staring at her mouth, how perfect her smile is, the way the bridge of her nose scrunches and her blue eyes sparkle, how she stares at me like she enjoys me being around instead of thinking I'm a creep who showed up at her school. God, and now I'm starting to get nervous. Bringing her here isn't my idea of a good time, but I'm going to try my best to see that she has one.

I shrug at her question a little late, steeling myself from her flirtation. Distractions are dangerous as hell walking into a creature haven with two humans, and the last thing I need is to get swept up in her smile the whole time. She's free to have fun.

Me? I can't risk that.

Leaning forward, I say, "Cian, the owner of The Haven, is a troll. He can be possessive if you let him, but he's harmless. He's been running this safe spot for creatures since before we were born. If you act nervous, he might not let you in, so act like you belong."

Callie squeezes Lily's hand. "I won't let anything happen to us, okay?"

I clear my throat, trying not to smirk. Confidence looks sexy on her, but that same confidence might falter the moment she comes face-to-face with an ogre or something not hiding behind a human façade. "It's kind of my job to protect innocent people, so you're good to go with me."

Lily pushes her door open. "Perfect, I might actually live to see tomorrow with you guys. Now, let's go. I'm ready to dance."

CALLIE

"You meeting your brother here, Mason?" A man with a dark beard and shorter than five feet stands from the stool he perches on. He rolls up the sleeves of his moss green, button-up shirt. "I didn't think you'd be back so soon."

Mason shakes the man's hand. "Not a lot to do on leave." He turns to me and Lily. "Cian, I want you to meet my friends, Callie and Lily."

Smiling, I offer my hand to the troll, but he just stares at it, making me all sorts of uncomfortable. You'd think my hand was disgusting or something. Awkwardly, I shift and drop my arm back to my side while flicking my gaze to Lily.

"You shouldn't have brought them here," Cian says to Mason, ignoring us. "Outsiders make the patrons nervous. You know that."

"They're not outsiders. They're with me, and we're here to have some fun if that's okay with you." He doesn't sound so convincing. It's almost as if he wants the troll to turn us away.

Cian's eyes soften, especially when he turns to study us for a moment. "You two need to be careful, you hear? If there's any trouble, you both have to leave even if you don't start it. Creatures come here to be themselves. This is their sanctuary."

I nod. "I understand."

Cian opens the door to the club, and music swirls around us. Lily sways to the beat before we even enter. Her lighthearted excitement is contagious, because it melts the serious expression right off Cian's face. But that's Lily for you. Her energy and charm can change the attitude of the grumpiest person.

Leaning down, she kisses his cheek. "Thank you. This place is amazing!"

I grin at her. "We're not even inside yet."

She waves her hand at the dance floor. "I don't have to be to know."

We leave Cian laughing in the hall and enter the club. Mason leads the way through the half-empty dance floor, the music and lights almost identical to the night I came. The small crowd of dancers parts as we head to the VIP lounge. A few people stare at us, sending a shiver through me. I automatically reach for Mason, linking my fingers with his to squeeze his hand. He meets my eyes, his head tilting slightly, and then he surprises me with a smile. He spins me once on the dance floor, and I full on giggle. I never thought he'd loosen up, let alone dance me through the small crowd of creatures I wish I could project into to hear exactly what they're thinking with all their obvious stares. Mason ignores the looks, as does Lily, and I train my gaze on the colorful lights flickering across the floor.

We reach the door to the VIP lounge and Mason holds it open. The place is empty apart from a couple sitting at a booth in the corner. They ignore us as we make our way to a bar-height table with three barstools. A server with blue spiky hair and a nose piercing saunters into the room and stops in front of us. Her hands sparkle with what looks like body glitter, but I'm not so sure that's what it is. She presses her palms on the black table, sending the sparkling powder into the air.

"Anything to drink?" she asks.

Mason leans on his elbows. "Surprise us, Maddie."

The server raises an eyebrow, grinning at Mason like they're longtime friends. "Trying to show off, I see." She turns to me. "Don't let this guy fool you. He's not much of a risk taker. He must really like one of you."

Lily tips her head back and releases a loud laugh, reminding me of our conversation about Mason liking me.

Mason leans on his elbows, a faint rosiness sweeping across his face. "Just trying to give my friends the whole creature experience."

Lily kicks me under the table, and I realize just how intently I'm staring at him. I can't help it, though. Under all the brooding, I-must-save-the-world, everyone-is-out-to-hurt-you,

you-are-asking-for-trouble serious face, he's pretty cute. Hot.

Maddie catches me staring as well and winks. "If you want to give them a real creature experience, let me dust them."

If that's not the strangest thing I've ever heard, I don't know what is. I tilt my head to the side. "Dust us with what?"

Straightening her back, Maddie lifts her hands from the table, leaving behind two glittery handprints. She opens her palms to me and blows the glitter dust at me without warning. Fear widens my eyes, and I'm afraid she just blew some sort of drug in my face. A tingling sensation crawls over my skin and down my neck and then to my chest. *Oh, my God.*

Confusion courses through my mind as I try to open my mouth. I'm frozen, not even able to blink. The only thing still in action is my racing heart, and I consider jumping out of my body at this very second to get away.

"Whoa!" Lily hops from her seat and shakes my shoulders. "What have you done to her?"

A scream burns in my throat. I concentrate on moving my fingers, but it doesn't work. This is the worst feeling in the world, not being able to move. Shifting my eyes to Mason, which fortunately still move, I expect him to yell at Maddie, but he doesn't.

Slowly reaching out his hand, he brushes the hair hanging in my eyes away from my face. It's like he wants me to feel this way. Anger sneaks up on me, and the moment I figure out how to escape, he's going to get an earful. "It's only a little pixie dust," he says. "Relax."

Pixie dust? Maddie's a pixie? The silliness of what he said

helps slow my heartbeat down. Mason did promise he wouldn't let anything or anyone hurt us, so this is only temporary. Being frozen in place is scary at first but now I'm just annoyed.

"Oh, me next!" Lily pokes my nose while laughing. The only thing I can do is glare, and I'm not even sure I'm doing that.

Maddie laughs, opens her hand to me again, and blows more dust in my face. This time, a cloud of green glitter engulfs me. The tingling sensation disappears, and I slouch forward, falling into the table.

"Ugh!" It's the only reaction I have to getting frozen in place by a strange glitter cloud. If I say what's really on my mind, I'm sure it'll cause some trouble, and I don't want any-body to think I don't belong here. It was a joke. Mason was right. I need to relax. "That was so weird."

"For a second, I thought you were going to attack me," Maddie says.

I totally was. "You surprised me is all," I say instead.

A smirk plays on Mason's lips as he reaches across the small table and rests his hand on mine. His dark eyes hold my gaze, and it feels like he's staring into my soul again. "You have to be prepared for anything in this world." I hope this doesn't turn into what I'm starting to think will be a typical Mason move, trying to teach me a lesson.

Maddie flicks Mason's arm. "Really, Mase? Don't scare them. We're a harmless bunch."

Lily stands quietly with a smile playing on her lips. Every-thing about this situation amuses her. I don't think Mason could scare her even if he tried. It's clear with how she bounces on her feet next to Maddie, practically ready to shake her to get her to throw pixie dust on her next. Fear is the last thing on her mind.

"You don't see what I see, Maddie." Mason's lips tilt downward, his expression turning serious again. I want to touch his shoulder and tell him he is the one who needs to relax now.

"And maybe they won't either." Maddie glances at the door as the conversation takes a somber turn. "I'll be back with a few things." Opening her palm to Lily, she blows a cloud of glitter on her. "Don't go anywhere."

Lily freezes mid-laugh. It's a lot more hilarious when you're not the one frozen in place. I laugh, tilting my head back, and touch her nose like she did to me. Her eyes remain happy and excited. She's picture perfect, frozen in time, and I tug my phone from my pocket and snap a photo.

Mason frowns while leaning his elbow on the table. It wipes the smile from my face.

I lean closer to him. "Take your own advice and relax. We're here for some fun."

His shoulders droop, looking defeated now that Maddie left after pixie dusting Lily. "No, you're here for fun. I'm here to protect you."

MASON

It took everything in me not to yell at Maddie for dusting Callie without warning. For a minute, I thought she'd project right out of her body, but when she didn't, I had hoped she'd learn a lesson about how fast something can happen. It didn't work, though. She managed to let it roll off her shoulders and keep on smiling with Lily, who leaves me uneasy with how innocent and eager she is acting about all this.

"I never asked for your protection, Mason." Callie crosses her arms. She glances at Lily. "Look at her. She thinks this is amazing. Are you afraid we'll tell someone?"

The thought didn't cross my mind until now. I've never been concerned about humans discovering the creature world, because the council keeps everything in check, but now I wonder. I barely know them. The council would intervene if they thought either would jeopardize the community, and in that case, if the council didn't learn about Callie's ability, I'd never get to see her again. And if they did find out, she'd never get to see Lily again, and probably not her family, either.

"No," I say, even though it's not what I'm thinking. "I'm afraid you'll trust someone you shouldn't."

"Are you saying we shouldn't trust Maddie?" Callie flicks her gaze to the door.

"You shouldn't trust people you don't know. That's common sense."

"So, I shouldn't trust you?"

Please, keep trusting me. "Maybe." I want Callie to trust me, I do, but it's important for her to realize that no matter how friendly a person is, they could have hidden motives. She doesn't understand how desirable her ability is. How despised it could be.

Callie's serious blue eyes hold my gaze. Apart from the low hum of the music through the wall, the hard reality of everything settles between us, destroying the mood. The only other people, an elf couple, get up and stroll back into the club. Casting the same doubt in Callie, the doubt that had once been instilled in me by my mom, is one way to kill a good time.

A few uncomfortable minutes of silence later, Maddie opens the door and saunters in with a tray of drinks, lessening the awkwardness boiling between Callie and me. Lily remains smiling in place, but her brown eyes now shine with concern.

Callie hops up and turns to Maddie. "Release her, please."

Opening her hand, Maddie blows her pixie dust over Lily, and she drops to the floor. I don't get up to help Callie lift her friend, and I don't move when Callie tugs Lily past Maddie toward the door. I need to think things through for a few minutes without them clouding my judgment.

With an uneasy smile, Maddie sets the tray of crystal goblets on the table in front of me. "Did I ruin your date?"

Yes. "No, don't worry about it, Maddie. It's not even a date anyway."

She turns toward the door. "Anything else, Mase?"

"Keep an eye on them, will you?" I ask.

She nods. "That'll cost extra."

I pull out my wallet and hand her three twenty dollar bills. "Dust them if they try to leave."

Maddie winks. "You got it."

11

~Too Much Trouble~

CALLIE

"WE'RE NOT LEAVING, are we?" Lily yells in my ear.

I strain to hear her over the music. "That was the plan."

She grimaces, her brown eyes gleaming with disappointment, and a frown crosses over my own lips. Straightening my shoulders, I peer around for a moment before stopping at the edge of the dance floor. I refuse to let Mason get under my skin. He can't possibly be right about not trusting anyone in this world. It's like he's trying to push me to the fringes, but my ability is drawing me to the center of everything. He can control me as much as I can control my ability, which isn't saying a lot.

He'll be sorely disappointed when he realizes it.

Lily grabs my hand and spins me in a circle. "It's not the plan anymore."

I give in to her smile. We didn't come all this way to sit in an empty room for a few minutes before running away like we don't belong. I belong here as much as any of these people do.

Lily dances around me, and I sway my hips to the rhythm of the music. The near empty dance floor doesn't stop us from acting like no one's watching. Actually, I can feel a dozen pairs of eyes on us. It's thrilling, being the center of attention, and nice that it's not because a jerk is about to break up with me.

A guy a year or two older than us slides up behind Lily and wraps his arms around her waist. He whispers something into her ear, and she tilts her head back, giggling. I spin, glancing at the small crowd as I dance. I meet the eyes of the soul sucker from last night before he turns his gaze away. He sits alone in a corner booth, now staring at his empty plate.

I dance closer to Lily and say, "I'll be back. If you get tired, I'll be at one of the booths."

The guy dancing with her smiles at me. "I'll take good care of your friend." Something about his words sends a shudder through me. I'm not so sure I want him taking care of her.

I touch Lily's hand and draw her closer to whisper, "Go to Mason if there's any trouble."

Lily nods while letting the guy twirl her away. I saunter across the dance floor to the soul sucker and slide in the booth across from him.

He shifts his eyes from the plate to peer at me in annoyance. "I'm not in the mood to make friends."

Friends? No. He's insane if he thinks I want to ignite a friendship with him. I came over here against my good senses to confront the boy who almost sucked my soul out of existence and then went after me. "Who said I want to be your friend? You tried to eat me."

Confusion puckers his brows and then his eyes widen for a split second. The color drains from his skin. Rubbing his hand over his faux hawk without really touching it, he slumps on the table. "I think I'd remember you. Now, please leave me alone. That kind of accusation could get me in serious trouble. The council has really come down on my kind, and I'm just trying to live my life."

The council? Mason spoke of them before. I think it's who he works for. Either way, it's not my problem. "Maybe you should be more careful then."

He lets out an exasperated breath, jerking his head up to peer at me more closely. His brows remain knitted together. He either doesn't recognize me or he can't see who I am in my skin. Either way, I know he saw my soul when I was projecting and thought I was a ghost. Maybe my soul looks differently when it's attached to my body. I've never thought about it. To me, I look like a transparent version of myself. Who knows what other people see.

I lean across the table. "You don't recognize me, do you?"

"Should I?"

"I guess you'd only know it was me if I didn't have my body."

His forehead wrinkles, his eyebrows shooting up with realization. "You're the projector." He shifts his gaze to search the room. "You shouldn't be here."

I turn to glance over my shoulder. Lily dances exactly where I left her. "People need to stop telling me what to do."

"Are you alone?" he asks.

I tilt my head back to Lily. She's the only girl on the dance floor. "That's my best friend. I left Mason sulking in the VIP lounge."

The soul sucker crinkles his nose. "You should tell your friend to come over here. The fairy she's with likes collecting trophies. If she's around him long enough, she won't be able to leave him."

"What is that supposed to mean?" Dread settles heavy in my stomach. The way he says it, it sounds like the fairy would hold Lily against her will.

He plays with his shirt sleeve. "There are two types of fairies. The ones who help humans and the ones who like to help themselves. Asher is the latter." He stops fidgeting. "He's proud of his irresistibility. Humans who find themselves attached to him get sick when they're away, almost like they're addicted."

I jump up before he finishes. The idea of some fairy guy charming my best friend into becoming obsessed to the point of addiction freaks me out. I don't know what I'd do if something were to happen to Lily because of me. *This world is a dangerous place for humans...*

Pushing Mason's words away, I head to the dance floor to grab Lily. I freeze on the sidelines, my heart slipping right from my chest to my feet. Lily's missing, and so is the fairy. Panic cascades over me in a freezing wave, and I cover my mouth to stop a scream from ripping free. I had only taken my eyes off Lily for a minute. She couldn't have gone far.

Fear cuts a deep wound into my heart, and it takes everything in me not to cry. Mason couldn't have been right about everything, could he? Everyone looks so innocent and normal. But obviously they're not or my best friend wouldn't have disappeared with a damn fairy to who knows where.

Spinning around, I search the room for signs of Lily. The place isn't that big. I should be able to spot her from where I'm standing. I clutch my knees and close my eyes. If there was a good time to project, now would be it. It's the only thing I know how to do that gives me infinite access anywhere I want. Without doing so, I may never find Lily. It's worth the risk of exposing myself.

Dizziness washes over me, and I concentrate on freeing myself from my body right in the middle of the club. Heavy hands latch onto my shoulders, breaking my concentration. I turn, expecting to see Mason, but it's the soul sucker. Mason broke his promise to protect us, and now Lily might pay for it. *You told him you didn't need his protection. You'll be lucky if he ever talks to you again.*

"You have to help me! She's gone." My voice quivers, panic threatening to consume me. I'm so stupid. Careless. I deserve whatever happens to me if Lily winds up some fairy addict.

His vivid green eyes lock with mine. "Okay, okay. Just don't project here. I see what you're doing, and it's a mistake."

"How else am I supposed to find Lily? She could be any-where." I close my eyes.

"She couldn't have gone far. It's not like Asher's going to open a door to the fairy world and drag Lily in."

What? "Are you kidding me? They have their own world?"

"Calm down. You're drawing attention. People are going to think I'm bothering you."

"Don't tell me to calm down, soul sucker." My low voice cuts through the music.

His hands loosen on my shoulders. "I'm trying to help you, *ghost girl.*"

"Just call me Callie." I ball my hands into fists while think-ing about what an inappropriate time this is for introductions, but he's right. He is trying to help me, and he obviously knows more than I do about crazy, girl collecting fairies.

"I'm Jax."

I knew his name, but I've been so stuck on what he does to survive, that I haven't really thought about it. I turn to face him. "Please, will you help me find her? I promise not to call you a soul sucker anymore, okay?"

He nods. "There's only one other exit besides the one guarded by Cian. It's through the kitchen."

I don't hesitate. Dashing away from Jax, I head toward the swinging door behind the bar. The bartender doesn't even glance my way as I thrust the door open and run into the kitch-en. I race past an old man stirring something in a pot on the stove, but he doesn't say anything either, just looks up once and continues cooking.

An exit sign glows over a door, and I push it open. Lily stands on the top step, making out with Asher, his hands tangling in her short blond hair. The door slams behind me, and they both pull away from each other. Lily smiles when she sees it's me, and Asher's eyes shift past me as the door opens again.

I twist to look at the door, expecting to see Jax. A cloud of silver dust rains over the three of us, blocking the view of the door. The tingling sensation grabs hold of me, and I stare with wide eyes as Maddie shakes her head, turns away, and leaves us frozen in the darkened stairwell.

MASON

"Just go out there and apologize," I say out loud. No matter how much I argue with myself, I can't force my legs to stand up. I hate admitting I might've gone a little overboard with the whole everyone is out to get you mentality. Trying to ruin Callie's perception of the creature world before she even has a chance to experience it wasn't my intention. It's just that I've never known anyone who couldn't take care of themselves. *Who says she can't?*

Music blares from behind me as someone opens the door, drawing my attention away from the condensation dripping from the goblets onto the table. I don't turn to look. It's been less than ten minutes, and if it's Callie, I don't want her to think I've been on the edge of my seat, waiting for her to come back, even if I was.

"Callie told me you were here. She ran off looking for her friend. I didn't want to get involved, so I figured I'd let you know her friend disappeared with Asher." Jax's voice cuts over the music.

Without thinking, I fly from the chair and push past him and onto the dance floor. I search the room, treating the situation like I do when asked to track down a creature for the council. Cian wouldn't have let them leave without me. Humans must be escorted in and out unless they take the other exit, which is highly possible since the cook won't stop anyone.

"Callie?" I call, swinging the kitchen door open.

Maddie runs into me, and I grab her arm before she topples over. Anger sweeps over her face for a split second until she realizes who I am, and then she points her thumb over her shoulder.

"I did what you asked, but this is it, Mason. I'm not a babysitter." Without another word, she waltzes past me and back into the club.

Relaxing a bit, I pause and look around the kitchen for what I need to take care of the pixie dust without Maddie's help. I snatch a couple bottled waters from an open case under the stainless steel counter and head toward the back door. Maddie promised me she'd dust Callie and Lily if they tried to leave, but she never promised to reverse it. If she were planning to, she'd have followed me back here. It takes hours for pixie dust to wear off, but fortunately I know a little secret.

A bare light bulb hanging from the ceiling lights the stairwell. Shadows cascade over the floor and walls as three figures stand frozen on the landing and first step. Callie's wide eyes shift at the sight of me. Strolling up to her, I stop a foot away and set the bottled water at my feet.

I cross my arms without attempting to release them. This might be my only chance to talk. "You're lucky I had Maddie keep an eye on you. This could've ended differently if I hadn't."

Callie stares at me, still frozen by the pixie dust. She'd probably have a few descriptive words to throw at me if she could, but I'm going to take the opportunity to force her to listen. It's tempting to toss her and Lily over my shoulders and leave. It'd cause a hell of a lot of suspicion if I were caught in the parking lot, though.

I stare behind Callie at Asher, who watches me in silence. Lily's back is facing me, but I have a clear view of the fairy. He's only a year older than I am and is well known in the creature community because he's the nephew of my boss' partner.

Asher moved into the city from the Creature Council's compound a few weeks ago and has already made a name for himself by revealing what he was to a human. She turned obsessed to the point where she was ill without him. Asher claims he didn't know the effect he'd have, and the council believed him. It took three different enchantresses to help the girl through withdrawals before they manipulated Asher out of her memories completely.

He swears he loved the girl, and he wasn't messing with her, but the council takes matters between creatures and humans seriously. Humans who get caught up in the creature world are always at risk of being hurt or worse. Bringing someone into this world isn't to be taken lightly. It's why I'm cautious with Callie. It's why I want her to be careful with Lily, too.

Pulling myself from my thoughts, I pick up a water bottle from the floor. I step forward and twist the cap off before I pour the water over Asher's head first. When the pixie dust washes away, he flies down a few stairs to put distance between us.

He holds up his hands. "I wasn't doing anything wrong."

I shift my gaze to Lily's back and then to Asher. "That's what you said with—what was her name?"

Asher's face reddens. "Leave Delilah out of this."

Guilt pings in my mind as I strike a nerve. I shouldn't feel bad for Asher, but his reaction kind of makes me think he was really telling the truth about loving the girl. Stories change the more they're told, so maybe I've only heard the twisted version.

"Sorry, man." I lean on my heels. "I just don't want anything happening to my friends."

"Maybe you shouldn't have brought them here." Asher climbs the steps. He touches Lily's arm. "Everyone here had their eyes on them. I should be the least of your worries."

I clench my hands into fists. "You're right. I've made a mistake."

"I'd suggest you watch your back and theirs, but I'm sure you already do." Without another word, Asher pushes past me and heads back into The Haven. I stare at Lily and Callie and wonder what I've gotten myself into and if I'll be able to get us out of it. Better to think about these things now before it's too late.

CALLIE

If I could reach out and slap Mason, I would. He just stares at me without attempting to release me from Maddie's pixie dust, probably enjoying the fact that I can't do anything. I'm sure the words, *I told you so*, are coming shortly.

He stands there, his forehead creasing, watching and thinking, waiting for me to perform a move I can't possibly make. After a minute of silence, he finally says, "You're not going to do anything stupid if I release you, right?"

You had better prepare yourself, Mason. You're in so much trouble for telling Maddie to do this, I think to myself because I can't open my mouth.

He waits another moment before bending down to grab another water bottle at his feet. Moving past me, he heads to Lily, who I can't see behind me. I listen as the water splashes on the concrete stairs. Lily gasps and sputters, now released from the pixie's magic. She shuffles in front of me, sending drops of water splashing on my legs but it's not enough to wash away the dust. Without saying anything, she leans her back on the wall near the door.

How Mason can go from cute and friendly to downright infuriating is beyond me. I want him to be cute, smiley Mason all the time. I wish I could tell him that. Heat crawls up my neck to my face, and I imagine hopping from my body to spite Mason. My ears pop before I have a second to think things through, and I find myself standing a few inches away from my body.

"Callie!" Lily screams.

I gaze into my blank eyes, fear creeping over me. The pixie dust still holds my body in place, and I look utterly terrifying. My dark hair veils part of my face, my lips hanging slightly

open. If I didn't know any better, I'd have thought I was looking into my dead eyes.

Mason presses his hand over Lily's mouth. "Shhh! Someone might hear you."

"So, what," Lily mumbles. "Look at her."

Oh, God. No, please don't look at me—at least not my
body. This is so embarrassing.

Mason stiffens. "Do you know what could happen to Callie if someone were to discover what she could do? There are
people out there who kidnap and kill for less. They'd use her to
spy on whoever they want. You'd never see your friend again."

Lily yanks Mason's hand away. "You're serious? I thought
you were being dramatic, trying to scare Callie to keep you
around."

Mason frowns. "Is that what you think? I want her to keep
me around because she likes me, not because she's scared without me."

If I could feel my heart, it'd be sliding into a puddle with
the rest of me on the floor. Mason's so hot and cold, I wasn't
sure if I was imagining something more when he smiled, or that
Lily was making it all up in her head.

Of course, why else go through all this trouble for me? At
least I hope it's because of that.

I glide closer and hover a few inches from Mason. He
reaches out and runs his hand over my ghostly form. I imagine
what his warm fingers would feel like as they brush over me. I
wonder if the air feels differently where I stand.

Lily waves her hand in front of my blank eyes. "Callie? Get

back here now. This isn't funny anymore. I'm getting scared, and you know that it takes a lot to freak me out."

"She's here," Mason says, nodding to me. He runs his fingers over my ghostly cheek, and I can imagine him pushing the hair from my face.

"Okay, this is seriously creepy and all sorts of wrong, and I usually appreciate this kind of stuff, but—" Lily swipes her hand through my ethereal form. "Get back to your body now so Mason can protect your ass."

I hold my hand up, ignoring Lily. She can use a dose of panic after what she put me through. We're in this stairwell because of her in the first place. I think Mason realizes this, too, because instead of asking me as well, all he does is raise his hand up to hold in front of my outstretched hand. His eyes soften as he watches me move. Lily shifts from foot to foot next to me, peering over her shoulder every few seconds to watch the door.

I press my translucent hand to Mason's, a tingling sensation shocking my fingers like I've hit a wall—but it's his hand. I can feel the firmness of his fingers as my aura touches him. A jolt of electricity rushes through me, and I draw my hand away. I can't believe I felt Mason. And I'm positive he felt me, too. His mouth hangs partially open before he reaches out again, this time brushing through me, and the tingling sensation doesn't return.

I frown, hoping it wasn't a freak incident.

"Callie, you need to go back to your body," Lily pleads, begging me. "Please, please, please."

I turn my gaze to my best friend. She holds herself, her lips turned downward, and her eyes shine like she's ready to cry at any second. Lily might be fearless, but when it comes to me, she worries. Mason's words got to her, and I can tell by her crinkling forehead, that she's questioning what we're doing here and why I introduced her to this world. It makes me question it myself.

I glide back to my frozen body, the pulling sensation drawing me in like I'm stuck in a magnetic field, and I reconnect. Darkness grabs hold of me, but a second later, I open my eyes to water streaming down my face, soaking my sweater. Gasping as I orient myself to the sudden weight of my body, I inhale a gulp of water. Coughs heave my chest, my knees buckling under me as the pixie dust washes away.

Mason embraces me, stopping me from hitting the floor. He holds me upright in his muscular arms for a minute before I find my footing. I gaze into his dark eyes, stuck in his stare, and it takes Lily clearing her throat to get me to let go of his arms.

I peer past Mason at Lily. "I think I'm ready to go. Are you?"

She nods. "Yup. This was enough excitement for one day. I can't believe I made out with a fairy."

I can't stop a nervous laugh from escaping. "I can't believe you left me to do so."

She shrugs. "Didn't you see him? Hot."

Mason rubs his hand over his forehead. "Let's get out of here before someone else comes. I might regret this, but I think you two need a few more lessons about creatures."

"So, you're not going to try to convince us to forget everything we've learned?" I ask.

He holds out his hand for me to take. "What's the point? It's too late for that, anyway. I honestly don't know what I'm going to do with you."

I want to ask him why it's too late, but instead I say, "You think I'm too much trouble." I can see it in his eyes. The way he looks at me like I'll suddenly cause his world to implode. In this moment, staring into his eyes, hearing his words, I realize the burden I'm unintentionally forcing on him. "It's okay to leave me to find my own way, you know."

Taking my hand in his, he slides his fingers through mine. "I can handle trouble. Lots of trouble. Definitely your kind of trouble." Uh oh. He's doing that soul staring look again, the one I can't resist losing myself in. "What I can't handle is knowing that you could possibly fall into the hands of the monsters I fight against, and it'd be my fault."

"You sound like a whole lot of trouble, too," I say. "Plus, I'd never join people who were out to hurt others. You don't have to worry about that."

He laughs, not a funny laugh, but a strained I-think-you're-crazy laugh. "I don't want to find out if that's true or not." He motions Lily to go through the door to the kitchen. "Come on, let's get out of here. We don't have to make any plans now."

"Plans for what?"

"How you're going to survive in this world."

12

⌁Gloom and Doom World⌁

MASON

KEEPING CALLIE AND Lily close, I guide them past the line of creatures hovering in the hallway as Cian greets each one before allowing them into The Haven. Sweat breaks out on the back of my neck from the humid air created by so many bodies in such a small place. The incoming patrons we pass by stare, and I ignore them and exit into the lobby leading to the stairwell.

A few creatures linger in the lobby, and a woman whistles from a chair in the corner, causing Callie to tighten her grip on my hand. Some creatures like their presences to be known, and this particular woman, who happens to be a succubus, clearly only wants to mess with our heads. If she planned to hunt us, she'd have already been out of her seat before we could even enter the stairwell.

I push Lily to move faster, but she hesitates at the door. "You go first."

Callie releases my hand and hooks her arm with Lily's. "Don't be afraid. We have every right to be here."

I consider mentioning that not everyone would agree with that, but instead I move past them and open the door. I motion them ahead after I see the empty stairwell, and Callie drags Lily down the stairs.

We reach the level Lily parked on, and Callie pushes the door open. She freezes in her tracks, letting go of the door. It slams shut behind her, cutting us off from each other. Lily turns to face me, her eyes wide, and I bound past her and open the door.

"What the hell? What are you doing here?" a masculine voice asks.

"None of your business. Now, please, stay away from me." Callie's voice echoes through the half full parking structure. She stands a few feet away with her hands on her hips.

Brendan moves from a black truck. "None of my business? Feels like it is. I didn't know you came here."

She steps back as he strolls closer. "I told you to stay away from me. You can't act like you have a right to anything involving me. You were a jerk. You humiliated me. I don't want anything to do with you anymore. Got it?"

Racing from the door to Callie's side, I grasp her shoulder, pulling her closer to me. She responds by sliding her fingers around my elbow and burning a death glare at her ex-boyfriend.

Brendan straightens his shoulders when he realizes who I am. "Seriously, Callie? This guy? I should've known." His gaze flicks from me to Callie before he raises his hand and points at me. "Stay out of our business, dude. This is between me and Callie."

Out of habit, I reach for my weaponry belt, but I'm not wearing it. I wasn't expecting to come to the city or having to defend myself. My weaponry belt helps dissuade disgruntled creatures, because not all of them have magical powers. But, I don't exactly need it against a shifter.

Narrowing my eyes, I concentrate on Brendan's aura. "It is. She's under my protection. Any harm done to her is an action against the council." Shifters love intimidating people. They can be hot-headed and aggressive, but most only threaten without following through. I'm not sure about Brendan yet.

In one swift step, he moves forward to look down at Callie by my side. "Babe, I think it's time we talk. Obviously, we both have been keeping secrets about what we are."

"You mean the fact that you're not human?" Callie asks, not letting Brendan's sudden closeness get to her. If her words weren't full of accusation, I might think she'd tell me to get lost to go home with someone she has history with. What kind of history? I'm not sure. Bad history. He was the one who triggered her projection. She might have never done it if it wasn't for him. Maybe not. It's not like projection is something passed down like being an enchantress or being a nightmare inflictor. I can only guess why Callie is what she is. It's pure luck. Good or bad depends on who you ask, I suppose.

"If I had known you knew about all this, I wouldn't have broken up with you. I love you. It was just getting too complicated. And with college—but you know." Well, that was unexpected and an unpleasant surprise.

Callie grips my arm harder. "Know *now*. I didn't know about any of this until you—" She crinkles her nose, realizing her admission. We both tense. Lily stands awfully quiet behind us, and I'm not even sure Brendan notices her.

Brendan lifts his chin at me. "Wait, he's the one who told you about all this, didn't he?"

Shaking her head, Callie says, "It doesn't matter. You've showed me a side of you I didn't want to believe you possessed, and I have no interest in trying to work things out. You humiliated me, Brendan. Just stay away from me."

His gaze flicks to mine. "What exactly did he tell you, babe?"

"Nothing, just leave."

Brendan reaches his hand out to touch her, but before he can even lay a finger on her, I tug her away. His eyes shift to where Callie's hand slides into mine. I squeeze her trembling fingers but don't turn to look at her. I don't know what she's thinking, but she's clearly nervous.

"But Callie—"

"Stop, Brendan. Get out of our way," she says.

Brendan shoves his hands in his pockets. "I just want to

talk. Let me talk. You don't know that guy or what he does."

"I know exactly what he does, and I'm sorry, but I don't want to talk to you. There's a lot of things I'm dealing with, and I—I can't do this right now. You hurt me."

A sudden scream rips through the parking garage, coming from behind us, and I spin to look at Lily. Pain swells through my face from an unexpected sucker punch to my nose. The surprise attack leaves me unprepared, and something hard bashes into my stomach, knocking the wind from me. I drop to my knees, hunching over to protect myself. Lily screams again.

I force my eyes to open, and through my blurry vision, I watch as a shifter tosses Lily over his shoulder and heads in the direction of Brendan's black truck. *What the hell?*

"Are you crazy, Brendan? Make your cousin stop," Callie says.

"You're seriously going to trust that guy over me? He kills people like us," Brendan says.

"You don't know what you're talking about," she says. "Now, let Lily go. She doesn't know anything."

"Stop acting like I'm some sort of monster. What has this guy told you?" Brendan punches my hurt shoulder, forcing me back. It takes everything in me not to attack him. One, I'm on leave. Two, I really shouldn't have brought Callie and Lily here. And three, I don't think I could successfully take on two shifters while I'm unarmed.

"Release Lily and go take a walk or something before I call for backup," I say.

Brendan laughs. "Going to try to hide behind the council?

Good luck proving anything. You're the one who brought them here. I think I heard Callie threaten to expose my secret for breaking up with her."

"What?" Callie asks.

Another set of footsteps shuffles around the parking garage. We're being surrounded. I don't know what Brendan is planning, most likely just trying to scare Callie for showing up with me, but I definitely don't want to find out. This could go all sorts of different ways—Callie could reason with Brendan, leave with him, makeup—whatever. Or she could reveal her own secrets. Either way, those are all terrible options in my opinion, but people make bad decisions out of fear, and Callie's panicking.

"Just come with us, Callie," Brendan says. "You don't need to be around someone like him."

She huffs. "Like him? You mean someone better than you?"

Brendan sneers. "You b—"

Before he finishes his sentence, Brendan flies through the air as someone tackles him, knocking him off his feet. I recognize the shimmery life force of Jax. I never thought I'd ever be this thankful to have an incubus back me up. Callie dashes toward Lily in the arms of Brendan's shifter friend, and the shifter drops Lily to grab hold of Callie's hair. Hearing her scream kicks me into action. I don't care if the council tries me for treason or shuns me, I'm not standing around while Callie gets hurt. Lunging forward, I race toward the towering shifter. His sinewy arms bulge with muscles from his transformation, and he'll be even bigger before I get to him.

He pushes Callie away, and she tumbles to the ground, skidding on her palms to break her fall. Lily yanks her off the ground, and they run toward Lily's car. I hope they leave without me. It's what I want them to do. I can protect myself.

The world slows as I concentrate on the shifter's glittering gray aura. He swings his arm out, but I duck and collide into his stomach, slamming him into the side of the truck. It shakes on its chassis, and my shoulder and arm smack into the metal door next to him. Pain rips through me, clouding my vision with black stars, fire engulfing my healing goblin wounds.

Stumbling back before the shifter can push me off, I clutch my hurt arm. He falls forward, the sound of his palms slapping the concrete echoing through the air. The shifter swears as I rush him before he has a chance to get up. I tackle him, digging my fingers into the back of his neck to restrain him by sheer force. But with nothing to bind him, I'll be sitting here all day. Any number of creatures could come from The Haven to aid this asshole.

A bungee cord drops next to the shifter, and I raise my head to meet Callie's angry gaze. Wind blows through her dark hair, and she stands with her chin up and her eyes narrowed. She looks like she can take on the world if she tried, and for the first time since I've met her, I know she might have a fighting chance.

She just might survive in this creature world after all.

CALLIE

I clasp my hands together to stop them from shaking. I've never been so scared in my life. In the two months time that Brendan was my boyfriend, I never thought he could be psychotic. I didn't know he wasn't human, either. He always had a short temper and a bad reputation for fighting, but he was cute and always nice to me. It's like someone flipped a switch on the boy I knew and thought I loved. It's terrifying to think I could still be with him. The Worst Breakup Ever was a gift.

Brendan's hot-headed, wannabe macho behavior pisses me off. How dare he tell me who I can associate with? Like I care if he regrets breaking up with me. There's no way I'd ever get back with him. What was he even thinking having his cousin try to take Lily to intimidate me into leaving with him, trying to play it off like Mason's the bad guy? That's basically kidnapping. Something I didn't know he was capable of. What would he have gotten out of it apart from scaring me? He's sick.

"Should I start billing the council for my assistance?" Jax asks from behind me. If it wasn't for the soul sucker, who knows what would've happened.

Mason shakes his head. "I'll pay you personally. I owe you."

Jax shrugs. "Glad I could help." He turns to me. "I have some rope in the bed of my truck. Can you grab it?"

I turn away from Mason as he finishes knotting the bungee cord on Brendan's cousin, Trevor. Jax nods toward a white truck parked next to Lily's Camry. Lily presses her face to her window, watching me jog closer. I reach into the bed of Jax's truck and pull a rope from the mess of tie-downs he piled in the corner.

Waving my hand, I motion Lily to get out and follow me.

She hops from the car, clutching a tire iron she found in the spare tire compartment in her trunk where I found the bungee cord. She strolls next to me with her makeshift weapon clutched in her hand for dear life. I wish I had one, too, but she needs it more.

I toss Jax the rope, and he binds Brendan's hands. Brendan lies unconscious under Jax's weight, but I see the rise and fall of his chest so I know he isn't dead.

"I need to borrow your truck, Jax," Mason says, yanking Trevor to his feet. Brendan's cousin doesn't resist, knowing he's lost. I bet he wishes he didn't try to help Brendan in the first place. Trevor graduated last year and is in his second semester of school at the local university on a football scholarship. I wonder what will happen to him now. I feel bad Brendan dragged his cousin into this, but Trevor should've known better.

"This was a joke, man," Trevor says. He's realizing his mistake. He looks at me from the ground. "Come on, Callie. Tell them. Brendan's just mad you've been hanging out with—"

Jax shoves his hand into Trevor's back, cutting off his words. He tightens the rope before standing up to dig in his pocket. He tosses a set of keys to Mason. "Want me to help?"

Mason shakes his head. "I'll call my partner. Can you do me a favor and ride with Callie and Lily back to my place to wait for me?"

"We don't need him to ride with us, Mason. I need to get home anyway." Lily stands next to me without saying a word, but I know she's thinking the same thing.

"Someone could follow you. Do you want to put your family in danger?" God, this world is full of such gloom and doom and fear. Mason has a point, though.

"Of course not." I never thought about the possibility of someone following me back to my house. It's hard to shake the fear threatening to send me into full blown panic. Is this how life's going to be now? Am I always going to have to worry about who's watching or who knows about me? I can't live like that. "But I have to go home at some point. My parents would freak if they think I'm missing. Not to mention Lily's mom."

Mason pushes Trevor toward Jax to let the soul sucker handle forcing him into the back of the truck. Reaching out his hand, Mason takes my hand and holds it against his chest, his eyes pleading with me. His heartbeat thrums against my palm in strong, assuring beats.

"It's just for a few hours. I'll make sure you're both safe at home tonight, okay?" His chocolaty eyes lock me in place. I can't do anything but try to peek into his thoughts through his intense stare.

The gentleness of his touch contrasts with the fierce strength of his muscular build, and I can't stop from thinking how hot he is in this moment. His protectiveness is endearing, though the last thing I want is a knight to save me. I hate feeling like I need to be saved.

His mixed signals make me wish I knew for sure if I'm more than a job to him. If things continue this way, I wonder if he'll step back and stop looking at me like he thinks I'm the most amazing soul he's seen. The last thing I want is to be work to him.

"Please, do it for me," he pleads, an edge to his voice. "I really don't want something happening to you, Callie." It's like he's answered my silent questions. Out of everything in the world he could've asked me to do it for—Lily, my family, even myself, he asked me to go to his house for him and his own personal reasons.

A tingling sensation slides from my core to my legs, weakening my knees. His words shouldn't touch me so deeply, but I can't help the excitement they ignite in me.

Lily clears her throat, forcing me to pull myself together before I melt into a puddle on the ground. "He's right, Callie. This whole thing has me freaked out, and you know when I'm freaked out, it's something huge. We can tell our parents we're going to dinner and then studying at Coffee Addicts. We have those English projects, remember?"

The last thing on my mind was the stupid English project, especially because my English partner happens to be standing in front of me, and I'm not sure he'll even show up to school anymore.

"Please, Callie." The way Mason says my name sends a storm of butterflies through my stomach.

"Okay," I whisper.

Mason wraps his arms around me, surprising me, and I breathe in the fresh scent of his shirt. I don't know if it's because he's caught up in the moment or what, but I sink into his arms anyway just to feel what it's like—and damn it if it isn't hard to step back. I might not if I didn't feel two pairs of eyes watching us.

Mason slips a key into my hand. "Make yourself at home and don't answer the door for anyone but me."

Jax helps Mason put Brendan in the back of the truck. I follow Lily and hop into her car. A minute later, Jax slides into the backseat of the Camry without a word. This has to be awkward for him considering I basically called him out and shamed him for accidentally feeding on my soul. Pulling down my visor, I glance past Jax and peer at Mason in the mirror as he paces in a circle while talking on the phone, probably to the partner he mentioned. I wonder if he'll ever introduce me to her—or any of his friends for that matter. I wonder what they'd think of me. *Why do I care so much? All these feelings could be in your head.* But I feel them in my soul, too.

Jax leans between the seats to look at Lily. "You okay to drive? We need to get out of here before any other shifters show up."

Lily nods without a word and starts the engine before reversing. She doesn't have to tell me how scared she is. It's such a rare expression to see on my best friend's face, but when I do see it, I recognize it. Jax must see it as well.

"You think more will show? Mason would be outnumbered." The thought of more people like Brendan showing up to confront Mason leaves me on edge. He's only in this mess because of Brendan's sudden jealousy over a breakup that was his idea in the first place. I thought I'd be a lot more upset and hurt over everything, but his attitude erased basically all good feelings I had for him. It helps that I've become distracted by my ability...and Mason. I bet Brendan wouldn't have looked twice at Mason if he didn't intervene on my first day back to school.

"Don't underestimate your boyfriend. He's a trained killer and can handle himself, probably more so than I can," Jax says.

"He's not my boyfriend." I don't know why I feel the need to clarify. It's not like it matters. "And I don't want anyone to die."

"Get used to it, *projector*. Death might be a regular occurrence in your future."

"Is that how it is for you, *soul sucker*," I snap. The last thing I need is for someone else to throw terrifying predictions in my direction.

Lily blows out a breath next to me. "You two are making me nervous!" She grips the steering wheel, her knuckles turning white. "You both have names, so use them." Her gaze flicks to Jax in her rearview mirror. "And if you dare refer to me as *human*, you better be prepared for a wrath unlike anything you've ever encountered in this gloom and doom world you swear will kill us all. My *name* is *Lily*."

Laughter bubbles from my throat as Lily turns from terrified to menacing in a matter of seconds, surprising Jax. Leaning back, he crosses his arms and draws his gaze out the window, watching skyscrapers zoom past. Lily navigates the streets to the bridge that'll take us over the river and back toward Mason's apartment.

When we're a few miles away from The Haven, she loosens her hold on the steering wheel and says, "I'm sorry for snapping back there, but this is a tense situation."

"And your words aren't exactly reassuring," I add to Jax.

He shrugs. "They're not meant to be. You're obviously new to how the world really works, and you can't keep your head in the clouds much longer. You do want to survive, right?"

My brows pinch together. What kind of idiotic question is that? I might like going ghostly, but it's not a permanent state I want to be in. What I want is to gain control over my ability, learn what I'm supposedly up against in this world, and figure out how to protect myself while having a little fun. It's not that much to ask for, is it?

I brush my hair behind my ears. "I am surviving."

He meets my gaze in the mirror. "Maybe strive for more."

13

⌒Breaking Protocol⌒

MASON

"SERIOUSLY, MASON. YOU'RE supposed to be on leave. Don't you ever stop working?" Kat jabs a syringe of sedative into Brendan's arm for easier transport. "You couldn't let these guys slide? They're not even under investigation."

I point at Brendan. "He tried to kidnap someone." I might be exaggerating a little, but I'm annoyed at the entire situation.

Kat hoists him over her shoulder. The curve of her muscles flexes as she tosses him in the back of her van. I've always been impressed that Kat's stronger than I am. "What the heck? He's so young."

Shrugging, I use the tranquilizer she gives me on Brendan's friend. Neither shifter put up a fight once they were bound. They probably knew that once they're detained by an agent, there's no point in fighting. It'll guarantee harsher punishment from the council if they do.

"So are we, and we know better." I drag Brendan's friend over to Kat. My shoulders and arm aches, and I'm sure I'm getting a black eye.

Kat pulls the guy in and slams the door. "What happened to the victim?"

"Victims." I rock on my heels.

"So, what happened to them?"

I contemplate lying, but Kat would see right through me. We've been working together for months, and we rely on each other. I can't risk putting a strain on our partnership, since I must trust her with my life, and I need her to trust me with hers.

"I sent them to my apartment with a friend of mine."

"You what? Why? You know the council likes to talk to the victims to make sure they're okay. What if they've been traumatized? They might need medical attention." Kat nudges my shoulder. "What's up with you, today? It's unlike you to break protocol."

I clench my jaw for a second, trying to figure out how to tell Kat the partial truth without giving too much away. "I want to keep them out of this if I can. It was a mistake for me to take them to The Haven in the first place. They're both human."

"*You* took them there?" Her voice echoes through the night

air.

I glance around the empty parking lot of the strip mall. There was no way I was staying at the club with the two shifters in Jax's truck. "It's not a big deal, Kat. The girls knew Brendan. He was pissed off they were with me, but I can't just let him or his friend go. They're unpredictable. I'm afraid they'll do something stupid to retaliate."

Kat glares at me. "That's why you let them slide, but I've already called this in to Dmitri."

"Kat."

"Don't try to reason with this, Mase. You know, you've been on leave less than a week, and I feel like I don't even know you anymore."

Her words sting worse than my healing shoulder. "I'm the same guy, but it's complicated. I swear I'll tell you everything but not now. I can't risk the council getting involved in my friends' lives."

"See! What friends? We know all the same people, but you've been on leave for all of a second and now you're hanging with some mysterious *human* crowd." She groans, clenching her fingers into fists. "If you didn't want them involved, then you shouldn't have taken them there. You should've kept them as far away from creatures as possible. You're smarter than this." Kat places her hands on her hips. She's not going to drop this. The best I can do is make her see reason.

I kick the ground with my boot. "You don't think I know that, Kat? One day, you'll learn that you can't control everyone and everything."

"And maybe one day you'll learn you can't do whatever the hell you want just because you can." So much for reason.

She struts to the driver's side door and flings it open. "Don't call me for any more favors, Mason. I'll take them to the council for an evaluation but expect a phone call from Dmitri. You can tell him what you want, because I'm not risking my reputation to help some people I don't even know, who you won't even tell me about for whatever lame ass reason, I'm sure."

This is as good as it gets with Kat. I don't want her jeopardizing anything on my behalf anyway. What kind of partner would that make me? "That's fine, Kat. I understand."

Her face softens. "I expect you to have your act together before our next assignment when you're off leave or this isn't going to work anymore. Who knew goblin venom could affect your good senses?"

Ouch. I don't respond as I turn and head toward Jax's truck. Glancing over my shoulder, I say, "Take care of yourself until then."

Kat hops into the van, the engine rumbling when she starts it, and I peer through the back window until she disappears. Kat and I have a love/hate relationship, and we drive each other crazy more than half the time, but she's my partner. In the end, I want her to be safe even if she annoys me.

I pull my phone from my pocket, a little afraid to see if I have any missed calls, but my phone only displays my lock screen. Calling my landline, I wait as it rings a few times before my answering machine picks up. Calling my house instead of

Callie's phone guarantees she's safe in my apartment.

"Hey, it's me, Mason." I don't know why I refuse to say Callie's name. Paranoia isn't my friend. After a few seconds with no answer, I say, "Hello? Someone pick up."

The line clicks. "Hey, when are you coming here? Do you realize you have no food?" Callie giggles as she listens to someone in the background. She sounds more relaxed than she did when she left me, and I'm grateful for that.

I sigh, relief washing over me. "I'll bring something."

"Hurry up, 'kay?" Callie's voice lowers. "I was getting worried that something bad happened to you."

I can't help the smile crossing my face. I wasn't expecting to hear her admit she was worried. It reminds me how she hugged me back earlier. "See you soon."

CALLIE

I curl my legs under me on the couch. Lily sits in front of Jax on the floor, staring deeply into his eyes like the world will end if she looks away. Okay, so not really, but they've been staring at each other without blinking for at least two minutes as he tries to teach her the impossible.

Music hums from Mason's stereo, and I cover my mouth to stop from laughing. A tear streams down Lily's cheek because she's concentrating harder now than even on one of Mrs. Padilla's English assignments. After another minute, Lily blinks her watery eyes. Straightening her shoulders, she blows a breath of air through her lips and then reaches up and pokes Jax's nose, causing him to smile.

"I still can't see it." Lily leans closer to Jax, getting in his face. "You're a terrible teacher."

Jax is convinced he can teach Lily to see auras, but I'm pretty sure he just wants her attention. If it were that easy, I would think everyone would be able to do it. Lily loved the idea of being able to see me without my body, and it'd surprise me if she didn't learn the ability with her determination. I bet she could fly if she tried hard enough at this point. If she did, we'd really be in this together.

Jax opens his hand and places Lily's over his. Their palms don't touch but hover an inch away from each other.

"Do you feel that?" Jax asks.

Lily's nose scrunches. "I only feel our body heat."

"Exactly."

Lily laughs, pulling her hand away, and then flicks Jax on the shoulder. His smile widens—the kind of smile you only give to someone you're trying to impress. Who knew he was capable of ever lightening up. But Lily does that to people. She's charismatic and easygoing. I have never met someone who didn't like her.

I tilt my head toward the ceiling. "He's messing with you, Lily. You won't ever see his aura."

She huffs. "You don't know that."

"I think I kind of do." I chuck a couch pillow at her, and she tosses it back at me. Jax glances between us, his eyes crinkling in the corner, and I wonder what his deal really is. "Tell her, Jax."

Jax clasps Lily's hands and looks into her eyes. "I think you can do whatever you put your mind to."

I roll my eyes as Lily's laughter echoes through the room. Even though Jax sounds so cheesy, I can tell by the way Lily watches him, she's enjoying every second of it. If he was looking at me the way he's looking at her, I wouldn't be able to stop from blushing.

I close my eyes. "Like how I can imagine myself projecting and just do it?"

"Is that how that works?" Jax asks.

"Yeah," I say.

"Callie?"

"What?"

"Callie, you projected."

I open my eyes. *What the hell?* This is getting out of control. If I can't even think about projecting before it happens, I'm going to be in a lot of trouble. Fear seizes me, and I don't move but hover a foot away from my body.

Lily scrambles to her feet and rushes to my side. She lifts and drops my hand, and then pulls my eyelid up to peer at my blank stare. She grimaces and punches my arm. "What's happening to her?" Lily asks Jax. "It's like she can't stop herself."

He wipes his forehead with his sleeve. "Like with anything, the more she does it, the easier it'll get. If she's doing it without even concentrating, I'm guessing she needs to practice awareness." He sounds like he's talking from experience.

Lily pokes my arm. "You hear that, Callie?"

"She's to your right." Jax raises his hand to point.

Gliding forward, I stand in front of him. He stiffens the closer I get, and when I'm inches away, he holds his breath. I bend and run my hand over his face, smirking while making him uncomfortable. He gasps, and a tugging sensation crawls over my hand. With wide eyes, he crab walks backward, afraid of my presence.

I move closer and step into Jax so he can hear me. A million emotions course over me—fear, anger, hunger, lust—as his thoughts ring through my mind.

"Please, make her stop. Please, I can't stop myself. I'm going to kill her."

"Calm down," I say. *"You're not hurting me."*

"But I will. I survive by consuming people's life forces, Callie. You're basically holding my mouth open and pouring food in—and by food, I mean you."

"Jax?" Lily's voice sounds through the fog of Jax's thoughts and emotions. "Are you okay? What's wrong?"

Jax doesn't answer.

"Get out of my head, Callie," Jax says.

Guilt rushes over me at the desperation within his plea. I step forward to leave Jax's body, but something hooks onto me, stopping me from moving. A loud pop snaps in my ears, the world flickering in and out of focus as Jax blinks. His body latches onto me and won't let go.

"Jax, I don't want to freak you out, but I'm stuck."

"Stuck? What do you mean?" His voice cuts through the room.

"You need to let me go. You're holding onto my soul."

"I don't even feel you, Callie. It's not me." Jax continues to talk out loud. "Just concentrate and project out of me like you do your own body."

Taking a deep breath, even though I'm not really breathing, I concentrate on escaping. Jax doesn't respond to my internal command. Without control over my soul or his body, it feels like I'm trapped in a mind prison. I see what Jax sees and feel all his emotions, but that's it. It's terrifying.

"*I can't.*" The words echo through Jax's mind.

"Well, you better try harder."

Lily moves to Jax. "I hate this one-sided conversation. What's wrong? Why isn't she returning to her body?"

Jax rubs his eyes, blurring Lily before us. "There's a small issue."

"*A small issue?*" This is more than a small issue. I'm trapped in the body of someone else, and I don't have control. It'd be different if I possessed him, but I'm chained to his mind with the inability to do anything.

"*Calm down. Your fear is freaking me out. I can't think,*" Jax thinks just to me.

I can't close my eyes or take a deep breath to settle my nerves. I'm not sure what else to do to stop the panic from swelling in my soul. What if this is it? What if I'm officially a part of Jax, and I never get back to my body again? What if he starts consuming me until I vanish from existence?

Oh, God, please don't let this be it.

A knock sounds on the door, interrupting my thoughts. Jax glances at Lily and then the door but neither move to answer it. He draws his gaze to my body slumped on the couch where I left it. Jogging to the couch, he hoists my body over his shoulder and carries me toward the bedroom door.

"*Where are you taking me?*" I ask.

"*You look dead. I'm not leaving your body on the couch for someone to find.*"

"*It's probably Mason.*"

"*I'm not risking it.*"

Another knock echoes through the air. "Callie, it's me. Open up."

If I could stick my tongue out at Jax, I would. "*Told you.*"

Jax sets my body down on Mason's bed. Clothes clutter the floor near the dresser, and a flat screen TV hangs on the wall above an entertainment stand. A few photos of people I don't know take up the top of the night table, and a glass case with a few weapons sits on the other side of his bed.

Voices echo from the living room, and a second later, Mason hovers in the doorway to his bedroom with Lily on his heels. He glances from Jax to my body on the bed, and then tilts his head up to look at the ceiling.

"Where's Callie?" Mason asks. He peers around the room and then turns to search the living room for my spirit. "Did she leave?"

Jax shoves his hands in his pockets. "You didn't tell him?" he asks Lily.

She throws her hands up. "I didn't have the chance."

"Someone spit it out." Mason crosses the room and sits on the edge of the bed. He touches my cheek for a second before gripping his comforter.

Jax rocks on his heels. "She's stuck, dude."

Mason frowns.

"Stuck?"

"Look at me."

Mason narrows his eyes, studying Jax. The color drains from his face as he realizes what's going on. "Are you kidding me? I don't believe this!"

MASON

What are we going to do? *Think, Mason, think.*

I run my fingers over Callie's arm like I can somehow will her to return to her body. If she's really stuck in Jax, I won't have any other choice than to go to the council for help. Callie's parents don't know about me, and they'd flip out if I tell them their daughter is once again brain dead. It'd direct too much attention toward me, and I know the council would intervene. I don't know what they'd do, but I'm sure I'll lose my job for keeping Callie's secret.

"This is bad. How did it even happen?" I peer past Jax's aura to peek at Callie's light pink essence streaking through his glittering gray life force.

"She doesn't know," Jax says. "Neither do I. She got too close to me. I warned her."

"If she can't return to her body, we'll have to get her medical attention or her body will die."

Jax's green eyes flash blue. It's like Callie's trying to push through to take control of his body. "The council will think I stole her soul. You know how they arrest first before questioning. I can't risk getting in trouble."

"I wouldn't be able to help you, either. I'm pretty sure I'll be out of a job." Sighing, I push to my feet. I wouldn't even know where to start explaining this.

Lily slides in front of Jax and grips his shirt. "Are you listening, Callie? We're going to be in serious trouble if you don't figure something out!" Her cheeks redden, fear and anger lacing her words.

Jax's gray aura shifts to pink. "You're not helping!" His voice rises as he places his hands on his hips. "You know the last thing I want is to ruin everyone's lives. I can't focus on body jumping with everyone on the verge of panicking."

Lily steps back. "Callie?"

Jax covers his mouth for a second. "Oh, my God! I'm possessing him." Callie's aura shines brightly, forcing Jax's to hide. It's strange watching Jax pace the room, knowing that it's not him controlling his body. "I'm sorry, Jax. It was an accident." He, or should I say, Callie, plops on the bed. "Stop yelling. I'm trying."

Jax and Callie have an internal debate about what's happening, and as I watch Jax's eye color flip between green and blue, an idea hits me.

I clear my throat. "I might know of a way to get Callie out without involving the council."

"How?" Callie asks through Jax.

"The same way wraiths are extracted from humans. You need to be exorcized."

She sucks in a breath, the gesture strange on Jax's body. "Won't that kill me?"

"I don't think so."

She shakes Jax's head. "There has to be another way."

I drop my gaze to the floor. "I'll give you an hour to figure it out. If you don't, I'm going to make a call. Letting your body die because you're too stubborn to let someone help is not how this is going to end."

Jax's aura shifts. Callie's spirit fights to remain in control while Jax's soul fights back to push her away. Callie's aura fades into Jax's, and Jax stands up. "She has a lot of fight in her," he says, clearly back in control.

Lily wraps her arms around herself. She's been quiet almost this whole time. "She'll fix this. Don't underestimate Callie. She's strong."

I hope she's strong enough to save herself.

14

～Possessed～

CALLIE

MASON'S CRAZY. ONLY demons need to be exorcized from people, and I'm definitely not a demon, if demons are even real. The thought leaves me on edge, thinking about how someone could even do that. I'll figure out a way to escape. I just need to concentrate. It doesn't help that Jax can't seem to let go of my soul, either. He'd disagree, but I know he's subconsciously holding me here.

"I need your help, Jax."

Jax's thoughts shuffle through a hundred images I can't make sense of—some of them petrifying.

"*What do you want me to do, Callie?*" Jax thinks.

I'm silent for a minute. "*Can't you push me out? I know you can suck souls in, but what about pushing one away?*"

He stares at his fingers. "*I've never tried.*"

"*Now's the perfect time, don't you think?*"

"What is she saying?" Mason asks. "Your eyes keep shifting to the same color as Callie's."

"Can you take Lily and go do something? We can't concentrate with you two hovering around." Jax meets Lily's eyes for a moment. With a quick nod, she leaves the bedroom to hang out in the living room.

Mason doesn't move. "Anything I can do?"

Jax sits at the end of the bed. "Callie's going to be okay. You can trust me with her."

Mason exits the room without arguing. If I could feel my heart beating, it'd be racing as I stare behind him. His hot and cold attitude confuses me. One minute he's annoyed, treating me like a burden, and then the next, he's protective. I wish he'd let his guard down and let me in. I want to know the real him.

"*Can you quit it?*" Jax thinks.

"*Quit what?*"

"*Your feelings for Mason are slipping through. He seems nice and all, but it's confusing me.*"

"*You're not the only one.*"

Jax doesn't respond as I watch the world through his eyes. He glances at his reflection in a wall mirror above Mason's dresser like we'll somehow find the answer looking back at us. Nervously, he pats the sides of his faux hawk. The longer he stares at himself, the more I realize something I hadn't noticed. Not only can I see through Jax's eyes, but I can see the world the way he does. A faint mist radiates from his skin—a luminescent silver—and within the silver lies streaks of pinks.

"I can see our souls," I say. *"They're faint, but I can definitely see them. Why am I so faint?"*

"Because it's my body." His voice echoes through the room.

"I wonder if you let me possess you again, if it'll be easier for me to break away."

He sighs. "What if I can't regain control?"

"But what if you can push me out?"

"Fine. Just hurry up."

Jax closes his eyes. The insides of his eyelids shine red from the light of the room. Concentrating the best I can, I remember what it's like to have the weight of a body holding me down, what it's like to take a deep breath, what it's like to feel clothes against my skin, the chill of the air conditioner, not only feeling everything but being in control.

A wave of dizziness cuts through me as my ears pop. My senses regain control—the weight of the body, the smell of food wafting through the air—all of it overwhelming since a moment ago I was limited to just my hearing and sight. Who knew how much I'd miss my sense of smell and touch. Hunger burns in my—I mean, Jax's stomach—and I shift uncomfortably when I realize he has to go to the bathroom.

Snapping my eyes open, I face the stranger in the mirror. I could never get used to being someone else. All those times in the past I thought it would be amazing being someone else are now officially void. I like being me. I miss being me.

I expect my wish to come true but nothing happens. I'm still trapped in Jax's body, and it's getting more uncomfortable the longer I remain in control. I shift on the bed, crossing my legs, and then I uncross them just as quickly.

Fire burns in my cheeks. "I can't do this."

"*Try again.*"

While closing my eyes, I suck in a deep breath and then exhale until my lungs burn. I need to want it enough to do it. Unfortunately, all I really want to do at the moment is go to the bathroom. I stand up and pace for a minute.

"*Come on, Callie. You can do this. Just project out. Do it. Do it, now,*" I say to myself.

"*Keep going. I think it's working.*" Jax's voice hums in my ears.

I try to concentrate again, but I can't. I can't stop thinking about going to the bathroom, and there's no way I'm doing that in Jax's body. The first time I'm going to see a boy naked is not when I'm occupying his body, especially to pee. My cheeks burn at the thought of having to acquaint myself to the male anatomy and no—just no. Not like this.

I squirm. "I can't. Your body has to go to the bathroom really badly."

"*You better not make me piss myself, Callie.*"

I dig my nails into my palms. "No promises. Why did you wait so long to go? This is your fault."

"*Give me control, Callie,*" Jax says.

"I'm not staying in here while you go to the bathroom. You're crazy." My voice rises through the quiet room.

Anger and determination rush through me. "*Callie, now!*"

The world spins as Jax rips control of his body from me. The sudden loss of power sends a searing pain through my soul, and I cry out as Jax runs from the room. Lily and Mason sit on the couch, eating pizza, and their eyes widen in surprise.

"*Hold it, Jax! I don't want to be in here!*" This isn't happening. I can't shut my eyes, and I'll see everything Jax sees. We just met. Going to the bathroom with a stranger isn't what I had on my agenda for today. Oh, jeez. Please. Why can't he just hold it? This is a best friend level experience, not one to be shared with a boy I never intended or wanted to see naked.

"You don't have a choice, Callie," Jax says out loud, striding across the room to the bathroom.

After he closes the door, things get real and fast, and panic and embarrassment sweep through me as he unbuttons his jeans. He doesn't even have the courtesy to close his eyes as he tugs the zipper down at lightning speed.

No. No. No. "*Let me go!*"

Burning pain smolders through my soul, and I rip free and fly back through the wall. I land soundlessly on the floor outside the bathroom and scream. The pain fades as I adjust to my ghostly form and calm myself down. I search over my translucent body, double checking that I'm still all there, and then I jump to my feet.

"I'm free." I dance around the room. "I did it!"

"Callie?" Mason's voice cuts through my excitement.

Gliding up to him, I touch my fingers to his chin and kiss him. A jolt of electricity zaps through me as my ghostly form feels his solid body. I pull away and press my fingers to my lips. Mason sits frozen in place for a second and then he mimics my gesture. He felt my kiss, too.

Lily clears her throat. "You're freaking me out, Mason."

He shakes his head, drawing his intense stare away from my essence. "She's no longer stuck."

Flying to her feet, Lily dashes toward the bedroom to find my body. I bound behind her, jumping one step ahead of her, and thrust myself back into my body. I don't even have to concentrate to connect again. My body sucks me back in, and the world goes dark.

And it stays dark.

The heaviness of my own weight grips me, exhaustion and pain sinking deep into my skin down to my soul.

I can't wake up.

I can't do anything.

MASON

I sit next to Callie's sleeping body. Her pink aura sets her skin aglow. If she were near death, I'd be able to see it. I've seen enough people die to know. A life force seeps away before it disconnects altogether and fades into nothing.

Callie's vibrant aura shines with life and beauty and everything that makes Callie who she is. I could stare at her soul forever, soaking in everything that she is only to hope she shares a tiny bit with me. When she kissed me without her body, though a strange and unsettling sensation, I realized just how much I feel connected to her. That she's more than a girl with a rare ability I feel obligated to protect. I want to know everything about her. I want to be with her. Kiss her. Feel her warmth against me and allow her to get to know me, too. Because I don't have to hide from her. I can't hide from her.

If only she'd wake up.

Her comatose state has me standing on the edge of hot panic and wonder. Why can't she wake up? Can she hear me? Is she aware of what's going on? I chose to go under a genetic alteration so I could be powerful and never be helpless. But I'm helpless now, sitting here, holding Callie's hand like I'll lose her when she just came into my life.

"Callie's strong, Mason. Never underestimate my best friend, okay? She's probably only exhausted from being trapped in an incubus," Lily says from the door, interrupting my thoughts. Unlike me, she fully believes everything is fine. It's like she knows something about Callie that I don't. Probably because she does after being friends for almost their entire lives.

"I won't leave her side until she wakes up," I say. "If she doesn't change by morning, I'm going to bring in a doctor." That is, if Dr. Harvey will help me without the council knowing.

Lily leans on the doorframe. "She's going to be fine," she assures me. "Also, I texted her parents that she was spending the night with me. They've never checked in, so I'm not too worried."

I rest my hand on Callie's as I keep my gaze on Lily. "You're welcome to stay, too."

Lily twists her lips to the side. "I want to, but my mom comes home tonight. I can't stay much longer."

Jax slides up behind her. "Want me to follow you home?"

Lily smiles. "I'd like that."

I get to my feet, even though I want to remain by Callie's side, and follow them into the living room. It's been hours since Callie managed to free herself from Jax, and I hope she wakes up soon. I can't hide her for days. Her parents will realize she's missing.

Opening the door, I peer out to make sure the coast is clear. "I'll call you the minute she wakes up."

Lily's eyes glass over. "The second she wakes up."

"The second," I repeat.

Jax slides his arm over Lily's shoulders and guides her to her car with a wave over his shoulder to me. I wait for them to leave before I shut the door and return inside.

My cell phone buzzes from the kitchen table, and I scoop it up and head back to my bedroom. Tossing a few pillows on the floor next to the bed, I ease onto them, getting as comfortable as I possibly can. I could sleep on the pull-out couch, but I want to be here when Callie wakes up. I'm not sure what she'll remember, if anything, and I want to talk to her about today. About her kiss.

The gesture replays in my mind again. The sensation was incredible, unlike anything I've ever felt, what a million emotions would feel like in tangible form—electrifying and warm and unforgettable. I want to know why she did it—if she was just happy to be free or if it was something more. I want it to be more, but I know she has mixed feelings about me. I'm the guy who stalked her to see how dangerous she was to the world. The last thing I expected was to be so drawn to her like I am.

And something about the kiss, not only that she did it, but that she could do it lingers with me. If she's able to manifest in her corporeal form, I can only imagine how things will be when she gets her ability under control.

My phone buzzes again, forcing my thoughts of Callie's kiss from my mind. I have four missed calls—one from Hunter, one from Kat, and two from Dmitri. Clenching my jaw, I glare at the names to decide who to call first. The reason for Callie being here nearly slipped my mind. Dmitri deserves an explanation as to why I sent two teenage shifters to him tagged as kidnappers, and he's the one I should be calling first, but I'm not in the mood to discuss work-related topics. Same goes for Kat. Brendan should've already been processed by the council by now, and she probably wants to update me.

I hit Hunter's number and listen to it ring.

The line clicks. "Hey, Mase. Are you home?"

"Why?" I couldn't sound more annoyed even though Hunter hasn't done anything to deserve my sullen mood.

"Can I stop by?"

I peer at my alarm clock. It's almost midnight. "Tomorrow. I'm half asleep."

He sighs into the phone. "Dmitri called me. He's worried about you. Said you arrested two shifters and had Kat bring them in. He said one was the guy who tried to fight you the other night at The Haven when you ran off with the incubus.

Are you okay?"

A million responses stay locked in my throat. I haven't thought of what I'm going to say to the council, and I don't even know what Brendan said to them. I'm sure he spun a web of lies so thick that there's no way I'll be able to prove otherwise without revealing anything about Callie. Unless he already told them about her, then I'm screwed.

"I'm fine. Just have some things to work out." Sitting up, I glance at Callie. I wonder if she can hear me.

A scraping sound cuts through the line like Hunter's adjusting the phone. "I also talked to Mom. She told me you have a girlfriend."

I frown. Of course she would. She was excited to stumble upon a girl in my apartment. I know she has always worried that work was consuming my life, and it has been.

"She's not my girlfriend...yet." I purposely don't mention Callie's name.

Mumbling voices buzz in the background on Hunter's end, and then Nadia's voice rings through as she says, "But you like her. You can't hide it from me. Alyssa saw a glimpse of your future. You can't keep her from us forever. I will meet her."

I can't help but laugh. "Yeah, I like her and because I like her, I'll keep her away from you all as long as I can."

Nadia giggles. "We won't embarrass you too much."

My smile disappears. "That's not what I'm worried about."

Nadia breathes into the line. "Oh, no. She's—"

"Human," I finish for her.

"Mason..." Nadia's voice trails off.

I clear my throat. "Don't give me that. You're with Hunter. He's human."

"He's also a skilled fighter with years of combat training and experience."

My gaze trails from Callie's closed eyes to her lips, and I study every inch of her as I think about an argument to get Nadia off my back. Callie curls and relaxes her fingers, and a small gasp escapes from her lips.

"And she can learn. She's unlike anyone I've ever met." I watch Callie's eyes flutter. "So, back off. I have to go."

"Don't hang up, Mase." Hunter's voice echoes through the line again. "We can talk about it. If you really like her, we can make sure she's safe."

"Bye, Hunter." I hang up without responding to him. He might think he knows how to keep a human in our world safe, but once he realizes she's not some ordinary human, he'll have no idea. I don't even think he could persuade the council to stay out of Callie's life. It worked for him and Nadia, and they made it happen for Evie, but Callie has so much to offer our world. They'd have a lot to fear from her as well.

"M-Mason?" Callie's voice pulls my attention to her.

I crawl toward the bed and take her hand in mine. "You're safe. Just relax. You've been through a lot."

She shifts to her side. Her endless blue eyes blink away tears. "I feel like death."

"Let me get you some water."

She squeezes my hand. "No, please, just stay with me. I'm scared."

She rolls over and pulls my arm so I climb into bed next to her. Her cold hand sends a shiver down my back. She slides her arms around me, burying her face in my chest, and I wrap my comforter around us.

"Mason," she whispers, her eyes still closed.

"Yeah?"

"Thanks for being here."

I couldn't imagine being anywhere else. "It's nothing."

She presses her forehead to my chest, and my heart picks up pace. "I heard what you said on the phone." She says it so quietly, I almost don't hear her.

"You don't have to worry about my brother."

"It's not that." She tilts her head back to look up at me, her lashes casting shadows under her eyes.

"I meant everything I said." And I did.

She closes her eyes, a smile playing on her lips. "I feel the same."

15

⌒Beautiful Soul⌒

CALLIE

SUNSHINE STREAMS THROUGH the crack in the curtain, brightening a new day. I roll over to face Mason still asleep on the bed next to me. Every part of me aches, my body stiff like I haven't moved in hours. I ease off the bed and shuffle to the bathroom in the hall.

Splashing cold water on my face, I wash my sleep away and make sure I'm not trapped in some weird dream. My reflection shows how awful I look with my ashen skin and shadowed under-eyes. I look as bad as I feel. Fighting to get out of Jax's body wrecked me both mentally and physically. I wonder how much of my soul I lost while doing so. I'm sure possessing a person who survives by consuming a life force has consequences. I can't think about that now, not when the night curled in Mason's arms remains fresh in my mind. The only other person I've ever shared a bed with beside my family was Lily. And this was different.

After I clean myself up the best I can, I head to the kitchen to satisfy my growling stomach with a piece of cold leftover pizza, the only thing in Mason's fridge besides some water bottles. Nausea rolls through me like I have a serious hangover—one comparable to last New Year when Lily's mom allowed us to help ourselves to the few bottles of champagne she received from one of her clients for Christmas. I grimace, taking another bite, hoping the carb overload will stop my sudden need to throw up.

Perching on the arm on the couch, I stare at the blank TV. The ringing of a phone cuts through the quiet air, drawing my attention to my cell phone sitting next to my bag on the table. I shove the last bite of crust into my mouth and unlock my phone.

A text message from Brendan sends fear down my back. He's not exactly the person I wanted to see flash across my screen. With a shaking finger, I click on the notification to read his message.

Need to talk. Meet me? I expected a giant paragraph wishing the most awful things upon me, but I guess Brendan's full of surprises.

I consider not texting him back.

My phone chimes again with another text message from Brendan.

Please. I'm sorry. Have to explain.

I sigh and write, *Can't 2day. Busy.*

I don't even have the chance to set my phone down before he replies, *Tmrw?*

I quickly type, *I'll let you know*, and then toss my phone into my bag. If Brendan wanted to talk, he could call. It'd be easier to listen to him than to have to see him in person because of what he did last night. I don't want anything to do with him. I'm afraid he's too hard headed to take no for an answer, so I'll have to do my best to avoid him until he realizes how awful he's acting.

"How are you feeling?" Mason stands in the doorway to his bedroom, drawing my attention away from my phone. His dark hair sticks up on one side, and he's still wearing his clothes from yesterday.

I brush my messy hair with my fingers. "Terrible."

He frowns as he crosses the room to me. Touching my cheek to move my dark hair from my face, he takes a moment to search my eyes. I lean into his hand, his fingers smooth despite the few scars decorating his skin. His forehead creases in the middle, just studying me, and I clench my fists to stop my hands from reaching up to touch his hand.

He drops his hand back to his side, leaving a spot of warmth running from my cheek down my neck. "If you don't feel any better by tonight, I'll call in some favors to get you checked out by a doctor."

I nod. "I think I'll be fine. I just need a hot shower and another nap."

Mason motions for me to follow him back into his bedroom. He pulls a T-shirt and some basketball shorts from his dresser and hands them to me. "Clean towels are in the bathroom cupboard, and there's a drawer of necessities under the sink. I can toss your clothes in the washer if you drop them outside the bathroom door."

I suck in my bottom lip. This isn't how I imagined spending my day. It's awkward for me to impose on Mason, but I'm enjoying his company. Memories from last night trickle into my mind—the conversation I overheard him have, how sweet he was to watch over me, and how safe he made me feel when I felt like my world was coming to an end.

"Can you text Lily and tell her I'm okay?" I ask.

"Already did last night," he says. "But I'll text her again."

Smiling once more, I keep my eyes trained on him until I close the door completely. Hot water steams the air from the shower, fogging the mirror. The heat sinks into my bones before I even step in. I slip from my clothes and pull a towel from the cupboard to wrap myself in to crack the door open to hand my clothes to Mason.

Music from the living room hums over the water, and I let myself get lost in my thoughts. I don't know how I'm going to live my life now, pretending I'm normal. How will I go home and look my parents in the eyes like everything is okay? As much as this crazy world full of things made from my nightmares scares me to death, I can't turn my back on it. I can't find the strength to stay away. Because in this strange, new world, I've met Mason. And deep in my soul, I know he's supposed to be in my life whether or not we're together. It was fate that I stumbled upon someone who can see my soul. It is fate that won't let me leave.

MASON

I throw Callie's clothes in the washer and then sit down at my dining room table. I can't avoid talking to Dmitri forever, and I prefer he didn't show up at my door. Staring at another missed call on my screen, I force myself to hit *Call Back*.

The line doesn't even ring before Dmitri picks up his phone. "You're ignoring me."

Yeah, and? Dmitri never circles around the subject. "I'm avoiding everyone."

"I need an explanation for what's going on. If you're in trouble, I can help you." Dmitri's deep voice reminds me of my own dad. I haven't seen him in years, since he left my mom when she put her job before our family, and I almost tell Dmitri what's going on. Almost.

The faint noise of the shower, knowing who's behind the closed door, stops me. "It isn't council business. It's personal."

"I'm not telling you as a council officer."

"Everything's fine, really."

Dmitri clears his throat.

"What?" I ask.

"I had to release the two shifters you had Kat bring in. They weren't under investigation, and you didn't provide any satisfactory evidence to start a case against them. You should've answered your phone last night."

Anger builds in my chest. "They tried kidnapping my friends."

"Kat mentioned that, but you didn't follow protocol. You should've brought in the victims, Mason. You still can, you know."

I shake my head even though he can't see me. "No, I know what happens to victims, and I want them out of this. They're not the ones who are a threat to the community. Those guys you released are."

"They claim it was a misunderstanding," Dmitri says.

"More of a threat, but whatever. I needed to make a point."

"About a girl?"

I sigh. "Nadia told you."

"You wouldn't answer your phone for me, so yeah. It's unlike you to act out without good reason, and if the shifters are targeting a girl, we need to intervene. She needs to file a report and proceed through the proper channels. I hope you've told her this. Young shifters are impulsive, and we need to do what we can to keep everyone involved safe."

I don't respond. I know all this. But the problem is that Callie shouldn't be in the spotlight or have any attention drawn to her.

Dmitri clears his throat. "Are you even listening, Mason?"

"I wish you'd trust me and start an investigation based on my word. Brendan attacked me, too. I have the black eye to prove it"

"He's not exactly injury free, either. I hate to say this, but without a victim, there isn't much I can do. But I need you to stay out of trouble and avoid contact with Brendan before he files a complaint against you."

I scratch my head. "You know what? It's fine. It's none of the council's business anyway. I don't need you all to take special interest in my relationships."

"Mason," he says.

"It's fine. I get it. I know the rules."

He sighs. "Just be careful, will you? Your position doesn't only make you vulnerable."

I want to yell into the phone that I'm aware of Callie's vulnerability, but I close my eyes and take a deep breath to calm my nerves instead. The last thing I need is for anyone to tell me the possible outcomes of any relationships I have. I know the risk.

The shower shuts off, and I know Callie will come out any minute. She doesn't need to hear any of this. "Anything else, Dmitri?"

He's silent for a few seconds. "Take a few extra days off. I want you to really think about everything. Maybe then you'll trust us enough to ask for proper help instead of trying to take things into your own hands."

I frown without arguing. I don't need more time off, a week is plenty, but I have to take advantage of the free time I have to spend with Callie. There's a lot to do to prepare her. Because keeping her out of things for much longer isn't an option, not with everyone getting in my business. She needs to gain better control of her ability so she can fake being normal.

Callie exits the bathroom, wearing the too big clothes I gave her. She dries her dark hair with a towel and beams a smile at me. Her face glows with color, her skin slightly pink from her shower. After dropping the damp towel on top of the washer in my small kitchen, she strolls to the couch and plops down.

She pats the seat next to her. "I feel so much better."

I sit down, bumping my leg into hers. "Good enough to go out?"

Her smile widens as she stares at the clothes I lent her. "You want to take me out after everything?"

I hold her gaze. "If you let me."

"Somewhere casual."

"I think you wear those better than me."

She rolls her eyes, her cheeks reddening with blush. "Yeah, okay."

I laugh. "No, really."

Her blue eyes stare at me with such intensity I can't turn away from her. Her cool fingers twine with mine, and she leans closer. Her dark, wet hair veils her face and the scent of my shampoo wafts around me.

Brushing her hair behind her ear, I almost close the space completely. She sucks in her bottom lip for a second, looking so sexy, I can't resist kissing her. I tilt my head down, and she meets me the rest of the way, pressing her full lips against mine. I cup her face, kissing her more deeply. She lets go of my hand and slides her fingers over my shoulders and to my neck.

Her tongue slips into my mouth, sending desire through

me. Her kiss tastes like my peppermint toothpaste, and I pull her onto my lap, feeling her thighs press the outside of my legs. I run my fingers down her arms to her waist and wrap my hands behind her back, feeling her smooth skin as I play with the hem of her shirt.

Her breathing quickens as I kiss her jaw and trail my lips down to her neck. Her fingers dig into my shoulders, and she lets out a small moan. I smile into the crook of her neck, my heart pounding so hard I'm sure she can hear it rattling my rib-cage.

A buzzing sound hums through the air, and Callie reluctantly pulls back. She kisses me once more before sliding off my lap. "It could be my parents."

She stands and crosses the room to the table. I drink her in as she sweeps her hair over her shoulder. My eyes trail from the curve of her neck to the subtle sway of her hips. She peeks over her shoulder and smirks when she catches me staring.

The look doesn't last long. The second her gaze falls on her screen, the flirtatious grin melts from her face, and she stiffens. Fear darkens her wide eyes, her mouth opening and closing as she tries to find her breath.

I jump to my feet, jogging across the room, and she holds her phone up, stopping me in my tracks.

"He's at my house. Brendan is at *my* house." Her phone displays a picture of Brendan and a young boy with eyes the same shade of blue as Callie's. "He said he's not leaving until I talk to him. What if he hurts my family? They trust him."

I squeeze her trembling fingers. "He'd be breaking council

law. They don't take actions against innocents lightly."

"Aren't I innocent? Why didn't they do anything after last night?" she asks. "I thought he'd be locked up or something. Isn't that what you do?"

I cringe. "I broke protocol by not taking you in. Without a formal complaint, they had no reason to hold him," I say with an edge to my voice. If Brendan does anything crazy it would be because I didn't do my job. Callie would never forgive me.

Tears well in her eyes. "I need to go home."

Her home is the last place I want her to be. "We need to figure out what he wants first."

She tugs her hand away. "I don't care. I don't want him there. I don't want to bring my family into this."

"Callie..." My voice trails off because her reason makes perfect sense.

She brushes past me and grabs her wet clothes from the washer. "Don't. I'm going home, and I'm going to give Brendan time to say whatever it is he needs to say without you there. I don't know if it's because he's jealous or because of your job or whatever, but apparently just the sight of you sets him off, and I don't need that right now."

I straighten my shoulders. "You expect me to let you face that psycho alone?" Letting her go there would be stupid on my part. I could make a call and have Kat head over there to bring Brendan back in.

She raises her finger at me. "You can't make these decisions for me. I know you think it's your job, but my life isn't some job. Brendan isn't some monster trying to hurt me. He's just acting a little crazy because he's not getting his way or whatever. I'll talk to him and make him see."

"You don't understand the type of creature you're dealing with."

She steps into her shoes. "This isn't about him being a creature, and you can't stop me from going home to make sure he doesn't do something stupid around my family. So drop me off or don't."

She storms out of my apartment, leaving me in stunned silence. I rush to get my shoes on, grab my weaponry belt, phone, and keys, and then I head out the door. Callie is already halfway down the block, so I hop in my car and catch up to her.

I roll down the window. "Get in, Callie."

She ignores me.

I park next to the curb. "Please, just get in. I'll take you home and stay out of it for as long as it's safe."

She places her hands on her hips. "Promise? I have enough to worry about with the whole body jumping that I don't need to add boy drama to the list."

I lean over the seat and open her door. "Yeah. Now, get in."

She slides into the passenger's seat and turns to me. "And I meant what I said. My life isn't a job."

I raise my hands up. "I know that."

She huffs. "Good, because I'm really starting to like you, and I just want to make sure you don't feel obligated to stay around."

"Can I make something clear to you?" I ask.

She sucks in her bottom lip and nods.

"Staying around you isn't in my job description. It goes against everything I've been taught. If I wanted to keep you safe, I'd leave. I'd let the council handle everything."

"I'm afraid I'll start turning into a job to you. You're so adamant about protecting people."

"I protect innocent people from monsters. But you're not those people, and you don't need protection from monsters. You might not realize it, but your ability will scare a lot of people. And it's those people I want to protect you from. They're the people who'll think you're the monster innocent people need protecting from."

"But I'm not a monster," she says.

I grab her hand. "I know, and I want you to remember that. I'm here because I like you, and I don't want to lose you because people might not see what I do. Actually, most can't. They can't see how beautiful your soul is."

The corner of her lips pulls up in a small smile. "You think my soul is beautiful?"

I nod. "Like you."

Callie's phone beeps again, stealing away a moment I was hoping would last forever—her smiling at me, looking at me like I'm not the most hated guy in the creature world because of my job. She's seeing me for me.

She sets her phone on her knee. "I need to get this over with."

"I still wish you'd let me take care of things."

She leans back in her seat. "I'm the one he should be afraid of, remember? Maybe that's what I need to do. Make him fear me."

"Let's hope not."

I can't shake the bad feeling whirling through my stomach, but if I don't agree to do what Callie asks, I'm afraid she'll do something crazy—or worse, that Brendan will do something insane.

Callie rests her hand on my knee. "Sorry if it does. My family's important to me."

I pull away from the curb. "And you're important to me."

16

❧ Something Unthinkable ❧

CALLIE

MY STOMACH TWISTS in knots the closer we get to my house. I wipe my sweaty palms on the athletic shorts I'm wearing of Mason's, and I wish I'd just kept my dirty clothes on instead of letting Mason put them in the wash. If my parents see me before I have a chance to change, they'll know I didn't spend the night at Lily's. I'll be grounded forever. *That's the least of your problems.*

Rage sweeps over me, thinking about Brendan. How dare he think he can control my life like this? He acts like it's my fault he broke up with me or that I'm not sitting around crying, waiting for him to take me back. I can't believe I even fell for him.

When Mason nears my neighborhood, I motion for him to pull to the curb a street over from my house. The last thing I want is to risk being seen with him. I meant it when I said I'd face Brendan alone to get him to stop harassing me.

"My house is the next street up," I say. "I'll text you if I need you."

Mason stares past me, his eyes clouded with his own thoughts, and then he nods. Before I have a chance to open the door, he reaches out and grabs my hand. He slides a tiny syringe into it, and I study it before meeting his serious eyes.

He closes my fingers around the syringe for me. "If he tries anything—and I mean anything you don't want him to—jab him with this. It's a tranquilizer. He'll drop within a minute or two, and it'll give you a chance to run."

Fear courses through me, causing me to inhale a long breath. "I—I—" The words stick in my throat. "You think Brendan will really try to hurt me? What if he sees this?"

Mason touches my chin. "He won't suspect you have it, and I honestly don't know. He has no problem trying to hurt me, so I want you to be careful. He might try something stupid, but he might not. He could really just want to talk to you."

"Until he realizes he doesn't like what I have to say." I groan into my hands. Maybe this is a mistake. But he's at *my* house. My family can't know about any of this.

"You sure you don't want me to hand deliver a message?" Mason asks.

"Definitely not. I can just imagine the damage you'll both inflict on each other and my house."

Mason frowns. "I—"

"It's okay. I know anything you did wouldn't be intentional, but I think you have enough injuries as it is, and I don't want you getting hurt worse...even if it's part of the job."

My words melt the frown from his face. "As much as it kills me to let you go home to face a hot-headed shifter, you do have it in you to do so. I know it."

My heart rams against my ribcage, and my mouth dries. As much as I'm trying to be this big, bad brave person, I'm not. I don't like confrontation. I skipped out on my own body to avoid confrontation with Brendan, but I shouldn't be this afraid of anyone. I don't know why I'm allowing Brendan to have such control over me. *He doesn't. You're not going to let him.*

Nodding once, I shift to open the door. Mason leans closer before I move and brushes my dark hair out of my face. He kisses me, his warm lips soft against mine, and I touch the scruff on his cheek. I pull away, and his brown eyes lock me in their gaze.

He lowers his eyebrows. "Be careful. Brendan can grow muscle and height to overpower you. If he wanted to surprise you, he could change his appearance altogether."

My mouth falls open. "Seriously?"

"Yes, and I promise to teach you more. Creatures are tricky. It's how they survive in the human world. They're capable of blending in. Brendan's family is known to shift into other people, but some shifters out there change into animals or even other creatures."

My head swims with the information as I fling open the door without taking my gaze from Mason "I don't know how long I'll survive in this world."

"I'll help you."

I get out before he can convince me to stay. "I can't spend the rest of my life depending on someone. The only help you're going to give me are the skills I need to take care of myself, okay?"

He raises his eyebrows. "That was the plan."

Stepping out without another word, I close the door and head in the direction of my street. My cell phone chimes with a text message from Lily. I turn off the volume before clicking the message open.

Feeling OK?

I consider ignoring her text, but instead reply, *Almost. Heading home. Brendan's there.*

What?

Talk later.

My phone buzzes again with another message, but this time I do ignore it and shove my phone in my pocket. I'm closing in on my house and can't allow myself to be distracted.

As I turn the corner to my street, I peer around my neighborhood for anything out of place. My house is halfway down a cul-de-sac, so I usually notice when there's a new car in my neighborhood.

My driveway's empty, meaning my parents are gone, but Brendan's truck sits at the curb, facing the wrong way. He sits on a bench on my porch alone, and fear settles in my heart. He stares at his phone without looking up. I'm tempted to call Mason to tell him to come. If my brother is inside, then I won't have to worry about him. Something holds me back, though. Brendan would most likely hurt Mason. No one should face my stupid ex's wrath.

I sneak behind our bushes, next to the block wall, so he doesn't see me coming. Peering around the edge of the bushes, I catch Brendan watching me. So much for surprise. The weight of the small tranquilizer in my hand helps calm my racing heart. If something happens, I pray that Mason was right, and it can save me.

Brendan's gaze sweeps from my feet to my messy, still damp hair as I shuffle in his direction. "Max said you were at Lily's."

"I was." I don't miss a beat.

He rubs a hand over his red hair, shaking his head while smiling but not in a funny way. His eyes say everything I need to know about him. He doesn't believe me and thinks I'm an idiot for trying to fool him. His smile widens until he bares his teeth at me. "You're lying."

I keep my face expressionless. "Who cares? You're acting crazy. You know that right?"

He stands up, towering over me. Mason's warning about Brendan's ability to change even his height replays in my mind. I suddenly can't remember if Brendan was actually this tall. The information is getting to me. "Whatever. It doesn't matter."

"You're right. It doesn't. My life and whereabouts are none

of your business. You lost the right to question me." I motion toward his truck. "Now, I want you to leave. You should've never come here."

Humming under his breath, he cracks his knuckles, trying to intimidate me. I think my words got to him. "I still want to talk."

Without thinking, I jab my finger into his chest. "Quit it, Brendan. You don't scare me. I'm done talking to you. Leave me alone or I'll—" I pause to think for a second. "Or I'll file a formal complaint with the council."

He steps closer, his figure blocking out the sun, and he forces my finger to dig harder into his chest. "Go ahead and do it. My dad already pulled me from Northern Bell because of what you made your new little boyfriend do."

"Mason had nothing to do with this. It's your damn fault, Brendan."

"My fault? All I wanted was for you to give me another chance, but that stupid wannabe creature got into your head and ruined me for you."

I blink. "Mason ruined *you* for *me?*"

He growls, the noise reverberating deep in his throat like something you'd hear from an animal. "I don't even care about you anymore. You were always an uptight bitch—all high and mighty. But we have three months left until graduation, Callie. You need to fix this. I mean it."

"Maybe you shouldn't have attacked me and hurt Mason. You scared Lily." My voice rises through the air, surprising me. I clear my throat and lower my voice. "It's not my fault you're a volatile shifter with a thick skull. There's no way I'm helping you return to Northern Bell. I'm glad you're gone."

His face reddens. "I never told you I was a shifter, Callie. Who told you?"

"No one. I guessed." He knew I knew he was a creature after finding him at The Haven. It's why he wanted to get back together. Why does it even matter how I know? The fact doesn't change anything.

"I know it was Mason. I never slipped up around you, and it's not something you could've guessed. Someone would have had to have told you. I know you aren't really part of the creature community, Callie. You're human."

"How do you know? You kept being a shifter from me. Why is it hard to believe that maybe I can hide my creature self from you, too." The longer I stand here, the angrier I get.

"Because I'm not stupid."

He reaches out and snatches the front of my shirt. "I want you to tell me the truth. I know it was Mason."

Fear slices through me as I try to pull back, but Brendan's tight hold doesn't let me get away from him. He strolls back with me until I stumble off the porch and into the bushes. He pushes me until my bare calves scratch on the branches. The force causes me to drop the tranquilizer. It hits the ground with a thud.

Brendan's gaze follows the sound to the syringe. "You're trying to set me up."

Faster than I can react, Brendan lifts me right off my feet and shakes me like it'll somehow make an admission fall from me. Rage burns away his mocking expression, filling his eyes with enough darkness to send panic deep into my very essence. I suppress a scream, afraid to draw attention from my brother or grandpa, who I know are zoned out in front of the TV on the other side of the wall. I can hear it through the window. But the distraction could save my life.

Before I can get enough air into my lungs to scream, Brendan slaps his hand over my mouth while forcing me away from the bushes. My eyes dart to the discarded tranquilizer, but there's no possible way I'll ever be able to reach it.

A laugh erupts from his mouth, startling me. "You know it's against the law to give away a creature's secrets to someone not involved in our community. Once I tell the council, none of this will matter. You won't get to see Mason ever again. I know what they do to people like him. Traitors."

I breathe in and out of my nose. Technically, Mason didn't break any laws. I overheard his mom talking to him, but I already knew Brendan wasn't human because I saw him in The Haven. But, if I choose to stay away from the council, I won't be able to tell them the truth. They'd lock Mason up like Brendan says. He'd do it to spite me.

So, this means I have to stay good on my threat. I'll not let Mason face punishment on my behalf. If only I knew what that meant for me.

Yanking away, I scrape my elbow on the wall, putting distance between me and Brendan. "That won't happen. I'll make sure the council knows the truth."

His smile sends a chill through me. "How? The council

doesn't know you exist."

Brendan reaches out, wraps his hands around my neck, and lifts me off my feet again. His strength crushes my throat, and I can't breathe. I kick my legs, fighting the best I can, but I barely tap his knees. I should've never threatened him. I should've just told him I'd fix things. Now, he's going to do something unthinkable to save his own skin and ruin Mason's life.

My eyes burn, bulging from their sockets from the lack of air. I struggle, trying my best to get him to loosen his grip long enough that I can gasp. I just need one breath. I need to escape.

My ears pop, and the weight of the world flies off me. The pain melts away as quickly as it had come, and I gasp, realizing I'm not actually breathing. I'm nowhere near my body.

From a few feet away, I watch in horror as Brendan squeezes the life out of my body, his wicked blue eyes sending a chill through my spirit.

I can't save myself now. I can't do anything to stop him.

MASON

It takes everything in me not to drive around the corner to watch Callie from a distance. I turn on the radio and listen to music, staring at my phone, waiting for her to text. If I don't hear from her in a minute, I'll check on her myself to make sure she's okay.

My phone buzzes with a message from Lily.

Are you w/Callie?

I twist my lips down and instead of texting her back, I call her.

"Mason!" Her high pitched voice cuts through the line.

"What were you thinking taking Callie home?"

I stare out my rearview mirror. "She didn't exactly give me a choice."

"Is she okay? What's going on with Brendan? You're taking care of him, right?" She assaults me with question after question without giving me the opportunity to answer any of them.

I blow static into the phone. "Calm down. I'm down the street from Callie's. She thought my presence around Brendan would make things worse."

"And you listened to her?" Anger laces her words. "Some protector you are. I thought you liked her?"

It's my turn to get angry. "That has nothing to do with this."

"It has everything to do with this. Brendan being at Callie's house right now is your fault. Whatever you did got Brendan pulled from school. He is pissed and blames Callie."

"Why didn't you tell us sooner?"

She groans. "I just heard. I tried texting her, but she's ignoring me now. You need to check on her."

I toss my phone on the seat without hanging up and pull away from the curb. I should've seen this coming. This is more than Brendan being pissed that Callie isn't giving him the time of day. He's planning to retaliate because I had him taken in to the council. I guess his dad pulled him from school to keep him out of trouble, like he did at The Haven. It's all coming together now.

Rolling through the stop sign, I turn onto Callie's street. She didn't tell me her address, and there are a dozen houses on the cul-de-sac. I spot Brendan's black truck, but before I can accelerate, a guy jumps in the street, causing me to slam my brakes.

I park my car in the middle of the road and hop out.

"It's best if you turn around and leave, man. Take the opportunity to get a head start. That girl isn't worth you losing your position with the council, is she? This is between her and Brendan." The shifter, who I now know is Brendan's cousin, clenches his hands into fists a few feet away.

Sliding my tranquilizer gun from my weaponry belt, I aim it at the shifter's chest. "Move."

"This is a warning, and you can't do that if I'm not threatening you. I know the laws."

Nice try. I shoot the dart anyway. "No, but you're trying to stop me from doing my job."

The guy rips the dart from his chest and smashes it on the ground like it'll somehow stop the sedative from coursing through his veins. I expect him to launch at me, but instead he growls and runs toward Brendan's truck. He gets behind the wheel, honks the horn twice, and then slumps in the seat.

I listen to my surroundings. It's eerily quiet, and I'm afraid I'm too late.

CALLIE

Brendan drops me when my body slumps. He thinks he's knocked me out...or killed me. What he doesn't know about me might've saved my life. Not even taking a moment to check my pulse, he averts his eyes toward my house. A horn honks twice, and he peers over his shoulder.

Without hesitating, he bends down and hoists my body up over his. Panic washes over me, and I charge toward him, jumping into his head. He's insane if he thinks he's taking my body anywhere. I don't care if I get stuck again. He can't take me.

"Let me go!"

Brendan winces as my scream rips through his mind. He drops me again, and I try not to think about the pain I'll wake up to. Brendan covers his eyes with his hands and shakes his head, trying to expel the sound of my voice from his head.

"If you ever try something like this again, I will hurt you."

"What the? Callie?"

"Who else would it be? Now get out of here."

He glances down at my body. When I expect him to leave, he bends down, checks my pulse, and picks me up again. Anger swells through me. Brendan's hands shake, but he continues to throw me over his shoulder again.

"I don't know what you are, but try anything stupid, and I'll kill your body. This is starting to make sense. I knew a council agent would never go for an ordinary human, but I knew you weren't a creature."

His words sting, thinking that Mason is only interested in me because of my ability, but I push the thought away. I won't let Brendan get to me, and I'm definitely not letting him take my body. Blackmail isn't going to stop me.

"Let me go!" The world shifts, my ears popping from the sudden change from weightless to solid. I blink a few times as the realization washes over me. I've taken control of Brendan's body.

Fear rushes through me, but it's not my own. Brendan's emotions blend with mine. I gently set my body down in the grass and step to where I had dropped the syringe. Plucking it off the ground, I frown at it in my palm. I'm going to have to jab it into Brendan's arm while I'm in control.

"Don't do this, Callie! I swear, I'll leave you alone," he pleads with me, his emotions feeling sincere, yet I can't tell if he's only saying it out of desperation.

I stick his arm with the tranquilizer and ignore the stinging sensation crawling through this temporary body. Closing my eyes as dizziness washes over me, I concentrate on projecting from the person I now hate the most in the world. Brendan drops to his knees as he regains control and shadows edge his vision.

"Don't move." Mason stands twenty feet away.

Brendan loses consciousness, and Mason's the last thing I see.

17

⤳Bad to Worse⤳

MASON

I SLIDE MY tranquilizer gun back into my weaponry belt when Brendan falls face first into the grass near Callie's body. Rushing to her side, I pull her into my arms. I want her as far away from Brendan as possible.

Her eyes flutter open, and she moans. "You can't leave him. He'll hurt my family."

"They'll be fine for a few minutes. I need to get you out of here." I pick up my pace and jog her to my car. "Think you can drive?"

She licks her dry lips. "Yeah, I'm okay. Just a little

bruised."

Her fingers trail to the row of finger-shaped bruises spotting her neck. Fury pulses through me, my heart racing, as I think about Brendan putting his hands on Callie, hurting her. He'll be lucky if he even makes it to the council alive. Accidents happen—fast and unexpectedly. With him knocked out, it could be so easy.

I puff out a breath and set her on her feet, trying to get myself under control before she sees the murderer lurking within my eyes. Shifters aren't high on the risk-factor list with the council, but I'm starting to wonder why they aren't. *You can't kill him, Mason. Get yourself under control.*

Taking a moment more, I inspect the rest of Callie, making sure she's not injured anywhere else. When I don't see anything else apart from some scrapes, I hand her my car keys. "Lock the doors while you wait for me. I need you to go with me somewhere."

She nods before wrapping her arms around me for a second. I kiss the top of her head and nudge her to get into the car. I'll be on edge until we get out of here unseen. If anyone spots us, I'll have to call the council. I want to avoid it for as long as I can.

I jog back to Callie's yard and tug a zip tie from my weaponry belt. Binding Brendan's hands behind his back, I drag him across the lawn to his truck, constantly searching around for people, including Callie's family. Things would move a lot faster if my arm was completely healed, but now, I push through the pain, and Brendan doesn't deserve to be carried. I do nothing to avoid every rock and curb I cross over.

Adrenaline courses through me as I toss his body into the bed of the truck, and then I open the driver's side door and tug Brendan's cousin out. Binding his hands as well, I hoist him over the side and into the back, using a tarp in the bed to cover them.

I wave to Callie once I'm behind the wheel, and she pulls away from the curb to follow me. I navigate the empty streets toward the freeway, a million ideas clouding my mind. None of them seem good enough to give Brendan what he deserves while keeping Callie out of it. My only plan is to get these guys out of here.

Every few seconds, I flick my gaze to my rearview mirror to watch Callie. She maintains my speed and follows me off the freeway at an exit a few miles away from her house. I pull into the empty parking lot of an abandoned, out-of-business furniture store and peer into the bed of the truck at the two shifters before jogging to Callie.

"I have a friend who can manipulate people's minds. I'm going to call her to see if she can help." I rest my hands on the door. "She'll be able to plant some suggestions about Brendan into your family's minds, too. It'll stop them from trusting him."

"It won't hurt them, will it?" Her soft voice barely comes out as a whisper. If only I could pull her to me and take her away from here this second.

I shake my head. "Enchantresses are really good at what they do, especially Mira."

Callie nods without asking any more questions. Rushing back to the shifters, I take their cell phones and lock them in the truck with the keys. I leave them passed out and bound in the bed of the truck and slide into the passenger's seat when I realize Callie doesn't switch places.

"Know the way back to my apartment?" I ask.

"Yeah. Can you text Lily and tell her I need her to cover for me for another night?"

Pulling my cell phone from my pocket, I write Lily a text before tapping in Mira's phone number from memory. The silence between Callie and I feels heavy with questions left unsaid. If only I could manage to say what's really on my mind. I should ask her if she's okay, but clearly she isn't as she accelerates onto the freeway faster than even I drive.

Instead, I rub my fingers over her leg with one hand and clutch my phone to my ear with the other to listen to each ring.

"What's up, Mason?" Mira's soft voice comes through the line.

I can't help the sigh I release. "I need another favor." Mira's the one who helped me enroll at Northern Bell, and she did it without question. "I'm in some trouble, and I can't ask the council for help."

She's quiet for a minute. "I'm on an assignment with Nate. I won't be back to the city until Tuesday."

I frown. That's two days away. I should've known the council would have Mira and Nate out on a mission. They're gone more than they're here, and Mira splits her spare time between her family in California and the Enchantress Sisterhood.

"No chance you could make it back early? It's kind of important."

"Hold on." Her voice muffles through the line, like she's covering the receiver with her hand as she talks to someone.

"Mason?" A familiar, masculine voice sounds through the line.

"Hey, Nate. Think you can come home to help me?"

"What exactly have you gotten yourself into?"

I glance at Callie in my peripheral vision. "It's a long story."

"Well, condense it."

I sigh. "I met a girl—who's human." I pause for a moment, trying my best to skip over anything that would give Callie's ability away. "And, well, her ex-boyfriend is a shifter. I need Mira to make him forget about her."

Callie grips the steering wheel. "Brendan knows I'm not ordinary. I had to possess him," she whispers so quietly that I almost don't hear her.

When her admission sinks in, I clench my teeth. It's gone from bad to worse—downright awful. "Look, this guy is dangerous. He tried to kill her."

"And that's what we do with the council, Mase. He needs to be taken in."

I'm not getting anywhere with this. "I've tried, but I need to keep Callie out of things. They wouldn't hold the guy without the victim. Please, I really need help. It's not safe for Callie. She just learned about our world. She has a family."

"Oh, Mason." Mira's voice echoes through the line. "I'll

see what I can do. Maybe I can get in touch with one of my local sisters, but they might not want to help since it's against council regulations to intervene. Nate and I will try our best to come as soon as we can if we can't find anyone. In the meantime, stay home or something." That did the trick. Growing up in the human world, thinking she was human, Mira has a soft spot for people who discover our world. Playing on Mira's empathy should make me feel guilty, but I don't. I need the help she'll give me with no questions asked.

I blow a breath in relief. "Will do. Thanks, Mira. I owe you."

She laughs. "We're friends, Mason. I don't keep tabs on favors. Just stay safe and stay out of trouble."

When I hang up the line, I notice Callie's white-knuckled grip on the wheel. I can't imagine what she's thinking. Everything about the creature world is foreign to her—hell, I'm still adjusting my ideals to match the truth I was never told before I joined the council.

"We'll just lay low for a while," I say. "Brendan doesn't know where I live."

Callie sucks in her bottom lip. "Brendan knows I'll come running if my family is in danger."

"He also knows you can possess him if he tries anything."

"He's going to tell someone about me."

I wouldn't put it past Brendan. I just hope Mira can get here in time to do damage control. Relying on someone else sucks, but I don't know what else to do except threaten Brendan's life. If he doesn't take my threats seriously, could I follow through? It'd leave me in a dangerous position and out of the council's good grace. They couldn't manipulate my mind and put me back in human society like they can with others, not with my special ability. I'd probably lose my freedom altogether.

"If he does, we'll figure it out."

Callie exits the freeway and continues toward my apartment. She doesn't say anything for a while, lost in her thoughts, and I wish for a minute I could listen in. When my familiar neighborhood comes into view, she drops a hand from the steering wheel and rests it on top of mine. I should say something comforting. I should say anything to break the silence, but my thoughts whirl in a jumbled mess in my mind.

It's my fault she's in this situation. If I hadn't meddled my way into her life, hadn't tried to investigate by myself, Callie would still be safe. She might have found the creature world, but she wouldn't have been involved in it. *You don't know that. If it wasn't you who found her, someone else would've.*

"As much as I want to hide in your apartment until your friends come, I can't let Brendan ruin my life. I can't let you put your life on hold for me either, Mason. What'll happen to you if your boss finds out? Brendan threatened to tell the council you told me about him. He said it was against the law to tell a creature's secrets." Callie blinks tears from her eyes without looking at me.

Gazing out the window, I say, "Don't worry about me, Callie. I'll be fine. The worst that can happen is they'll outcast me. I'll have to figure out what to do with myself. I could go to college like my brother." I don't even believe the lies coming out of my mouth. The council won't release an altered human into society. Not with my past. If I'm not with the council, I'm against them.

"I'm not worth giving up everything you know for." She says it like it's a fact. "You don't even know me that well." Which is true. Denying it would make me sound crazy even though I do think Callie could be worth it. She could be a lot of things to me. It's those possibilities that don't send me running. Finding someone who puts up with my bullshit is worth the effort.

"No, but I want to know you. And wouldn't it be kind of pathetic if my job was everything I knew?" I suppress my urge to frown. In the last few months, my job has been everything. I could barely take a day off without wanting to patrol the city just to make sure nothing was happening. But since I've met Callie, I see the possibility of more. I like that possibility.

She laughs, the sound breathless, like she's fighting to stay serious. "You know what I mean."

"You were quite clear about it."

She fakes a pout that quickly turns into a smile, sending my heart racing. "Stop it. You can't make me laugh in a time like this."

"You feel better, don't you?"

She purses her lips to hide her smile. "A little." Turning into my apartment complex, she parks in my single-car garage. The leather seat squeaks as she swivels to face me, leaning forward to close the distance between us. I meet her halfway, and she brushes her lips against mine. It's feathery soft and short but nothing less than incredible. A kiss like hers leaves me craving a thousand more.

She pulls away with a smile. "Thanks for not abandoning me."

I gaze into her blue eyes. "That's the last thing I'd ever do."

CALLIE

A knock sounds on the door. Mason pushes from his spot on the couch and crosses the room to answer it. He peeks through the peephole and then opens the door. Lily rushes in, pushing past him, and flings her arms around me.

She breathes into my ear as she smothers me. "I was so scared. I'd have had to go after Brendan myself if he hurt you." She's not kidding. We'd do anything to protect and avenge each other.

Jax strolls in and shakes Mason's hand. I didn't realize Lily had called him, but I'm glad she did. I don't think she's safe from Brendan either, and if a guy who can suck the soul from someone wants to hang out with her to protect her and not kill her, I'm all for it. *What is happening to our lives?*

"This is a nightmare, Lily. You should stay far away from me." Tears spring from my eyes, and I sniffle against her shoulder. They're words she should listen to, but the last thing I want is to lose my best friend when I need her—but that's the thing. I might lose her because I need her. "I'm only alive because I possessed him. I don't understand why he's so crazy."

Lily pats my back. "You're the crazy one if you think I'm letting my best friend handle this alone."

My heart hangs heavily in my chest. "Thanks, Lily."

I swipe my hands over my cheeks and turn to face Mason and Jax, who talk quietly near the door. Mason notices me watching them and the conversation falls silent. He motions Jax farther into the living room, clearly done talking about me.

Jax takes a good look at me as I stand next to Lily with teary eyes. Reaching out his hand, he slowly brushes away the dark hair off my neck, pushing it over my shoulder. The face he gives Mason speaks volumes with the way his dark brows sink over his eyes.

A muscle in his cheek twitches. "And everyone thinks I'm the monster."

I pout my bottom lip out, pulling my hair back to cover the aching bruises on my neck, which isn't the only thing that currently hurts. My shoulders, knees, and calves also burn with pain. "If only they knew. You're one of the nicest guys I've met. You chose to help us when you could've walked away."

Lily hooks her arm through Jax's. "He's brave, too."

I hide my smile with my hand, watching Jax's ears burn red. He brushes invisible dust off his sleeves and rocks on his heels. "Not really. I just can't stand around and do nothing when someone's in trouble."

"Which is why he's volunteered to watch your family," Mason says.

Lily's eyes sparkle in the light. "With me of course."

She can't be serious. "No way. I want you here with me where I can watch you." Like I can protect her from the universe if things turn bad. It doesn't stop me from wanting to keep her in my sight where I'll know she's safe.

"I'll be fine. Plus, I'm so not going to be a third wheel to your slumber party."

Heat blossoms into my cheeks. I can't hide behind my makeup like I usually do because I'm not wearing any. Shifting my gaze to Mason, who keeps his face expressionless, I consider pushing Lily toward the room so I can shake her without anyone else seeing.

"You'd never be a third wheel," I say, trying my best to keep calm even though Lily put a whole bunch of anxiety-inducing thoughts into my head about spending the night in Mason's apartment. Last night was different because I was sick, but I feel a million times better. Not to mention we've kissed. A lot. I'm sure I'll be too nervous to even sleep.

Lily rolls her eyes. "Stop arguing. As your best friend, I'm telling you that I will do everything in my power to make sure this guy keeps your family safe." She pokes Jax in the arm.

Jax grins at Lily, the smile he gives her makes me feel like maybe things aren't so bad. "We should go."

I'm tempted to beg them to stay a little longer. The last place I want Lily to be is checking on my parents for me. What if Brendan shows up and tries to take her? What if he has more friends, and Jax can't fight them off? I don't know what I'd do if anyone got hurt because of me, but I have to trust they can take care of themselves.

Lily's smile melts into a frown, and she hugs me again. "It's going to be okay, Callie. I promise. If there is any sign of trouble, I'll call the police. It might be enough to deter Brendan long enough to get help."

Straightening my shoulders, I hold my head high even though I want to cover my face and cry. If Lily can handle this, so can I. I refuse to let my fear consume me. "Call me if you need anything, okay."

"I won't, though."

When Lily waltzes from the apartment, holding onto Jax, I turn toward the wall and hug myself for comfort. The sound of Mason closing the door clicks through the air, feeling more final than it should. Without looking at him, I feel his gaze on me. A shadow crosses the wall and then strong arms embrace me, Mason's heartbeat pounding against my back as he holds me from behind, resting his chin on my shoulder. It's enough to fissure my stone façade. My mouth quivers, and I sniffle, hating myself for crying. He probably thinks I'm a goner if something as little as the thought of something bad happening is enough to set me off. I bet Mason's never cried in his life.

I spin in his arms to rest my head against his chest. "I'm sorry. I can't stop."

His fingers rub between my shoulder blades. "Don't apologize. You're not doing anything wrong."

I laugh, hiccupping. "I bet you never cry, especially over something like this."

"Not true. If I was you, I'd probably be rocking myself in the corner," he says, his face oh-so-serious and sexy.

I pull back and smack his shoulder. "You would not."

He smirks. "Okay, so maybe not, but I'm not some emotionless fighter. I handle things differently when I'm faced with terrible circumstances."

"How?"

He rubs his hand over the back of his neck while keeping his other one against my back. "I focus on things I can control."

"Like your superpowers?" I ask.

That gets a good laugh out of him. Talking with Mason lightens my mood enough that my tears stop falling. With him around, things don't feel as unbearable. Things feel miniscule, like I can face them head on.

"Yeah, kind of," he says. "Which isn't a bad idea. I think it'll help take your mind off things."

He's right. Projecting might ease the fear in my heart. Not because it'll take my mind off things, but because I can go check on my parents myself without having to worry about getting hurt. Mason would protect my body for me—he'd keep me safe. I'll just pop in for a minute and come back.

When I don't respond right away, he says, "Why do you look like you're planning on doing more than practice in my apartment?"

"How'd you know?" I can't fool Mason, and there's no point in lying. He'd watch my soul leave his apartment anyway.

"Because if I were you, it's what I'd do." He studies me for a minute. "And if that's what you want, go ahead. I'll make sure your body is safe."

I kiss him. "Thanks. I'll be back soon."

Without another word, I project from my body and watch as Mason catches it. For the first time all day, I actually feel safe. I feel like things will finally be okay.

18

ᴄ⁓Fugitives⁓ᴐ

MASON

CALLIE JERKS UP on my bed, gasping and clutching the comforter. She's only been gone ten minutes, but I can't help thinking something went wrong. She sweeps her hair from her face, the wildness in her eyes vanishing as she blinks.

I relax. "That was fast."

"Well, there's no traffic getting in your way when you can fly through things." She swings her legs to the edge of the bed. "Not to mention I can literally leap twenty feet at a time. I wish I could show you."

Her description of what it's like to project actually sounds a lot more fun than I imagined. "Yeah..." I don't know if I'd be brave enough to abandon my body no matter how awesome it sounds. "So, everything okay?"

She nods. "Thanks for not protesting too much. I'm on edge."

"As long as your body's safe, you're safe, unless you come across creatures of the soul manipulation variety."

"Which are?"

I move to my dresser and pull out a book from my top drawer. It was a gift from my mom a long time ago—a manual of sorts from her time studying creatures. Half the information it contains reads like fiction, as most of it isn't true, but I still felt the need to keep it. It's the only book I have with a list of every creature my mom ever encountered. The Creature Council has nothing of the sort—at least at my disposal.

Sitting on the bed next to her, I flip open the book, skipping past the graphic images included to scare people into hating creatures. The organization my mom previously worked for spent decades killing and experimenting on creatures in the name of saving humanity, but in the end, they needed creatures to save them. It's what brought the Creature Council and the remaining members of the Human Preservation Agency together to make the council what it is today.

"There are different levels of soul manipulators. The most feared are incubi and succubi. They have the ability to consume life forces, but they're also pretty hard to kill. The best way to describe them would be parasitic. If you do kill one, they release a scent that'll make you consume their flesh, then they body jump and take you over."

Callie pales, swinging her gaze from the book to me. "Wait, what? You mean it's possible that body doesn't belong to Jax?"

"Don't worry about Jax. That's his body. The council monitors all incubi and puts restrictions on them. No creature is allowed to kill."

"Is Lily safe with him? He's not going to accidentally hurt her, is he?" The worry on her face makes it clear she's now doubting the safety of her best friend in the hands of someone who survives on other's life forces.

I shrug. "There's always a risk. I'm sure if things get serious, they'll discuss it."

She blows hair from her face. "Okay, what else?"

"This one isn't in the book, but there are nightmare inflictors, a creature who survives by turning your dreams into nightmares." I lean over and scoop a framed picture from my nightstand. I point to Nadia. "My brother's dating one. People volunteer to experience a nightmare from a nightmare inflictor, because it's supposed to be the scariest thing you've ever experienced."

"I can see the allure if you like being scared. Lily would love it." Callie flips a page and points. "What's a sin-eater?"

"A creature who redeems bad souls. Unfortunately, if you have a bad soul in need of redeeming, you also die."

"What a sucky ability." Callie flips another page. It's a picture of a tanzanite stone containing a wraith, one I taped in and added notes myself. "A wraith? That's what you thought I was, right?"

I take the book from her and close it. "Yeah, wraiths are the worst. They're spirits who refuse to move on and possess people to live a sort of half-life. They feed on brains to maintain their bodies."

Callie's eyes widen. "Wow, like a zombie?"

I twine my fingers with hers. "Zombie's aren't what you think. They're just reanimated corpses controlled by necromancers, which I guess is another type of soul manipulation. They could probably control wraiths if they wanted. But with wraiths, they're parasitic and extremely hard to get rid of. There's only one person who safely extracts wraiths from their hosts without killing the host at the moment."

"Was this person the one you would've called if I couldn't get out of Jax's body?"

I nod. "Yeah, Nate is like me in a way. We were genetically altered months apart. It's his girlfriend who's going to help you get your life back."

"I'm glad you know such good people."

I grin. "We've had our ups and downs, but in the end, we're all on the same side."

Callie leans her head on my shoulder. "You live such an interesting life, Mason. I wonder..." Her voice trails off.

I gaze at our hands. "What?"

She tightens her fingers on my hand, curling her thumb and index finger around mine. "Maybe we met for a reason. What if I can help people, too? Maybe you should take me to the council. It'd make things easier."

Her words surprise me. I don't think she realizes what that choice would do to her life. She'd have to give up her family and friends, her wants for the future, and she'd have to be willing to give up her life. Helping others comes with sacrifice, and it's not always worth it. The bad guys sometimes win.

"Don't make any decisions yet. You should at least finish high school."

"A little hypocritical, don't you think?"

"I always wonder what it'd be like if I did," I say.

A knock sounds on the door, drawing my attention to the living room. I'm not expecting company.

Hopping to my feet, I slide my knife from my weaponry belt. If this small gesture of uncertainty doesn't persuade her to rethink her thoughts about the council, I'm not sure what will. Having to grab a weapon just to open my door isn't exactly the most fun aspect of my life, but it is necessary.

I turn to Callie. "Stay here."

She stands and moves next to the door to watch me. The banging on the door continues, and I peer into the peephole and blow out a breath. Hunter and Nadia wait on the other side of the door.

I turn away.

"We know you're in there, Mason. Open up. It's important," Hunter calls out.

I sigh and unlock the door. "I'm busy."

Nadia glides into the room. "Are you out of your mind or something?"

Hunter grasps her shoulder before she can get in my face.

"Calm down, Nadia."

"How am I supposed to calm down? He kidnapped two shifters and left them bound and defenseless in a parking lot. The whole shifter community wants his head. You shouldn't be so calm. He's put my father in a terrible position." Nadia shrugs away from Hunter inhumanly fast and grips the front of my shirt. "Tell me you didn't do that."

I grimace. "I can't. I needed to buy some time."

Nadia thrusts her arms in the air. "For what?"

They won't leave until they have answers. "For Mira and Nate to come back to manipulate the shifters' memories."

"What have you done, Mase?" Hunter asks.

I don't answer right away. I thought I'd have more time before Brendan went to the council. He didn't seem like the kind to go running to tattle, especially since he knows he's in the wrong. But now, all I can think about is Callie. If Brendan plays the part of the victim, the council will have no choice but to bring me in. It'll leave Callie unprotected and in danger.

"Did the shifters mention a girl?" I ask instead of answering.

Hunter shakes his head. "Is this about the human? They didn't mention anyone but you."

"Don't say it like you aren't one." If Brendan didn't mention Callie, there was a reason, and I'm afraid to think about what he's possibly planning. With me out of the way, he'd be able to attempt anything he wanted. This is bad. "How long do I have?"

"Minutes," Nadia says. "Just turn yourself in. We'll get it

all figured out. We can help your girlfriend." Until Brendan tells them that Callie possessed him. Even an accidental possession could mean punishment, especially if Brendan plays the part. Too many people already have bad associations with me. Creatures hate me for my past.

I run to the bedroom and fling the door open. Callie stands there, wide-eyed, and when I grab a bag from my closet, she jumps into action and retrieves my weaponry belt while I toss some clothes in. Kneeling down in my closet where I keep my safe, I pull out all the cash I have. I keep some of it here and the rest of my savings in a safety deposit box at a bank downtown. It's what my mom told me to do in case something was to happen in the creature world. I never imagined it would involve me.

"Where will we go?" Callie whispers.

I hold my finger to my lips. "No one can know."

Slinging my bag over my shoulder, I lace my fingers through Callie's. We race into the living room where Nadia and Hunter stand in stunned silence. Callie squeezes my hand, her panic scrunching her brows, and I guide her past them without introducing her to them.

"Go start the car," I say to Callie. "If I'm not out in two minutes, find Jax. He'll take you somewhere safe." I hand her the bag of weapons, clothes, and money, and she races out without a second thought.

I turn to my brother. "I wasn't here, okay?"

"You're running." Hunter doesn't question the obvious.

I hug him. "Out of everyone, you should be the ones who

understand."

"Things have changed, Mason," Nadia says, crossing her arms over her chest.

I can't stop the glower crossing my face. "For you, maybe, but I'm not going to risk it. Take care of my brother. I'll call if I can."

Without looking back, I run from my apartment. I'm not sure if I'll ever see the place again—or my brother for that matter—but this is the only way I know how to protect Callie and myself. Even if I was able to explain everything to the council, it'll be my word against Brendan. I can't guarantee Callie and I would be okay in the end. I need us to be okay.

CALLIE

Drumming my fingers on the steering wheel of Mason's car, I wait outside the garage, ready to drive. With my luck, if I hadn't have pulled out, someone would've tried to trap me in.

I stare at the street in front of me, praying Mason comes soon. The last thing I want to do is leave him. Not only would my heart shatter into a million pieces if something were to happen to him, I'm also not sure I could survive on my own. I don't have the connections Mason does. I wouldn't even know who to trust apart from Jax, and he'll probably decide to stay out of it for his own safety. I can't drag any more people down.

A knock sounds on the side window, and I nearly fly from my skin. Mason opens the door when I unlock it and leans in. "I'll drive."

Hopping out, I bolt around the car while Mason gets behind the wheel. He's accelerating before I have a chance to buckle my seatbelt, and I brace myself as the tires squeal when he makes a sharp turn onto the main street leading to the highway.

"Text Lily. Tell her what's going on."

I glance at my almost dead cell phone for a second before typing, *Had to leave Mason's. Tell Jax that Brendan lied to the council. We're on the run.*

A text message pops up a second later. *Come here.*

I peer through the dark windshield. "Lily says we can go there."

Mason shakes his head. "Tell her she needs to leave, too."

Leave home now! Trust no one.

My phone rings, startling me, and I answer when I see Lily's picture. "You need to get out of there."

"What about your family?"

Tears blur my eyes. "I just have to hope that Brendan stays away."

Voices mumble through the line for a second before Lily says, "Jax said he'll call his sister to keep watch over them."

I blow a breath into the phone. "Tell him I'll owe him my life."

"Should we meet?"

I turn to Mason. "Should we meet up with them? Won't it be safer if we're all together?"

He twists his lips to the side for a second. "Jax would be helping a fugitive."

"No, Lily. It's safer if we don't. I have to go, though. My phone's about to die."

"Stay safe, Callie."

"You, too."

I hang up the phone as Mason zooms down the freeway. I can't stop thinking about the risk everyone who associates with me is taking. Mason said whoever is with him will be punished for helping a fugitive, but what about me? I'm not a part of the creature community. Holding me accountable seems unfair. Actually, it's just plain wrong.

I rest my hand on Mason's knee, and he covers my hand with his. I'm so angry with Brendan for putting me—us—through this. I just want him to pay. I want karma to take care of him so I don't have to. I hate not knowing what's going on or what to do. I'm facing all these invisible threats coming from a world I'm barely starting to understand.

Headlights shine past us. The dark road blurs as I blink away tears. It's taking everything in me to keep it together. Mason doesn't need the burden of keeping me calm.

Tears roll down my cheeks, but I angle my body in a way that Mason won't see them. "Do you have a plan?"

He doesn't answer right away. "I'd like to tell you I have everything figured out, but I don't. I don't even know where we're heading or if I should be taking you with me."

"My parents will freak out if I disappear," I say.

"I'm afraid to leave you. It might be worse than letting your family worry." Mason switches lanes.

He's right. While my absence would leave my parents' world upside down, I'll be alive—and hopefully safe. It'll give us time to figure things out and let things blow over. Maybe I could figure out a way to protect myself from any sort of back-lash from people discovering my ability.

"You're probably right. But I hate this. How can one single person get away with trying to ruin our lives? And what does he get out of it? Why does he want to?" I want so badly to body jump to find Brendan. I can imagine possessing him and not letting him go until I get answers. He couldn't hurt me that way. I could even...

I sit up straighter as an idea hits me. "Mason!"

He swerves, startled. "What's wrong?"

I bounce in my seat. "I have an idea. It's brilliant, really."

Mason shifts to look at me for a split second and then trains his eyes back to the road. "Go on."

"I want to project and find Brendan. I can possess him and pretend to be him. I'll tell the council the truth. He won't be able to stop me." I smile, thinking about it more. It could be so easy.

Mason's eyes don't light up like I expect them to. He presses his lips together and they disappear into a thin line. His brows furrow as he processes my plan. He switches lanes again, crossing over to the slow lane. He puts his blinker on but then speeds past the exit.

"Crap," he says.

"What? I think it could work.

He taps the rearview mirror. "It's not that. We're being fol-lowed."

My stomach twists into knots. Sweat beads on my fore-head, the air conditioning suddenly not cool enough, and I lick my lips, trying to moisten my mouth. My heartbeat pounds in my ears. Fear consumes my thoughts. I can't even bring myself to look in the mirror.

"I'm going to project," I say. "I can do it now. If you keep driving, I might get to Brendan in time to call the council off."

Mason speeds faster. "No. I need you to be able to run. If they catch me with your body, things will really get out of control."

"But I can fix this."

"Not if they find out about your ability. If they know about you, they'll make sure to have someone who can see souls on hand to make sure nothing is out of the ordinary. Possession is a serious offense. They wouldn't give you a chance to escape before they rip your soul from him and lock you up in an inescapable spelled rock." Mason holds my hand tighter, steering with his free hand. "I'm not worth that kind of fate. I'd rather wait it out and accept my punishment."

The thought of being stuck in some sort of spelled stone for all eternity scares me more than the thought of facing Brendan. I'd have no one to speak for me. They'd just assume I was some evil entity out to get people.

"What do I do then?" I ask.

"I'm going to exit the freeway to try to lose them. The moment I do, I want you to get out. I want you to run. Go somewhere public. Call my friend Mira and tell her what happened. Tell her as much as you're comfortable with. She'll influence your parents to relocate. She can help you start over away from this."

"What about you?" My bottom lip quivers at the thought of abandoning Mason. His plan pushes me away from him. What if it means we could never see each other again? This is so much more than protecting my life, my heart needs protecting, too.

"I'll find you again when everything is said and done." I'm afraid that would be impossible.

"What if they imprison you or worse?" I can't restart my life knowing that there's a possibility Mason's could be over. He's only known me a short while. He should be watching out for himself.

"The council doesn't hold people for long," he says.

Confusion creases my forehead. "Then what do they do?"

"They erase everything you know about the creature world and force you to start over in the human world." He swerves across a few lanes and exits the freeway. Something about his words doesn't speak the truth.

I grip the grab handle, stopping myself from bumping into him. "Mason, you're not an ordinary human. How can they change that?"

He doesn't glance at me. "I don't know, but it's the best I can hope for."

"So, you'll forget everything? Even your family?"

He runs a stop sign. "Even you."

I suppress a sob in my throat. This can't be happening. This can't be how our story together ends. It'd be like all of this was for nothing. I didn't start to immerse myself in Mason's world to have him taken from mine. I won't allow it. I won't allow anyone to intervene and change what I want my future to hold.

"Grab the bag, Callie. I want you to take it with you," Mason says.

My hands shake as I tug it from the backseat. "You might need it."

"You might need it more."

I clutch the bag against my chest. It contains a few thousand dollars and weapons I don't even know how to use. *God, I can't do this.*

Mason lets go of my hand. "Get ready. I'm going to stop at the corner. Jump out and run. You'll reach the Stargazer Mall in about half a mile. Make the call to Mira there. You have enough money for a hotel. You might have to pay extra to stay because of your age."

"Mason, please. I can't do this." I beg him with my eyes even though he stares at the road.

He slows down. "Yes, you can." The car jerks as he slams the brakes. Quickly leaning over, he kisses me on the cheek. "Take care of yourself. I'll figure out how to find you, I promise."

I hop out and sprint from the car, cold air rushing around me. Mason's tires squeal as he speeds off, leaving me to my own fate. Tears sting my cheeks, and it's hard to see, but I don't stop. I won't stop. I'll never stop until someone forces me to, but even then, I won't let them.

19

ᴄᴏ Treason ᴏ

MASON

I SPEED AWAY from Callie, my dreams of our future together fading as she disappears in my rearview mirror. I haven't seen the van tailing us since the freeway, but I want to make sure no one turns to follow her. I'm the one they want, but if they know someone was with me, they'd try to find her, too.

My cell phone rings, and I hit the throttle harder, picking up speed. I don't even have to look at the screen to know what it's about. I hit my Bluetooth to answer it through my stereo.

"If you don't turn yourself in now, I can't protect you, Mason." My mom's voice booms through the car. "Please, be reasonable. I want to help you."

"I didn't do anything wrong," I say.

"Then you have nothing to worry about."

I sigh. "It'll be my word against Brendan's. You know the community doesn't exactly trust me."

"But the council trusts you. I trust you. Please, come in."

My car jolts forward, and I swerve before the van nudges me again. "You're not exactly giving me a choice, Mom."

"Don't fight. It'll make it worse."

I grind my teeth. "I can't believe after everything we've been through together, you still choose your job over your family every damn time."

"Mason, that's not fair."

I hang up on her. I've spent far too much of my life following my mom's beliefs and orders, even when they were wrong. She might have changed somewhat, but deep down, her priorities don't include me. I don't know why I'm surprised—I should've learned from Hunter. She put him in a situation that nearly cost him his life.

The van bumps my car again. I doubt I could outrun it, and even if I did, I have nowhere to go. I gave Callie everything. I knew my fate would come to this. I knew I'd have to face the consequences of my actions—face the people I spend so much time protecting, to find out how they're going to repay me.

Easing off the brake pedal, I turn into the parking lot of a grocery store. The van pulls up behind me, blocking me in. I unbuckle my seatbelt and climb out of my car with my hands linked behind my head. Kat and Evie stand a few feet away with

Bree, another altered agent on my team.

I meet Evie's eyes. "What are you doing here?"

"Dmitri asked me to come." Evie steps closer to me. "We'll get this figured out."

Kat doesn't meet my gaze. She's still angry with me, and I'm sure it's not only because of the last time we saw each other. "You know they're talking about dismissing you?" Kat's voice echoes through the night. "Why can't you bring the human in and fix this. Prove that Brendan is acting against humanity. The shifter community thinks you're trying to destroy them."

Bree doesn't say anything. I don't know how much she knows. She leans against the van with her arms crossed.

I clench my fists. "I can't, all right. I just can't."

Kat saunters up to me. Her red aura, the same color as mine, shines brightly around her. Her short blond hair sticks up in the back, and her steely gray eyes burn imaginary daggers at me. She raises her hand and swings at lightning speed, but I raise up my arm and block her.

In a fight, we're matched equally, but she could take me out if she wanted to because she bottles her emotions and uses them to enhance her abilities. I can't do that, though. If I don't hone mine in and ignore them, it makes me sloppy. At least I know Kat well enough to predict her next move.

Evie steps between us before Kat has a chance to try to slap me again. "Control yourself. He's on our side. He's been our friend way longer than we've been in this community. If Mason says he can't, then he can't. He wouldn't put himself in this situation for nothing."

Kat's shoulders slump. "He's giving everything up for a girl."

Evie swings her gaze from mine to Kat's. "Watch it, Kat. You're talking to the girl who gave up everything to try to get out of this world with a guy."

"And look where that got you." Kat places her hands on her hips.

Evie's eyes widen, and her mouth tilts downward. If they weren't my friends, I'd let them fight so I could escape. But it doesn't feel right.

"Enough! Evie left because she didn't believe in the cause." I glare at Kat. "And as for me, no, I'm not doing it for a girl; I'm doing it because of who the girl is. All I ever wanted was to help the innocent and this is what I'm doing." I stroll past them to the van. "Now, let's get this over with, because if I'm the one being taken in, it means Brendan is still out there, putting the world in danger." I want to say putting Callie in danger, but I'm sure my teammates already know that's what I mean.

CALLIE

Sweat soaks through my shirt as I jog through the illuminated parking lot. The mall buzzes with life outside the movie theater, and I avoid eye contact with the people I pass. I slow down, afraid someone's going to think I'm being chased. The last thing I need is to draw more attention to myself.

Weaving in and out of cars, I make my way toward the theater. I clutch my bag under my arm, holding onto it for dear life. Sweat drips onto my cheeks, and I swipe my sleeve over my face. Mason thinks being in the public will keep me safe, but I can't shake the feeling that everyone is out to get me.

I fall into step behind a group of people my age, blending in the best I can. Cold air blasts my face the second I enter the mall. The hum of voices wraps around me, mixing with different types of music pulsating from each store.

When the group of teens heads toward the food court, I stop in front of the map. I've never been to this mall, and I'm dying to head to the bathroom to clean up so I don't look out of place. Laughter breaks out behind me, and I meet the gaze of a group of girls standing outside a store named Lola's. I force myself to smile.

"Don't project, Callie. Not here. Not now." Everything about this place sends shivers up my spine. There are too many people to watch and too many places people can lurk and wait to attack me. *Calm down. No one knows who you are.*

My knees shake, and I force myself to walk. If I stop, I'm afraid I'll end up on the floor in the middle of the crowded mall. All I'd need is to attract everyone's attention to me, especially since I wouldn't be able to explain why I'm carrying so many weapons and so much cash. They'd think I robbed a store or something.

I enter an empty corridor with the bathrooms stationed in the back, my nerves starting to relax. Instead of going into the main bathroom, I lock myself in the single stall family bathroom. I'd rather take a thousand glares from angry parents than have to constantly look over my shoulder.

I splash water on my red face before looking in the mirror. My hair sticks to my cheeks, and I use my fingers to comb it behind my ears before twisting it into a knot on my neck. The bruises from Brendan are darker than the last time I looked at them, and seeing them again sends such an intense hatred through me that a thousand thoughts of revenge swirl in my head.

My phone buzzes from my pocket, and I tug it free, praying it's a message from Mason.

It's Lily. *Where are you?*

I type back, *A mall.*

Send me your location. We're coming to get you.

Tears brand streaks on my cheeks. *Can't. Isn't safe.*

My phone chimes immediately. *They got Mason.*

Before I have a chance to respond, Lily calls. I pick up and say, "Mason doesn't want me to intervene. I'm supposed to call some of his friends for help, and then I'm supposed to wait for him to find me."

"Callie..."

"What?"

"Mason isn't like some ordinary person. He's been altered with special abilities. Jax said the council isn't treating this like they would normally do. Brendan's dad is asking for a firmer punishment, because he doesn't think Mason is looking out for the good of the creature community. He's accusing him of treason."

I lick my dry lips. "Mason said the worst that can happen is that they'll wipe his memory and relocate him with no knowledge of the creature world. His mom works for them. She'll protect him." I knew deep down that I was right when I questioned Mason. He's far from ordinary in this world.

Lily doesn't say anything for a moment. "Not this time."

"I don't understand."

"If they find him guilty, they'll attempt to reverse the alteration. It could kill him."

A wave of dizziness washes over me as my heart sinks into my stomach. "What can I do?"

"Tell me where you are. We'll come get you and figure it out then. We can try to reason with the council. Explain things."

She's right. I can't sit here, waiting for Mason's friends while doing nothing. If I have to reveal myself to the council, then I have to. I just hope Mason's wrong and they'll show me leniency. They couldn't possibly be any worse than Brendan—not if it's where Mason came from.

I sputter the name of the mall, my voice cracking and my heart hurting with each passing breath. A second later, my phone dies. I slide my cell back into my pocket and drop to the floor, covering my face with my hands.

Mason fought so hard to keep me safe, to keep me out of the creature world. His intentions were to protect me, but that task now seems impossible. I'm not meant to stay hidden. I'm meant to shout who I am to the world and face whoever would dare threaten me. I'm done hiding. I'm done running for my life and being scared. I'm just done with everything.

I pull myself together, swiping my hands across my wet cheeks. This isn't the time to lose it. Mason needs me to be strong.

Tugging the zipper of the bag open, I pull out and hook Mason's weaponry belt around my waist. I slide my arms into a way too big black jacket, and it covers the belt. The cash hides beneath two shirts, and I pocket a few hundred dollar bills in case something happens before slinging the bag over my shoulder and strutting from the bathroom.

A dad with his two toddler daughters zooms into the family bathroom when I exit, and I ignore the heated words under his breath. I don't have time to feel bad for his mundane situation. I have bigger problems to deal with, ones I'd gladly trade with him to be a little irritated that some teenage girl was hogging the bathroom he wanted.

The mall is more crowded when I stroll from it to wait outside the movie theater. I plop down on the ledge of a planter filled with flowers and watch the parking lot for signs of Lily and Jax.

Just when I'm about to give up, Jax pulls to the curb in his white truck, and Lily jumps out. I fling my arms around her, blinking tears from my eyes. She doesn't say anything as she motions me to the truck, and I slide in after her and lean my head against the cold window.

Jax pulls from the curb, watching me in his peripheral vision. "We'll make things right, Callie, okay?"

I purse my lips. "How?"

Navigating the streets, he darts his eyes from the road to me. "I have some friends who'll help us."

"I've dragged enough people into this. Just take me to wherever the council is. I want to talk to them myself."

"You sure?" Lily asks.

I brush fallen strands of hair from my face. "Never been more sure of anything in my life."

MASON

The Creature Council's compound, a haven for creatures and the headquarters of the council members, resides thirty minutes north of the city within a forest protected by magic. It's nearly impossible for outsiders to find, and even if they did find it, the magic of the forest itself would never let them in.

I lean forward and peer through the divider separating me from Kat and Bree. Evie sits quietly next to me. She hasn't said a word since we got in.

The gate to the Creature Council compound slides open, and we're greeted by Summer, a blond forest nymph. Bree drives forward, waving to Summer, and then navigates the concrete road leading to the main building, which contains a meeting hall, council member apartments, and a library.

Instead of parking in the packed lot, Bree weaves around the building, driving over the bright green grass to a small door in the back. Through the windshield, I watch the door fling open before Bree even has a chance to stop the van. Dmitri glides out with my mom on his heels.

I don't move to get up even though Bree, Evie, and Kat already stand outside the van. Resting my hands in my lap, I ignore Dmitri's onyx eyes. He looms well over six and a half feet, and his black hair hangs in his face. He looks a mess, unlike every other time I've seen the nightmare inflictor. A gold ring sparkles on his ring finger, and he unlatches my seatbelt and unhooks the restraints Kat insisted I wear for the ride just to annoy me.

Dmitri tugs me out. "Come on, Mason. You're still innocent until proven guilty."

"Do you think I'm guilty?"

"The whole community thinks you are, Mase," my mom chimes in. "It's why you're here. Running didn't help the matter either."

"I wasn't running from you," I mutter. While it would've been ideal to escape with Callie, I wanted to get her out of here. I'm not afraid of my fate with the council. While Brendan might have convincing allegations against me, and it's possible the unrest in the community might force the council to punish me, I knew what would happen if I were caught. They could do whatever they want, and I wouldn't have changed anything...except maybe drive Brendan a little farther away.

"Care to elaborate?" My mom's gold-rimmed glasses reflect blinding light from the building's outside lamps into my eyes.

"I was protecting someone." I cross my arms.

"A girl," Kat says from behind me. "What's up with both your sons risking their lives for girls, Dr. Sullivan?"

Dmitri clears his throat. Nadia is his daughter after all. "You three are excused." He turns to Evie before she can walk away. "Thank you for agreeing to help. I knew you'd make sure he'd make it here unscathed. Katerina already put in a request for a new partner."

Evie's sad, hazel eyes meet mine. "I understand where Mason's coming from. Make sure the council doesn't buy into everything the shifter says. He doesn't exactly have a clean record."

Dmitri nods. "You sure you don't want a position on my team? You could finish college first."

Evie shakes her head. "I like my life as it is."

Her words replay in my mind over and over again. I thought I liked my life, too. I took pride in helping people and creatures in the community. But now, I'm not so sure. *Maybe that's why you're not broken up over the possibility of losing your job...*

My mom slides her arm across my back. "Was the girl Kat mentioned Callie?"

I nod. "Brendan attacked her—nearly killed her, Mom. I couldn't let him get away with it."

"You should've brought it to the council's attention. We could've handled it for you," she says.

I scrunch my nose. "She's not a part of the creature community. She stumbled upon our world by accident."

"So, you're trying to keep her out of it," Dmitri says.

"Something like that. She's—"

A yell cuts through the air, stopping me from telling Dmitri and my mom a partial truth about Callie and how she's been gifted with an ability, but the words never make it from my mouth.

Sharp nails dig into my shoulders. Someone yanks me backward and away from Dmitri. The world spins as I'm thrown into the air, and I land on my back. Air rushes from my lungs, leaving me coughing and sputtering on the grass. I wasn't expecting getting assaulted within the compound, and the surprise attack leaves me incapable of fighting back.

A blade glints in the light, and I draw my focus to a familiar red-haired man. He presses a knife to my neck, my throat stinging, and I close my eyes. All it would take is one deep swipe for him to end my life. One second and it'll all be over. I have one second to think, but my mind draws a blank. All I can think is I'm not ready to die.

20

ᴖFight to Surviveᴗ

CALLIE

JAX WEAVES THROUGH the city like he knows it inside and out, never hesitating to figure out where we're going. He occasionally glances at Lily, a small smile playing on his lips, and I wonder how cozy the two have gotten already.

I touch Lily's knee, and she shifts away. "What?" she asks.

I scrunch my nose. "You okay?"

"Of course." The odd tone of her voice tells me she's not.

"Are you worried?" I ask.

Lily shrugs without answering. She is—probably as much as I am.

The hairs on my arms rise, and I start to feel claustrophobic in the truck. A strange sensation washes over me, the sudden need to hop out consuming me. I lean away from Lily and touch my fingers to the door handle.

"Are we almost there?" I ask Jax.

He turns his head to look at me, and I notice something horribly wrong. Jax's eyes match Lily's with their blue color. Sliding closer to the door, I try to suppress the fear creeping into my soul. Lily doesn't have blue eyes. She's complained nearly all our lives how she wished hers were blue. And Jax's eyes? I could never forget the beauty of their unusual bright green color.

"Yeah, a few minutes tops."

A shifter can change into anyone... The memory of what Mason told me about Brendan surges to the front of my mind. Panic nearly knocks me from my body as I sit next to two people posing as my friends. If Brendan and Trevor have shifted into Lily and Jax, and they're driving in Jax's trucks, then where are my friends?

My stomach twists into knots, and I think of a million horrible things that could've happened to Lily. I'll never forgive myself if she is hurt or worse.

And now, I'm stuck in a truck with my ex-boyfriend, who would love to see me pay because he can't handle facing the consequences of his own actions. I have no idea where we're going or what I'm going to do. *At the next stop, jump out. Don't think. Just do it.*

Jax—or whoever it is—continues along an empty street

and then slows down. Sweat breaks out on my back and neck. I'm afraid he'll turn down one of the alleys at any second, and I won't get the opportunity to run. If I can't run, I'll have to fight, and I can't possibly take on two people and survive.

He turns on his blinker just before an alleyway. I press closer to the door, putting an inch of space between my leg and Lily's imposter. The sudden movement causes her to jerk her head to look at me. The second I meet her eyes, I know I'm in trouble. Reaching over, she grabs my wrist, squeezing with more strength than Lily would possibly have. I cry out, afraid my bone will snap.

I swing my arm out and slap the shifter across the face. My shoulder bumps the door when the shifter posing as Jax turns. Unlatching my seatbelt, I shove the door open and fall out, hitting my arm hard on the curb while scraping my hands and hip on the concrete. Pain radiates through me, and I grind my teeth together.

The truck squeals to a stop, and I force my stinging hands to push me off the ground. A door slams, but I'm already running. I bolt away, crossing the street, and turn into an alley. I have no idea where I'm at, but I need to get off the street and hide.

"Callie!" Brendan's voice echoes through the night.

I suck in air through my nose and breathe out my mouth as my sneakers pound the concrete. Wind whips around me, making the stinging of my raw hands worse, and I feel warm liquid soaking through my jeans. The pain in my hip slows me down even though I try my best to ignore it.

When I reach the end of the alley, I exit onto another street. A car zooms by, stopping me in my tracks. I expect the driver to hop out and tackle me, but the car disappears around the corner. I dash in the opposite direction. If I can reach a busy main street, I could flag down help. I doubt Brendan will try anything stupid where other's can witness.

A car horn blares behind me, and I glance over my shoulder. If my heart could, it'd explode from my chest and run away. Not even twenty feet behind me is Jax's truck with Brendan and Trevor inside.

Brendan swerves, half driving on the sidewalk, and the engine roars as he accelerates. He's going to run me over. I never thought that getting hit by a truck could possibly be how I die. And if I do survive, I'm sure Brendan will take pleasure in slowly and painfully killing me.

Headlights bathe the sidewalk in a golden glow, the sound of the truck's engine drawing closer, and then I thrust myself into the wall, pressing my body as flat as I can against it. The side mirror of the truck grazes my back but doesn't knock me off my feet.

I release a breath and force myself to dash away. It'll only take Brendan a minute to turn around, and then he'll try to hit me again.

But I don't even have time to think about it.

A strong hand wraps in my hair and yanks hard. Falling back, I crash into a muscular chest. Pain bursts in my back as my attacker throws me to the ground. I glare into Brendan's blue eyes for a split second before my ears pop, and I project out of my body.

My body slumps on the ground. Brendan spins around, searching the street like he can catch sight of my soul. Bending down, he grabs my body by my hair, pulling me to my feet.

I leap toward him with everything I have. Letting him take me isn't an option. But instead of entering Brendan, I hit an invisible barrier that sends me flying backward as a jolt of electricity shocks me, sending pain into my soul. It's awful, not unlike feeling pain when Jax unintentionally tried to consume me.

Brendan's eyes widen, and he leers at my body. "Possession won't work with the protection of an elf spelled charm." He jiggles his wrist, showing off some weird, knotted leather band.

Someone clears their throat, and I turn my gaze to Trevor. He's wearing the same type of bracelet as well. Panic seeps into my soul, squeezing me, trying to snuff me out of existence. How can I save myself if the only thing I know how to do is useless?

Brendan pulls out a switchblade from his pocket. "I know you're here, Callie. Return to your body, or you won't have a body to return to." He holds the small blade against my throat.

I contemplate not doing as he asks. I'm already a living ghost. At least if I stay here, I can die without pain and suffering.

He presses the knife harder, and a small drop of blood trails down my neck, disappearing into the fabric of Mason's black jacket. "Last chance, Callie. My buyer would prefer to have you, but I'll still get paid for Lily, so I don't care."

What? He has Lily? Oh, no. Please, let him be lying. I don't even think about it as I reconnect with my body. The world shifts from black, and I open my eyes. Thrusting my hands up, I lock my fingers around his wrists. He releases me, nearly pushing me away. I fall to the ground, hitting my knees so hard on the pavement that I scream.

All I can think about is getting as far away as possible, even if I have to I crawl away inch by inch. Brendan shoves his boot into my back, forcing me to the ground, and I scrape my chin on the sidewalk. Tears burn my eyes, but I force them away. I can't cry. Not in front of him. I won't let him see my weakness.

Brendan kneels next to me. "You know, all you had to do was get my dad off my back, but you had to make things complicated. You ruined my life, and all for someone who has spent his life hunting people like us."

I blink the tears from my eyes. I don't think Brendan will ever hold himself accountable. His mentality is dangerous. Poisonous. The type of person who'll blame the universe before they even consider that maybe they were the one to mess up.

"I can still help you. I'm sorry, okay?" If I have to grovel, I'll grovel. I'm not below doing what I need to do to survive.

"You really do think I'm stupid," he says. "But you know what? I'm going to give you some advice because I did like you. As long as you don't make things hard and you're obedient, maybe the Feeders won't make you suffer too much."

My chest heaves as I try to find my voice. "W-Who?"

"They're the ones helping me get my life back while taking care of my biggest problem."

My skin cools, his words swirl through my mind. "I don't

understand."

He bares his teeth. "I'm not risking you turning me into the council. Without you, they can't hold me accountable, even if they do believe your wannabe creature. But who knows, maybe they won't. Either way, I'm set now."

"You won't get away with this. Mason knows people. They'll hunt you down."

"That's an idea you can hold onto. A little hope to carry when you finally realize how badly you screwed up. Did you know my dad threatened to disown me for provoking the council because of you? The only reason he didn't was because I lied about Mason. But, I'm sure everyone will figure it out soon enough. It'll be too late for you, though. The Feeders already have a buyer for you and your friend, and I'll have already disappeared." Brendan flicks his gaze to Trevor. "Put her in the truck."

I can't believe it. I can't even process it. Brendan sold me. He *sold* me to some group called the Feeders. Out of all the things I imagined him doing, I never expected to be sold like a piece of property. And I'm freaking out. I almost would rather die right here on this pavement than experience what unthinkable things will become of me in the hands of monsters who kidnap people. My life is over.

Trevor digs his nails into my arms and drags me a few feet down the sidewalk to the truck. He lifts me by them, my arms screaming in pain, and tosses me in the back of the truck.

I hit the cold metal bed next to Lily, and a sob rips from my throat. Her bruised cheek presses into the bed, and she doesn't stir. Whatever they've done to her has knocked her unconscious. Reaching out, I brush her blond hair from her face, noticing a tiny thumb tack jabbed into her neck just below her ear.

I'm going to be sick. "Oh, God, Lily. Wake up. You have to wake up," I whisper.

Someone yanks my hair, exposing my neck. My skin stings, and I close my eyes and project myself. I can't lose consciousness. Not now. Brendan might have control over my body, but I will never give him control over my soul.

MASON

"Touch him and you'll die." My mom's cold voice cuts through Brendan's dad's guttural yells.

His hand loosens on the knife, and I take the opportunity to swing up and punch him in the throat. The knife drops from his hand, clattering next to me. I thrust my legs up and catapult to my feet. I tackle the old shifter and wrap my hands around his neck and squeeze.

"Enough!" Dmitri pulls me off the shifter and hugs his lean arms around mine, locking his fingers on my chest. "You need to calm down, Mason."

"He tried to kill me." I stop fighting Dmitri's hold. "I know where Brendan gets it from."

Brendan's dad glares. "You attacked my son and nephew. They could've been killed because of you. You were targeting them."

I tense. "That's a load of crap and you know it. Brendan tried to hurt my friend. He nearly killed her. I was only trying to protect her from him."

"Liar!" he yells.

My mom steps between us. "Let's take this inside, Howard. This is a private council matter, and we don't take either of your accusations lightly."

Dmitri nudges me forward, forcing me to enter the building. He escorts us all to the elevator and down to the meeting hall in the basement. My mom unlocks the double doors with a set of keys like someone would dare enter the boring, empty meeting hall when a meeting isn't in session. The four council members sit at a blue-clothed table, meeting me with looks of concern on each of their faces. Even Thierry, the always-bored elf, actually pays attention.

Veronica Sanders, the only human council member, twists her lips downward when she sees me. Next to her sits Ana, a young enchantress, and finishing off the group is Jacqueline, the sin-eater my brother shares a love/hate friendship with.

Dmitri pushes me into a seat and stands behind me. My mom offers Howard a chair on the opposite side of the stage, and he watches me, like he's waiting for the opportunity to try to kill me again.

Veronica clears her throat. "We're all aware of why we're here today, so there's no need to reiterate accusations. All we want is to hear both sides of your story."

Jacqueline leans her elbows on the table. "Where is your son, Mr. O'Brian?"

Howard shifts on the seat. "I thought he'd be here."

"Well, we can't take your account of the situation considering you weren't there," Thierry says. He yawns into his hands before rubbing them over his bald head. "Why don't you call him?"

Howard tugs his phone from his pocket and clicks a few buttons.

"On speaker phone, please," Jacqueline says.

Howard hits a button, and the phone rings out, echoing through the small auditorium. After the third ring, the line picks up, and music hums over the speaker.

"Hey, Daddio? What's up? I'm kind of in the middle of something important." The sound of Brendan's voice sends me to the edge of my seat.

Howard frowns. "You were supposed to meet me at the compound ten minutes ago."

Brendan mumbles something to whoever he's with. "Sorry about that, Dad. Something's come up."

Howard brings his gaze from his phone to the council members, and then he directs his attention to me. "The agent was telling the truth, wasn't he?"

Laughter erupts in the line. "I didn't want to do it, but you forced me out of school, threatened to cut me off and shame me from the family. What else was I supposed to do?"

"Brendan..." His dad's words trail off.

I clutch the edge of my chair, ready to bolt out of the room. My gut screams at me to get out of here as fast as I can, because Brendan's planning something. He's smart. He wouldn't give himself away without a foolproof plan. This is much bigger than ruining my life. I don't think he was planning on ruining my life at all.

Someone bangs on the locked double doors, and Dmitri glides away from me when the thudding persists. I get to my feet, cross the room to Howard before anyone can stop me, and I yank the phone from his hand.

"Mason! Mason, they took Lily!" Jax's voice echoes through the air.

I swing my gaze to the incubus, his lip split, both his eyes bruised, and he holds his arm in a makeshift sling.

"The leech survived!" Brendan's voice blares through the phone. "I was bummed I wasn't going to get to see your reaction when you found out, but now I get to hear it."

A cold pool of dread settles in my stomach. Callie was terrified something was going to happen to her best friend, and now it has. She doesn't even know it.

"I'll kill you if you hurt Lily. I swear."

Brendan chuckles. The music fades from the line and the sound of a car door slamming cuts through his laughter. "I wasn't talking about your reaction to Lily."

Callie's screams rip through the air, and it's like everyone in the room stops breathing. "No. Please, don't do this." I never thought I'd find myself begging for mercy from anyone. Callie's screams rip through me right to my soul, threatening to tear me apart.

Callie screams again, the terror in her voice shredding me to pieces. I can't stand here and listen to this. I have to leave. I have to get out of here and find her, but I don't even know where to look.

"Dmitri, summon Evangeline," my mom says. "We'll have a team ready in five minutes."

"Hey, Callie," Brendan says, his voice fades in and out as he moves the phone. "I'm really not that bad of a guy, I swear. I'll prove it and let you talk to your little boyfriend."

Dmitri heads out the door, and my mom has her own phone to her ear. The council quietly mumbles among themselves, and Howard slumps in the chair with his face in his hands. Jax hobbles down the aisle toward me, his brows pinched together and his mouth open.

"Ma-Mason?" Callie's soft voice sounds weak. She sniffles into the line. "I'm so sorry, Mason. They tricked me. I should've called your friends like you told me. Now, we're being sold to the Feed—" Her words turn into a scream again.

The line cuts off, and I throw the phone against the wall, smashing it to pieces. I punch the air, rage roaring up my back, threatening to consume me. I've failed at doing my job. I've failed at protecting the innocent. I let Callie down.

"I didn't think the Feeders were still around," Jacqueline says. "I thought they went down when their leader was captured by the Human Preservation Agency."

Veronica sucks in a breath. "If we don't move quickly, those poor girls won't stand a chance."

Listening to the council members talk, I start putting things together. I've never heard of the term Feeders, but I know exactly who they're talking about. The wraith who nearly annihilated the HPA and brought them together with the council was selling humans to creatures—for food, entertainment, and worse. He was the leader of the group who was kidnapping humans. It looks like the monsters continued their jobs without their leader, and now Callie and Lily's lives are in their hands.

The double doors bang open, and Evie runs in behind Dmitri. She races to the stage and flings her arms around me. "I'll do whatever I can to help."

Howard drops his hands from his face. "You have to find my son."

Evie nods. "I need something of his."

"In my car." Howard jumps into action, and Evie runs after him.

I turn to face the council. "I can't promise I'll bring him in alive."

Veronica presses her lips together. "Do whatever you have to do to save those girls, Mason."

Jax stands up next to me. "I'm coming with you."

I don't argue, because Jax doesn't need to be in good fighting condition to kill someone. He doesn't even need a weapon when he can just consume someone's soul. He's definitely someone I want on my side. I want all the help I can get.

I'm afraid I'm going to need it.

21

❧Soul Sick☙

CALLIE

BRENDAN CARRIES MY body while Trevor swings Lily over his shoulder. A woman with six inch stilettos, wearing a short, navy blue dress, taps her foot as she waits for the shifters to approach her.

The moment I started screaming Brendan's plans, he stuck me with the spelled thumb tack to knock me out, and like the first time, I projected just in time. I refuse to leave Lily or my body, though. I'm the only one who can save us now.

The woman searches my body, lifting my hair, inspecting the tangles, and then she pokes each bruise, scrape, and imperfection. "I'm deducting fifteen thousand each for the damages. They'll need at least a week to heal."

Brendan huffs. "That's half! It's not my fault they fought back."

The woman clicks her tongue. "Would you prefer to hold onto them during the healing process?"

His eyes narrow. "No, but—"

The woman raises her hand. "Then it's settled."

She inspects Lily for a few minutes and then turns on her heels and struts toward an open door of a warehouse. She motions for the shifters to follow her. "You said they fought?"

"Yeah."

Trevor doesn't speak as he follows his cousin.

The woman peers over her shoulder, lifting an eyebrow. "The buyer I have interested will love that."

I glide behind them, searching the surroundings, memorizing every door and window to escape from and every item that could be used as a weapon. We pass a desk in an empty room, and I notice a phone and computer. The warehouse has a small stage set up in the middle of the room, with a cluster of chairs around it but nothing else.

I didn't think it was possible, but queasiness washes over me, and I become soul sick. My translucent hands tremble, and I start to fade. If I don't find even a morsel of bravery, a pinch of hope, I'm sure I'll disappear from existence. I won't die. I'll be nothing.

The woman's stilettos tap the concrete floor. She pulls a key from her necklace and unlocks a box on the wall, retrieving a keychain with a dozen keys. She saunters to the back of the room to a dark hallway, and then flips on a light. Twelve doors line the hallway, six on each side, and I assume these used to be offices. She stands in front of the second door on the left.

"Leave them here and go wait in the viewing room. Thomas will complete the transaction." The woman waves them away, and they leave without even a second glance.

As she unlocks the doors, someone sobs from within the room. Bracing myself for a second, I gather everything in me to glide through the wall. I peek my head in first, and if I had a body, I'd throw up. Four large cages, two on the back wall and one on each side, display two boys and a girl, all around my age. Plastic bottles, some with water and some with stuff I refuse to even think about, litter the cages along with dirty blankets crumpled in the corners. A ratty curtain covers a small alcove next to the cage with the girl, partially hiding a toilet and hose hung on the wall. The girl's messy blond hair hangs in her face, and she sits with her knees to her chest but doesn't move. She wasn't the one crying.

The cage across the room from her contains the two boys. The boy with curly hair covers the mouth of the other, stifling his cries the best he can. After a second, the crying boy regains control and falls silent. His wide gray eyes peer at the door, and he pales as the woman drags in my body.

She pulls in Lily next, and then she closes the door and locks herself in with us. She tugs the magical tack from Lily's neck, causing my best friend to jerk upright. Her screams pierce the air as she crabwalks backward away from the woman, and then she screams again when she sees my body.

"Oh, God, Callie." She crawls over to me and shakes me.

The woman's face transforms when Lily remains by my side. Her teeth elongate, the whites of her eyes redden, and she points a dagger sharp nail at Lily. "Get back."

Scrambling away, Lily moves to the corner of the room. She opens her mouth to say something, but then she catches the amber eyes of the girl in the cage. The girl shakes her head with sad eyes and motions with her finger to be quiet.

The woman's eyes turn away from Lily, and she saunters to my body and bends down. Flying forward and into my body, I connect back with myself before she can remove the tack. It's more important than ever to hide my ability, especially since I don't think Brendan told her because she looks like she's only interested in ordinary humans. I doubt body possession is a desirable trait, but I couldn't be more thankful he was more concerned about what he got for me than what damage I could cause. Projecting might be the only way to get out, and if I wasn't here, Lily would be alone. The thought of my best friend at the fate of these monsters makes me want to tear the place apart.

My body sucks my soul into darkness, and then pain radiates from me, and I groan. Everything hurts—my face, arms, neck, head, back, and shins. If I didn't know, I would think I've been hit by a car. *You almost were.*

When the fog clears from my head, I sit up and glower at the woman. She smiles, her sharp teeth gleaming in the dim lighting. She reaches down and pinches my chin. I swing out and smack her arm away, and she snaps her jaws at me.

I suppress the fear coursing through my veins. I won't let her intimidate me. "Go ahead, bite me."

The woman's face smoothes, and she chortles, the noise light and soft, a stark contrast to her now demonic appearance. "Feisty, aren't you?"

I grind my teeth. "You've made a huge mistake."

She taps her finger to her lips. "I'm not sure whether to admire your bravery or laugh at your stupidity, little girl."

I don't give her the chance to decide. I launch at her, crashing into her chest, and we skid across the room and hit the wall next to an empty cage. I grab her face in my hands and slam her head into the concrete, and she roars. Her hands ram my chest, knocking the wind from me as she shoves me off her. Her nails stab my clavicle, and I wince, shadows edging my vision. She's on me a second later, straddling me while I swing my arms the best I can to keep her from hitting my face.

The woman locks her hands around my wrist, yanks my arm to her mouth, and snaps down. I scream, tears burning my eyes. Sharp pain explodes as she rips a chunk of skin from my arm. She swallows my flesh, my stomach rolling at the sight. Dizziness washes over me, and I expect to project out of my body, but then the world flashes black. I fade in and out of consciousness.

Lily's screams tear through the air, pulling at my soul, begging me to stay awake, but I can't. Darkness grips me in its cold embrace.

The world melts away.

MASON

"I can't pinpoint their location. Wherever they are is concealed with magic. We're going to have to comb through the city," Evie says. She clutches Brendan's sweatshirt in her hands. "I keep glimpsing concrete flooring, like a warehouse."

I rub my hand over my face. "That describes at least a few dozen buildings."

She closes her eyes. "He was with a ghoul, now he's in a room with a stage, a desk, a computer." Her eyes snap open. "Everything is fuzzy."

"Keep trying. If they leave, you might be able to pinpoint them." Dmitri drums his fingers on the steering wheel.

Jax sits next to him in the front of the van. He leans against his good arm and trains his gaze on the road. Isla, a fairy with bright pink hair and skin with a luminescent sheen, perches on the seat across from me. The rest of the team includes Bree and Kat despite Kat's protests. She made it clear she's not doing this to help Callie but to take down the Feeders. She lost her boyfriend to the wraith who used to control the human trafficking group, and it might be one of the sole reasons she chose to stay with the council.

Dmitri navigates the freeway leading into the city. It looms in the distance, a bright beacon amid a dark night, and I try not to think about the horrors Callie might be experiencing. She could project to get away, but knowing her, she'd never leave Lily. She's fiercely protective of her best friend, and like me, she's probably ridden with guilt for putting her in this situation.

The city grows larger, the towering skyscrapers bright

enough to outshine the stars and then the cityscape disappears as we drive into it. I search our surroundings, concentrating on the auras of the people we pass by. I hope to spot Callie's pale pink aura, but I'm left disappointed. It wouldn't be so easy. Fate brought us together, but it also keeps us apart.

Evie releases a breath. "I got something."

I lean toward the opened divider between the cab of the van and the cargo area where I sit. "How far?"

She lays a map in her lap and draws a square. "It's somewhere in the middle of Fourth and Sixth and in between D and F." She shifts in the seat to glance at Isla. "From Brendan's perspective, I see three windows stacked on top of each other, so it isn't a tall building."

"Let's split up," Dmitri says. "We'll cover more ground." He pulls to the curb and kills the engine.

I'm out of the van first, and I help Bree and Isla out. Kat ignores my hand and jumps past me. I tug her arm so she must face me. "I'm sorry, okay?"

She yanks her arm away. "It's fine."

"It's not. You're mad at me. I want to know why. It's more than about Callie."

"You're just so selfish. We were altered together, we trained together, we fight together, and we've almost died together. You're my partner, Mason, yet you haven't been one since you met that girl. You should be able to trust me with anything, and you can't. I just—I can't work with you if that's how it's going to be."

I twist my mouth down. "You have to understand."

"I do. You don't trust me to keep whatever secret you're hiding."

"I—" I pause. "It's not my secret to tell."

Kat turns her back to me, and I race to step in front of her. "Just forget it, Mason."

I plead with my eyes. "I swear, when this is all over, I'll introduce you to Callie. It's better if she tells you."

She sighs before she hugs me. "You just better get her out alive."

Kat's words send a cloud of doubt hanging over my head. I'm worried enough that Callie is hurt and frightened, but it hasn't crossed my mind that I could possibly fail. *You won't fail her...*

But what if I do?

"Mason?" Dmitri's voice pulls me from my thoughts.

I force the doubt to flee my mind. "Yeah?"

"You okay partnering with Jax? I want Kat and Bree to stick with Evie, since she's vulnerable, and the last thing we need is to lose the only tracker we have." Dmitri hands out earpieces. "Don't act alone. You find something, you call it in, and we attack as a team." He's saying it to the group, but he doesn't take his eyes off me.

I nod. "Unless it's life or death."

Dmitri frowns. "If the enemy doesn't fight, do not kill them. If they do, the council's ordered automatic death sentences." He glances around our circle. "But, please, try to get them to surrender. Prisoners are useful, and I'm positive this isn't the only warehouse."

I adjust my earpiece and slide a weaponry belt around my waist. It's bulkier than the usual, with a few added items, like an extra knife and some elf enchanted charms. I peer at Jax, who has trouble clicking on the belt until Evie reaches out and helps him.

Jax meets my gaze, and I nod. Static sounds in my ear, and Dmitri's voice cuts through the line. "Stay safe everyone."

I stride next to Jax as he matches my pace even though he's limping slightly. We head down Fourth Street and turn right onto F Street, starting in the middle. Dmitri and Isla will keep to the perimeter of the area Evie marked on the map, and Kat and Bree will follow Evie's lead as she follows any and all creatures in the area. She can track anyone by a simple touch of something they have touched. It gives her a real time view of their surroundings.

City noise echoes through the air even though we're in what seems like an abandoned area. Trash clutters the street. The overpowering stench makes it hard to breathe without my eyes watering. Boards cover old businesses, and the ones that remain open, have closed up for the night hours ago.

A homeless woman rests her back against the cinderblock wall of a building. "It isn't safe to be wandering around these parts this time of night, boys. You'll go missing."

I stop in my tracks. "What do you mean?"

She grins, displaying a chipped front tooth. "Information comes with a price."

I glance at Jax. I gave all my money to Callie. The few ones in my wallet wouldn't be enough to buy information. Without even thinking about it, he tugs his wallet free and hands the woman a hundred dollar bill. Her eyes widen, and she tucks it into her pocket.

She sweeps her gaze around the street. "A demon disguised as a pretty woman lurks this neighborhood. She's not alone, either. I've seen even the strongest kids get taken. A few a week. The screams keep me up at night."

Jax crosses his arms. "And they don't bother you?"

She shrugs. "They feed me."

I concentrate on her aura, realizing she's not human. She's a succubus, the female counterpart of incubi like Jax. He probably knew it this whole time, but it's not like he could've just told me. I should've been paying more attention. If I'm not concentrating, I lose focus and stop reading auras.

I squat down and lean close to the woman. "See anyone new?"

The woman holds out her hand, expecting more money. She didn't really tell us anything we didn't know, except that a woman is running the Feeders now. Probably the ghoul Evie mentioned. Jax opens his wallet, but I shake my head.

"She doesn't know anything we don't already know," I say. "Save your cash. I'm going to call her in to Dmitri."

The woman waves her arms. "Dmitri Petrov? You're with the council?"

I click my earpiece. "Dmitri, come in."

"Wait! I can help you. I saw two shifters, young ones, drive by in a white truck. It was odd, though, because a spirit floated right along with it, like it was following them." The woman rubs her face with her dirty hands.

"Find something, Mason?" Dmitri asks in my ear.

I look at the woman without responding to Dmitri right away. "Where'd they go?"

"I don't know. The whole block is spelled."

"Mason, come in." Dmitri's voice rings in my ear again.

I turn away from the woman to answer. "Hey, yeah. I have a witness who saw Brendan driving Jax's truck. She said it vanished into thin air." I don't mention the woman is a creature. She's clearly guilty of something to be afraid of the council. I'll let her slide for now. I don't have time to detain her.

"Sounds like elf magic."

"That's what I thought. Any way around it?"

The earpiece buzzes with static. "I'll have to make a phone call."

I press my lips together. "We don't have time."

Dmitri doesn't answer. I jerk my head in the direction the woman saw Brendan disappear, and Jax follows me. I expect to hit a wall, but nothing happens. The street appears empty. I don't think elves can create another dimension, but I can't be sure.

A strange sensation crawls over my skin. Jax steps back, and I know he feels it as well. It's like the air thickens, stealing my breath away and fear strangles my heart. I can't suppress the need to run. *Calm down. It's the magic.*

"Mase, I got something." Evie's voice cuts through my panicking thoughts. "Look toward the light pole. You should see a white truck."

I blink a few times and peer at the four closest streetlamps I can see. I click my earpiece. "I don't see anything. It's spelled."

"Just head in that direction. Brendan's outside."

"How do you know?"

"Because he's watching you."

22

⁓The Real Monsters⁓

CALLIE

A RATTLING SOUND cuts through the darkness, coaxing me from unconsciousness. My eyelids shine red against the lighting. The ground shakes under my body, jolting pain through my arm, drawing the memory of the horrifying woman taking a bite from me forward in my mind. Shivering at the thought, I snap my eyes open.

Warm fingers twine through mine, and I squeeze Lily's hand as she twists to gaze into my eyes. Tears smear mascara down her cheeks, blending with the wet hair stuck to her face. She's wearing a simple black dress without shoes, and an unfamiliar gold charm bracelet glitters on her wrist.

I shimmy from the cage floor, pressing my back to the only solid wall of our tiny prison. I'm wearing an outfit identical to Lily's, wet hair and all. My stomach lurches at an unsettling thought. I don't know how long I've been out, but it's been long enough for our captors to have bathed me. My cheeks flush with anger, and I link my fingers through the chicken wire walls of our cage.

"Shhh!" A voice hisses from my right. I can't see the girl, but I know she's there. I saw her when the woman brought us in here. "She'll come back if you're too loud."

"Who is she?" I whisper.

"Miss Lana," a masculine voice says from my left, his voice low. "We don't know what she is, but Pete thinks she's a demon."

"Pete?"

"Hey," another masculine voice whispers.

Lily clutches my hand. "I'm scared, Callie. I overheard that woman telling a guy she had a buyer for us. We're being sold to someone." Sobs rake her chest, and I pull her into my arms without telling her I already know.

I breathe into her wet hair. "I'm not going to let that happen. Mason knows we're here. He'll find us."

"Hate to break it to you two, but the last person who tried to escape got eaten by Miss Lana," the girl says. "Even if you break out of your cage, you won't be able to leave."

I stare at my wrist. "The bracelet is spelled." I don't ask. I just know. They wouldn't give us such a pretty trinket without reason. I peer around the room again. "Are you all human?"

"What do you mean?"

Pulling at the wire, I try to yank it from the staples in the wood. "You heard me."

When a staple pops free, Lily snatches my arm, causing me to jump in pain. "Callie, stop. I don't want you getting eaten."

I sigh and lean back. "I was checking to see if I could do it. Should be easy enough."

"What would we be?" Pete asks, drawing my attention from Lily, still mulling over the question I asked.

I release a breath. "Never mind."

Lily shifts in the cage and leans closer to me. She presses her lips to my ear. "They don't know about the creature world." Well, if they didn't know, now they do. There's no way to deny that Miss Lana isn't human. Clearly, they think she's a demon, and who knows, maybe she is, but not in the biblical sense they assume...I think.

The door swings open, startling Lily. I wrap my arms around her shoulders and hug her. The woman, Miss Lana, saunters in and closes the door behind her like we could somehow escape. She flips her black hair over her shoulders and peers at each cage. Lily trains her eyes on the floor, but I keep a steady gaze, waiting for the woman to meet my eyes.

She lowers her eyebrows, placing a single hand on her hip. "Haven't you learned your lesson yet?"

I don't take my eyes from hers. "Why don't you open my cage and find out?"

The girl in the other cage audibly gasps.

The words even surprise me, but I can't take them back. I clench my jaw to stop the fear from rolling through me.

Miss Lana struts forward, her face distorting, and she bends down to glare into the cage with her reddening eyes. Her long nail cuts one of the metal links, and she bares her sharp teeth at me. I press my back to the wall, forcing my shoulders to stay straight.

"You're lucky I need you alive." She breaks another link with her nail. "But I have you for another week and some powerful people on my staff can heal you quickly enough."

I swallow but don't say anything.

She smirks. "That's what I thought." Turning on her heels, she click-clacks to the center of the room. "Because you've annoyed me, no one gets to eat dinner tonight." She snarls at me and then heads toward the door. She hits a switch, cutting the lights, and exits the room. A sliver of light illuminates through the darkness from under the door, and I release a ragged breath, a shiver shaking me to my soul.

"You couldn't just keep your mouth shut, could you?" the girl in the other cage snaps.

I touch my finger to the cut wire, and it pokes me. "I'm sorry. I'll make it up to you all."

"How?" It's the boy with Pete.

"I'm going to get us out."

The girl laughs.

"Shut up, Justine. I don't see you helping any," Pete says.

Lily leans on me. "You're leaving, aren't you?"

I nod in the darkness. "How often do we get checked on?"

I ask the others.

"In the day, every few hours. Never at night. There's a camera in the corner, but I'm not sure it even works," Pete says. "We're alone 'til dawn."

Peering into the corners of the room, I search for signs of a camera but can't see anything in the darkness. I shimmy down, lying on my back with my knees bent because the small cage doesn't allow me to stretch out. Lily tugs my shoulders until I shift to rest my head on her lap. She pets my hair, and a tear splashes on my forehead as she silently cries.

"I'm going to look around. I'll be right back. I promise I won't leave you," I tell her.

She sniffles. "I know."

I close my eyes, take a deep breath, and project from my body. I expect to hit a force field, like the one protecting Brendan, but nothing happens. I'm free to leave my cage in my ghostly form, and no one can stop me.

I peer around the dark room for a second before I stick my head through the door and search the empty hallway. Soft voices whisper in my direction from the viewing room, and I leave the holding room and leap the ten feet of distance back to where the stage was.

Miss Lana and a man with a long braid down his back stare at the computer screen at the rickety desk. I sneak behind them, expecting to see a video feed of the room, but they have what appears to be an information sheet of the girl in the cage next to mine. She frowns in her picture, looking into space like they drugged her. Leaning forward to get a better view, I read over the information about the girl, Justine, no last name. It has all her body information and some notes about her personality. It's unnerving these monsters keep files on all the people they kidnap, but at least it's not a video feed of the cages like I expected.

Miss Lana types in a few words. "We have three potential buyers coming in at ten for her. I hope to start a bidding war."

If I could feel my body, my heart would be racing. I'd probably puke.

"What about the new girls? Why aren't you putting them on auction?" the man asks.

The woman straightens her back. "Don't question me, Thomas. Lydia gave me a number I couldn't refuse. She's been looking for a human like the brunette for a while and was thrilled that she came with a companion. You know how she is with her collection."

"Something special about the girl?" he asks.

Miss Lana shrugs. "Don't know. Don't care. She tasted average. Lydia's paying the price of gourmet for fast food in my opinion, but she's the one who put the number out there to stop me from listing the girls."

God, this is so twisted. Who knew I could be relieved to hear I don't taste like fine dining. If I did, Miss Lana would've taken more than a bite.

I stroll around the desk to stare at their faces. The man's eyes sparkle in the light, like the idea of money lights them on fire. A smile crawls over his face, and he lifts his gaze. He freezes, staring right at me.

I fly back. He's an incubus. I know it.

He raises his hand. "We're not alone, Miss Lana."

I cringe and slide into the wall, only pressing into it enough to hear what's happening.

"What do you mean?"

I can't see him. "I saw a spirit."

"Think it's a wraith looking for a new host?"

"Possibly."

I peek through the wall and watch as Miss Lana circles the room. "Hello, wraith. Are you looking for a place to belong? I can offer that to you. All creatures interested in our cause are welcome here."

Thomas waves his hand in my direction from his place at the desk. "It's hovering in and out of that wall."

I step from the wall completely to face her as she moves closer. Of course these people think I'm a wraith. According to Jax and Mason, not many people know about projectors. The first thing a creature would assume is a disgruntled ghost, and with how evil the Feeders are, I'm not even surprised they want me to join them. If only they knew.

Before she has a chance to open her mouth again, a crashing sound echoes in from an open window. Thomas and Miss Lana freeze, looking toward the door, but neither moves from their spots. A yell cuts through the air, and I recognize the voice. It's Brendan.

"Put us on lockdown, now!" Miss Lana shouts.

Thomas presses a button on the desk. Two more people, a man and a woman, bolt into the room.

"Get ready to relocate," Miss Lana says.

Her words grip at my soul, causing fear and desperation to slice through me. All I can think about is getting to Lily and getting us out of here.

Thomas presses another button on the desk. The lights flicker and then cut off, and I'm left standing in utter darkness unsure of what I'm going to do.

MASON

Brendan appears out of nowhere, crashing into me, and we skid across the pavement. He grabs my shoulders, lifting and slamming me into the concrete. Locking my hands onto his arms, I dig in my fingers, pinching as hard as I can until he lets go.

He raises his hand, and the world slows as I concentrate on his next move. His fist hits the ground, an inch from my head, and he screams out. I swing my elbow up, striking his nose. Blood rains down on me from his face. Shoving him hard, I push him off me. He hits his back on the ground but jerks his knees toward his chest and launches back to his feet.

His muscles shift and his bones crack. He grows another few inches in height as he barrels forward. I jump to my feet and slide my knife from its sheath. In a swift motion, I jab it at him, catching his shirt but nothing else. He jerks back with a yell, his face scrunching with anger before he spins and bolts away.

He'll disappear the moment he passes the magical barrier, and I can't let that happen. I charge after him and jump on his back. The world zooms. He spins in a circle, trying to throw me off. I tighten my grip on his thick neck, and he runs backward, smashing me into a cinderblock wall.

Stars pepper my vision, the air whooshing from my lungs, but I don't let go. With one hand, he grips my hair, locking his fingers around my short strands. He's trying to flip me off him but can't get a good hold. I tighten my grasp with my healing arm, the pain non-existent with my adrenaline, and then I raise my knife to his neck.

Before I have a chance to swipe the blade, dread seeps into every pore on my body as he rushes toward the magical barrier. It bites me with a thousand imaginary teeth, and I can almost feel the blood seeping from every inch of me. It takes everything in me to hold on even though all I want to do is let go and run. I've never felt so close to death in my life. I'm almost certain if I cross the barrier, I'll die a horribly painful death.

I yell out. I can't help it. The sound of my voice cuts through the air, and I'm sure my voice can be heard for miles.

The world hazes, and I squeeze my eyes shut. Brendan runs through the magical barrier protecting the warehouse where the Feeders have imprisoned Callie. Shock lashes at me, the wavy air threatening to knock me unconscious.

My ears hum with white noise as my earpiece experiences interference, and I tug it from my ear. My chest tightens with every breath I inhale. It hurts to breathe. I'm suffocating even though I know the air is fine. But the magic weakens my strength, gets into my mind. If I don't fight it away and convince myself that this isn't real, I'll drop from Brendan's back at any second. I flex my cramping fingers, and my knife clatters to the ground.

I stop fighting, and Brendan halts in place. I'm now only

holding him with one arm, and he reaches up to grab me again. A bracelet on his wrist catches my attention, the golden beads glinting in the light of the moon. The pain and fear coursing through me dissipates the longer I stare at it. It's what I need to survive.

I jab my hand at his wrist and lock my fingers on the bracelet, ripping it free. Whatever elf made it didn't take the time to tailor it to Brendan. It probably cost too much. And for that, I'm relieved. I steal it right from him, and Brendan thrashes, knocking me away as his protection from the spell disappears.

He hollers and drops to his knees, covering his face with his hands. I tie the bracelet on my own wrist. Peering around the street, I expect to see an angry mob of creatures heading my way, but all I see is Jax's truck.

"Mason, where are you?" Jax's voice echoes through the night.

"You alone?" I ask.

"No, I have Brendan's cousin. He surrendered when he realized I was about to consume his life force."

"Take his bracelet. It'll let you in."

Jax appears next to me without Brendan's cousin. He lifts his eyebrows seeing Brendan curled in a ball in the middle of the street.

"I have to move him." I jog to Brendan and slide a pair of cuffs from my weaponry belt on his wrists. "Start your truck."

Jax moves to the truck and climbs in. The headlights illuminate the street, and I drag Brendan to the bed of the truck and hop in behind him. Jax drives forward, out of the magical barrier, and the hazy air clears. The moment we cross over, Brendan stops groaning. I stand in the bed, staring down at his cousin.

A cracking sound echoes through the air, and before I have a chance to brace myself, Brendan pushes me with his shoulder from behind. I fall forward and flip over the edge of the bed. The wind whips around me the second it takes me to drop to the ground, and my breath knocks from me, leaving me gasping for air.

Brendan jumps from the truck, his hands still cuffed in front of him, and I roll before he lands on me. He grips the back of my shirt and hoists me from the ground. The truck door slams, and Brendan swings me around, smashing me into Jax. He flies off his feet, landing with a thud on the asphalt. Brendan tosses me, and I tuck my head into my arms and somersault to ease the fall.

Instead of facing me, he rushes to his cousin, helping him up. I take the moment to scramble to my feet while sliding my spare knife from my weaponry belt. He's not getting away. His resistance warrants an automatic death sentence.

Charging forward, I point my blade at Brendan's back. He twists when he catches my shadow cross the wall and uses his cousin as a shield as I jab my knife out. His cousin wails, the blade sliding into his side. Blood soaks through his white T-shirt, and Brendan pushes the shifter toward me, deepening the wound.

With wild eyes, he bolts toward the truck. Jax pulls the trigger on his tranquilizer gun, a low pop sounding through the air. Brendan roars, yanking the dart from his chest. He charges toward Jax, still on the ground, and slides his hands around the incubus' neck before tugging him to his feet and off the ground. Jax flails in Brendan's arms. The shifter adjusts his grip, holding Jax from his head, digging his fingers into Jax's cheeks. My eyes widen at the same time Jax's do, the realization that Brendan is about to snap Jax's neck sinking in.

The world slows, and dark shadows edge my vision. I take a deep breath, pull my arm back, and throw my knife. It sinks between Brendan's shoulder blades. Jax falls to the ground at the same time as Brendan. I sprint toward Brendan, now convulsing, overtaken by pain and the sedative, and kick his shoulder to roll him over. He stares up at the dark sky, blood dripping from his mouth. The light flickers out of his eyes as I watch him take his final breath. His glittering life force disconnects from his body and then it vanishes completely.

Jax coughs from the ground, drawing my attention away from Brendan's lifeless eyes. "Call for backup."

I kick Brendan's dead body again, anger pouring through me. I thought killing the guy responsible for all of Callie's pain and suffering would make me feel better, but it doesn't. Nothing will until I find Callie.

23

❧Trapped❧

CALLIE

GLIDING THROUGH THE darkness, I listen to the voices
echo off the walls. I don't head to the hallway yet. I can't do
anything if I can't see. Holding a flashlight isn't even an option
in my ghostly form. If I'm going to get out of here, I need to
figure out how to turn the lights back on.

I hover in front of the desk and attempt to hit the panic
button that turned everything off, but my fingers only brush
through it.

"Come on," I say to myself. "You can do this." All it takes
is one push. One push and I'll help Lily. One push and things

will turn in my favor.

"Get out of here before I consume you, wraith." I spin to see Thomas standing a foot away from me. "You have no business sneaking around here."

His threat gets under my skin, and I launch at him, attempting to possess him. Electricity zaps me as I hit his magical shield. I eye the bracelet on his wrist, but before I can get a good look at it, a sucking sensation pulls at me. Pain explodes in my soul. The man gulps a breath of my essence, the sensation similar to when Jax consumed some of my life force.

I try to scramble back, but I can't. I can't move. I can't even fight him off. Every time I try to touch him, I'm zapped with hot electricity.

Panic seizes me. Lily's frightened brown eyes flash in my mind, and all I can think about is her thinking I've abandoned her. Her fate would be worse than mine, and I'll never forgive myself for putting her through this.

Thinking of Lily gives me the strength to fight back. I plant my soul firmly in place and tug back. Thomas' eyes widen, but he doesn't stop. He takes another deep breath, and I watch as a pink glow wafts from me and into his mouth.

"No!" I reach out and grab his wrist. Pain swells through my translucent hand, but I don't let go. I imagine my fingers tugging at his bracelet, and it's like I can feel the smooth leather band. The bracelet drops and disappears on the dark floor, and my hand grips onto nothing.

Thomas stumbles back, the realization that he lost the one thing protecting him hitting him hard, and he turns around and runs. He doesn't even get five feet away before I jump into him.

"*Oh, shit. This isn't happening. The bracelet shouldn't have come off. That damn elf failed. I'll kill him. Come on, move, Thomas.*" His voice trickles around me.

"*Hopelessness is an awful feeling isn't it?*" I concentrate on connecting with him, stealing his control, and then my ears pop. I blink in the darkness as the heavy weight of his body chains me to the earth. I clear my throat, moving around a piece of chewing gum with my tongue, and I spit it out.

"*Let me go!*" Thomas yells. "*I can get you a better body. A younger one. A nicer one.*"

Anger washes through me. "*You mean one of those poor kids you have locked up in cages? No. I think I'll keep yours.*"

Ignoring his screams and pleas, I force his fear to the back of my mind. I stumble back to the desk, unsteady in my new, bulky body, and then I feel around the desk until my fingers graze over a small button near the phone. I slam my palm on it.

The lights flicker before illuminating the room. I dash toward the hallway and slow down as Miss Lana stops in her tracks, her keys dangling from her fingers right in front of the door where she's locked up my body.

"What's going on?" she asks.

I clear my throat. "Something is malfunctioning."

Her red nails dig into the palms of her hands and blood drips from her hands. "Well, hurry up. The truck is ready. I want this room loaded first."

I let out a small breath. "Sure thing."

Miss Lana unlocks the door and flicks on the lights. Lily

blinks from her cage directly across the room. She clutches my body to her chest but doesn't do or say anything. Miss Lana waltzes across the room and stops in front of Justine's cage. She unlocks it and opens the door.

Miss Lana points at her. "It's time to go."

Justine doesn't move. Tears rim her eyes, and she blinks them away. "Please, no. Not yet. Please." She shakes her head, her blond hair whipping her face.

Miss Lana reaches in and grabs her arm, yanking her out. "Oh, shut up before I knock you out."

Justine stumbles away.

"Get her, Thomas," Miss Lana snaps.

I strut forward and grab Justine's wrist. She whimpers but doesn't resist. I steady her on her feet, the gesture causing Justine to pause and look at me. She tilts her head to the side for a second before turning her gaze to Miss Lana as she heads toward my cage.

When her back is to me, I reach out and tug the bracelet around Justine's wrist. It doesn't unclasp. Sweat beads on my forehead, and I continue to mess with it, but it's no use. I can't get it off her.

"Your pocket," Justine whispers. Her intense eyes stare at me.

I shove my hand in my pocket and feel a pair of scissors. A charm dangles from the handle, and I place them to the bracelet.

"Thomas, get over here." Miss Lana glares at me from over her shoulder. "This one's not moving."

I drop the scissors into Justine's hand and then shuffle across the room to my cage. I stare at my body, lying on Lily's lap. Miss Lana tugs my body, but Lily grips tighter.

"Thomas, grab the girl."

I open the cage door on the other side and yank Lily out. She cries, gripping my body, and I slap her hand to get her to let go.

I huff. "Go stand over there." I point at Justine.

Justine rushes forward and pulls Lily away before I turn back to Miss Lana. She presses her slender fingers against my body's neck to check for a pulse. She shifts to peer at me, her forehead scrunching.

She bends further into the cage. "She's alive."

A million thoughts rush through my mind. I can't let her get her hands on my body. I can't let her take it.

"*Don't do anything stupid, kid,*" Thomas says in my mind.

But it's too late. As his words circle my mind, I fling out my hands and wrap them around her neck. I yank her from the cage and toss her into the air with all my new body's strength. She slams to the hard concrete, her hair covering her face, and then she jerks her head up and stares at me with wide, red eyes. The surprise attack stuns her, and she doesn't move as I charge her. I land on her and backhand her across the cheek.

Her face distorts, her jaw cracking as her fangs descend. She whips her head up and tears her teeth into my flesh. My deep voice echoes through the room as I howl. Pain swells all the way up to my shoulder, but I push past it. I lock my free hand into her hair and pull her head down and away. She knocks it on the concrete with a loud crack. The pain seems to energize her more, because a second later, she's struggling, flailing her body under mine, gnashing her teeth in hopes of getting close enough to my limbs.

I lean down, pressing my weight against her. My arm crosses her chest, and she loses the mobility to attack.

"Lily! Lily, grab her bracelet!"

Miss Lana's eyes narrow, recognition scrunching her face. I hold tight as best as I can and peer up. Lily jumps into action and dashes closer. She cringes as Miss Lana growls. Frothy spit sprinkles my face, and I press my lips together to stop from gagging.

Lily bends down and tugs at the pretty beaded bracelet around Miss Lana's wrist. It doesn't snap like I expect.

"You better tell me how to get it off before I let her eat you," I say, my voice echoing through the air though I'm talking to Thomas.

"*You can't.*"

"Lily, we can't unhook it like this."

"Let us out!" Pete calls from the other cage. "Hurry."

"Help them. I'll hold her," I say to Lily.

Lily circles us, trailing her eyes over Miss Lana. "I don't see the keys."

I frown. I know where they are. "That's because I'm on them. If I move, I'll lose my grip."

Miss Lana doesn't stop struggling. The moment she has the opportunity, she will attack again.

Lily kneels next to me. "I'll try to get them."

"We should go and get help while we can," Justine says from the door.

It's tempting to send Lily away with her. "I don't know how much longer I can hold her."

"Long enough for me to get the keys," Lily says.

She shoves her hand between my stomach and Miss Lana. Pressure sends a shooting pain through me, and the lump of metal keys digs through my shirt as Lily yanks them free. She jumps to her feet, the keys jangling with the motion, and races to the cage with the two boys. She unlocks it and lets them out.

Sweat pours down my forehead, dripping into my eyes. I blink to clear my vision. Miss Lana stops fighting. She relaxes her shoulders while she tilts her head back to stare at the ceiling.

The sudden stop in movement forces my own muscles to relax. Before I have a chance to brace myself, Miss Lana slides her arm free and jabs her dagger nails into my shoulder. As pain explodes through me, I roll off, and she launches to her feet. Instead of rushing at me, she races toward the others. She jumps on the back of the closest person, the boy whose name I haven't learned, and takes a bite out of his neck.

Blood drips from her mouth as she chews. The boy wails, clawing at Miss Lana, and she snaps her jaws on his wrist. I charge at her, cringing at the sound of crunching bones. Colliding into her, I knock the boy out of the way. Miss Lana somersaults back to her feet and jumps on me. I scramble backward, but I'm too slow to get out of her way. She leans close and bites hard on my ear. The sound of flesh ripping burns into my brain. My vision shadows as I lose control of Thomas' body.

"Run!" I yell. Teeth gnaw my shoulder, and my legs wobble. "Leave my body. I'll only slow you down."

Thomas fights to take control of his body, my world fading in and out. It's like I'm pressing all my strength against a door, but it's cracking at his stronger presence, empowered by the desperation to live, like he's using an imaginary axe to break it down.

My ears pop, and I fly from Thomas. Without hesitating, I run to my body and reconnect. The darkness lasts what feels like forever, but when I open my eyes, Miss Lana kneels on top of Thomas, sinking her teeth into his shoulder again.

I crawl from the cage and bolt toward the open door. The empty hallway greets me, and I pound my bare feet on the cold concrete and head to the only exit I know of. A wail cuts through the air behind me, but I don't stop running.

I catch sight of Lily and the others racing toward the same door. Justine pushes the door open, and Lily and Pete help the wounded boy out. My heart thrashes, and I sweat despite the coldness of my body. Adrenaline dulls the pain radiating through me, and the open door to freedom cheers me on. I can't believe I'm going to make it. I can't believe I survived.

The door starts to close and I yell, "Lily, wait!"

Her dark eyes widen, and she waves for me to hurry. I breathe hard, pushing myself to go faster as the quick tap of heels grows louder behind me. *Ten more feet! Come on, Callie!*

I rush at the open door, the scent of fresh air wafting in. Lily stands alone, holding the heavy door open, and I jump the last few feet and crash into an invisible solid wall. Fiery pain bursts in my nose, and I fall back and slam hard on the cold concrete. I roll to my stomach and push up on my hands.

The glittering gold bracelet catches my eyes. I'm trapped. Without the spelled scissors to cut it off, I'm not escaping.

"No!" Lily screams. Someone pulls her away, and the door slams shut.

Sharp nails dig into my ankles, yanking me back, and I drop to my stomach. Miss Lana flips me over, rakes her sharp nails through my hair, and smiles.

MASON

"Help!" A voice screams from a block down. "Someone help us!"

I turn toward Jax, sitting on the bed of his truck. Dmitri and the others should be here at any second, but I can't wait for them. I don't have enough spelled bracelets to go around anyway. Jax hops from his truck and keeps my pace as I run into the hazy air.

A group of people shuffle around the front of a building. A guy lies on the ground, blood staining the street around him, while the others hold their heads. The magical barrier affects them like it did me, and I'm positive they came out of the warehouse.

"Lily!" Jax yells from next to me.

I search the faces of the people, stopping on Lily. Her blond hair partially covers her face, and she wears a simple black dress without shoes. Blood coats her arms and neck, and fear clenches my heart.

I run next to Jax, and he picks her up in his arms. She cries against his shoulder, her words distorted by her sobs, and then she brings her eyes to mine.

"Callie couldn't get out. You have to get her!" She releases another sob, resting her head on Jax.

I don't even think as I rush toward the door. Before I enter, I peer over my shoulder at Jax. "Get them out of the haze. I'll be back."

I yank the door open and enter the warehouse. Silence surrounds me, and I can't shake the eeriness of it.

A scream rips through the air, piercing my soul. I recognize the terror in Callie's voice. The sound reverberates through me, and I jet toward the back of the warehouse. I jump over toppled chairs, peering around while I move, and run straight for a dimly lit hallway.

Blood smears over the floor—too much blood—and I flail my arms to keep my balance as I slip across the slick floor. I enter the hallway and watch a shadow move across the wall and disappear.

"Callie," I call.

"Mason, stay back. She'll kill me if I project, and she'll kill you if you come any closer." Callie's voice sounds from the left, and I move forward. I'm not afraid of creatures. I'm not afraid to fight.

I stroll deeper into the hallway, my boots soundless from years of practice sneaking around. A door in the back opens, and I meet the eyes of a man and woman. I reach for my tranquilizer gun, aim it, and shoot twice. I hit both my targets, and the couple stumbles back and the door slams shut.

I release a breath. If they attempted to fight before the sedation took them out, I might have been in trouble. They did what I would do in that situation, running while they still could.

A whimper echoes from a crack in a door. I pause in front of it and listen.

"Please, don't," Callie says. "Please, n—" Her voice cuts off.

I push open the door, and it bangs against the wall.

The wild eyes of a ghoul glare at me from across the room. Blood coats her chin and soaks into the neckline of her dress. My gaze shifts to Callie, who lies lifelessly on the floor under the woman. She points her sharp nail at me and grins, displaying a mouthful of razor sharp teeth.

"Drop your weapon, or I will kill her." The woman drags her nail along the front of Callie's dress, ripping the fabric open for a clear shot of her heart. "You know a projector can't survive long without a body anchoring them here, unless you're willing to give up yours. I think I have a client who'd pay a fortune for you."

I grind my teeth as I kneel down and drop my knife to the floor. "Is that so?"

She runs her black tongue over her teeth. "Thinking of making a deal? I don't care who I take. You both are so special. Maybe I'll just keep the two of you for myself."

I swipe my knife back from the floor. "Not a chance."

The ghoul runs her nail up Callie's chest. Blood bubbles from the scratch, and I grip my knife tighter. I focus on the ghoul, and her sparkling magenta aura shines through. It'd take me two seconds to cross the room. Callie would be dead before I could even lay a finger on the monster of a woman.

She sighs. "I assume you're not alone."

I don't respond.

She drags her finger across Callie's skin again, cutting through the scratch she already made to deepen it, sending panic through me. "Which means I don't have a lot of time. So, here's the deal. Let me take the girl, and you may live. Surrender yourself to me, and I'll give her a head start, or fight and you both die."

I twist my mouth down, weighing my options. Callie's pale pink aura shines around her, and I notice a set of elf enchanted bracelets on her wrist. One keeping her unconscious, and the other, I'm not sure of.

The ghoul clicks her tongue. "Decide now."

I slide my knife back into my weaponry belt and unlatch it, dropping it to the floor before I kick it toward her. "She stays. I'll go." I hold my hands out to the ghoul.

She leans down, pressing her mouth to Callie's ear, and says, "You're safe now, but I'll come for you."

She grabs my weaponry belt and slings it over her arm, running her finger over each item and then slides a zip tie from a small pouch. She binds my wrists behind me and pushes me toward the door. I can't fight the man-eater with my bare hands. She'll bite them off if I even try. I just hope my team can get to me in time. I'll fight to the death before I surrender my freedom to a creature. In this moment, death looks rather good.

24

⮾No Second Chances⮾

CALLIE

I'M BOUND TO darkness. The heavy weight of my body presses down on me. No matter how hard I push against it, light refuses to shine through. My soul begs for freedom from this unbearable confinement, and I wonder if this is what it would be like to have my soul taken and trapped. I couldn't imagine an eternity of lonely darkness. What if this is my fate, though?

"Wake up, Callie." My voice echoes around me. "Open your eyes. You can do it."

Nothing happens.

"If you don't, Mason will die. You will die. A lot more people will die if Miss Lana escapes. This is what you're supposed to do. You can fix this. You can get your life back."

A spark of light zooms through the darkness, and I imagine my soul latching onto it. Heat washes over me, and my soul burns as this pinprick of light speeds me through a universe of black.

I scream. The pain sears me from head to toe, and the invisible tether I've used to bind myself to the light loosens. A heavy weight crushes around me, like falling into a churning ocean. I can't move. My thoughts turn to mush. All I can focus on is the flash of light and how it's fading.

"No!"

The world shifts, and the light grows and moves, and rushes toward me to swallow me whole.

I open my eyes. I'm back in the dim room with the cages, except this time I'm alone. Fear trickling through me, I gaze down at the small line of blood pooling on my chest as my body lies on the floor.

I can't believe I did it. I projected through whatever evil magic Miss Lana forced upon me in those dangerously beautiful bracelets. I bound through the door without looking back. I can't do anything for my body, but I have to find Miss Lana. I know Mason's with her. He lives to rescue people—it's his job—and I have no doubt in my mind that he'd do something as stupid as bartering his freedom for me, even knowing that Miss Lana would never actually let me free. He's giving me a chance, and I have to make the most of it.

As I head toward the back exit, the door swings open. A bald headed man holds Mason by his arm outside the door, and Miss Lana saunters away from him. Mason struggles in the man's grip, but he can't break free.

Miss Lana peers over her shoulder as the man drags him away. "Sorry, my little warrior. You'd have been better off fighting. At least you'll be with your girlfriend, right?" The door closes as she returns inside.

Anger rolls through my spirit, and I fly forward to ram into her electrifying protective shield. Heat buzzes over me, stinging my soul. She can't get near my body. I won't allow it.

My hands spark the harder I press against the radiant, powerful shield. But I can do this. I can break it. I have to.

Miss Lana freezes, stiffening. My ethereal fingers lock around her solid wrist. She tries to tug away, but I squeeze harder, bolts of light glittering between my soul and the charm bracelet. I scream, pain zinging through me, and I blink in and out of existence for a second, fear washing over me. But anger replaces my fear and I rip the bracelet free, scattering golden beads everywhere.

I force my way into Miss Lana and connect to her. An evil so dark, it nearly thrusts me back out, settles on my soul.

I watch the world from the red tint of her eyes. She bends down to pick a bead from the floor. *"Damn it. I'm going to kill that elf."* She doesn't realize it was me who snapped the bracelet. She thinks I'm still trapped in my body in the room. *"Good thing I can put that agent up for auction. He'll probably get more money than the projector—I wonder if I should keep her for my-*

self...she'd be useful if I could break her into complying."

Her thoughts wrap around me in vile hate. I push against the inky dread threatening to consume me. Everything in my soul tells me not to possess her, but I can't think of anything else to do.

"Stupid woman, underestimating me," I say.

Miss Lana freezes in her tracks. The second her thoughts quiet, I force my soul on hers and push her into the black pit of her mind. A hunger so fierce, so distracting, grabs hold of me, and I clutch my stomach. The world shines a tad brighter as my vision adjusts to the red veil covering everything. I curl and un-curl my fingers, poking my new palms with my nails, and I roll the dull ache in my shoulders.

"Don't move." The deep voice slithers through the air, and I halt in my tracks. "Surrender and I won't kill you. You are under arrest by the order of the Creature Council."

I lift my gaze from my hands and meet the endless black eyes of a scarily tall man with shiny black hair and skin so chalky white he's nearly colorless. My new heartbeat rattles ir-regularly in my chest, like it's beating once, skipping a beat, and then drumming twice before continuing the pattern.

"Mason's through the back door," I say.

He glides inhumanly fast toward me. "Give me your hands."

I step back. "Wait, you're going to let her live?"

His brows lower in his head. "Hands out, now. We have confirmation you're behind this. You'll be tried by the council." He thinks I'm trying to play innocent.

My breath quickens. The thought of Miss Lana walking out of here scares me to death. What if the council doesn't convict her? What if she fights and kills more people if I leave her body? What if she escapes and comes after me again? I can't live with the uncertainty.

This woman—this vile, barbaric woman—doesn't deserve a second chance to live. I'm not leaving her fate in the hands of strangers, in the hands of a council of people who wanted to arrest Mason for trying to protect me.

"No," I say. "She can't live. I won't let you take her alive."

I pull the knife from Mason's weaponry belt still hung over Miss Lana's arm. I close my eyes, terrified of the pain I'm about to inflict on myself, but I don't see another way. I'm doing this for Lily, for Justine, for all the others this woman has tortured and killed. I'm doing this for those who could have been taken in the future. I'm doing this for me. I'll carry her death for the rest of eternity, so I can try to find my place in this world without the fear that has been hanging over my head. One life in exchange for many is worth it to me.

I raise the blade to my heart and jam it in using the monster's strength. Pain burns through me, and Miss Lana screams in my mind. Her presence pushes at me, crashing against me, and as the pain threatens to knock me out, she thrusts me from her body.

I stand feet away from her and watch her writhe on the ground. A moment later, she stops. Her red eyes stare through me, and I know I've killed her. I didn't know I was capable of murder until this moment. It's such a thing I pray to never have to do again no matter who or what they've done. I just—I couldn't live in this world if she was still in it. Not after today. Not after everything she's done. Where this leaves me and my soul now? I have no idea. Just being able to live without Miss Lana around is all that I can hold onto.

I leave her with the creature and bound back to my body. It calls to me, slowly sucking me back to it, but before I reconnect, I concentrate on the bracelets. Electricity zips through me, and for a split second, I feel whole—complete, very much alive. A mixture of pain, relief, anger, and hope washes through me, and the bracelets snap under my ethereal touch.

I get back into my body, letting myself be consumed by my emotions, and then my ears pop, and I open my eyes. I groan as the weight of my flesh hugs me, but I've never been so happy to be back in my body. I made it. I'm finally safe.

Footsteps echo through the air, and the door opens. I rub my hands over my eyes and then look at the pale creature with black hair.

I might be safe now, but I don't know if I'm free. If I'll ever be.

MASON

The elf grabs my wrists, and I thrust my head back, slamming it into his face. He wails, the bellowing sound resonating through the crisp night air. I spin with my arms still behind my back. I might not have a weapon or the use of my hands, but I still have a lot of fight in me. I knew the ghoul wouldn't make good on her word, and I'd have been stupid to trust her—hell, I wasn't even sure if I'd make it out of the building before she tried to eat me, but I wanted to give Callie the best chance I could by distracting the woman and getting Callie out of the line of fight.

I charge at the man, lowering my head and shoulders, and I crash into his gut, knocking him off his feet. I kick him over and over until his body stops moving. Elves have many talents—they wield powerful magic allowing them to do anything as long as they can get their spelled charms or talismans in place. They're also fantastic at evasion and tracking—it's where Evie's abilities came from—but, not all elves are fighters. This one is clearly behind the spells of everything, but he can't fight to save his life.

I search around the alley for anything I can use as a weapon. The ghoul stole my weaponry belt, and I can't fight her with my hands bound. I'd run, but Callie's inside. I can't leave her. I didn't come this far to give up.

A truck with a shell idles a few feet away. Its headlights illuminate the alley. I turn to gaze at the closed door. It's taking the ghoul longer than I expected to return. Worry rolls in waves through me, but I suppress them. She wants Callie alive. It's the only hope I have that pushes me harder.

I head toward the bed of the truck and reach up as far as I can to pull the tailgate down, but my arms still can't reach. A pile of crates lies a few feet away near a dumpster. I jog to them and kick one over. It gives me just enough height to unlatch the tailgate. It drops open with a bang and then hands lock onto my wrists.

A woman screams as she clutches my arms. She was hiding in the bed. I pull away, dragging her with me, and she falls from the truck in a heap on the ground. It's the creature I tranquilized earlier. She must've been protected like the elf against the full effect of the sedative.

Her eyes roll as she tries to push up to her feet, but the tranquilizer hasn't completely worn off. I kick out, knocking her leg with my boot, and she topples over. I run to the back of the truck and peer inside the covered bed. A small basket of talismans and charms with a few other things, like wire cutters, duct tape, rope, and a knife sits in reach.

I knock the basket over by swinging my arms a few inches. Perching on the tailgate, I grip the knife the best I can. I shove the knife between my hands, my wrists stinging. I hope to catch it on the zip tie, but with the awkward angle, it lodges between my bound hands.

The woman moans and gets to her feet. She glares, her brows puckering in anger, and then she locks her fingers around my ankles and pulls. The air whooshes around me as I fall from the truck and land hard on my back. The knife sinks into my skin, sending a wave of fire up my arms, but the force snaps the zip ties. As the woman reaches down, I roll and then swing my arm free and jab the small knife into her side.

Instead of fighting, she runs, clutching the knife handle, leaving me alone.

The door behind me creaks open, and I spin to face the ghoul. I don't have a weapon, but at least my hands are free. But it's not the ghoul who greets me.

Dmitri hovers in the door, his onyx eyes searching the area around me with his weapon drawn. He lowers his hand and glides forward to me.

"Callie's in there." I move past Dmitri, but he grabs my shoulder.

He presses his lips together. "I found her possessing a ghoul."

I let out a breath as relief washes over me. "Where are they?" I want nothing more than to face the ghoul and look in her sadistic eyes so she knows she's lost.

"Callie's out front with the team. She's beat up, but I think she'll be okay." Dmitri turns away from me to the elf on the ground. He touches his fingers to the elf's neck, and then pulls his handcuffs free from his belt and binds him before turning back to me. "And the ghoul is dead."

My mouth drops open. "You killed her?"

He shakes his head. "Callie did while she possessed her."

I nod. "Oh." Callie could've let Dmitri capture the ghoul while she was controlling her, but she didn't. I don't blame her either. It'll upset the council because I know they wanted to use whoever we caught to find the rest of the Feeders, but it doesn't always work out the way we plan.

I think about what he's told me. Dmitri saw Callie possess the ghoul. He watched her kill her as well. Those actions alone make Callie a threat. The council will want to interrogate her. The thought curls around my heart, and I think about all the ways I can get Callie away.

"What happens now?" My voice comes out low, and I'm not sure Dmitri heard me.

He doesn't respond right away. "We search the rest of the

warehouse. Kat and Evie have taken a group of innocents to the hospital. After that, we'll go to the compound."

"Was Lily with them?" I ask.

He shakes his head. "She's with Jax and Bree. Callie, too. They wouldn't leave with the others without you."

I rub my hand over my hurt back. It's wet with blood, but the cut doesn't feel deep enough to cause any real damage. "Callie's vulnerable, Dmitri. She has a family, too. She's human."

"She's been gifted with a special ability."

"People can't know about it. They'll use her."

Dmitri nudges me toward the warehouse. "I'm not going to lie to you, Mason. The council will find her appealing. Just imagine what she's capable of. She'd also make a dangerous enemy."

"She just wants to finish high school, Dmitri."

He opens the door, and we enter the warehouse. "Well, let's see how things go. We'll make what Callie wants a priority, but it's important she knows her options. You know as well as I do that she can't continue living like she has."

"Why not?"

"She told me she doesn't want to."

25

❧Capable of Killing❧

CALLIE

LILY CLUTCHES MY hand, leaning her head on my shoulder, and I rest my head on Mason's. His hand touches my knee, and he drums his fingers on my cold skin. I stare straight ahead, watching dozens of headlights flash by. I can't close my eyes. Every time I do, I envision the room with the cages.

I shiver.

I hate how weak I felt at the warehouse, even when I know I was at my strongest and fought my hardest—hard enough to win. I want to feel brave and courageous. I can't keep living like I'm only surviving. In this twisted world, I need more than that.

I'm capable of more.

I'm afraid of myself, too. Because I'm capable of anything. I'm capable of killing. It's not even like I had to do it to survive. I did it because Miss Lana made me feel weak. She made me question if I was meant to be in the creature world. She made me feel less than human and creature.

The road clears as we head away from the city. After what feels like eternity, the car slows and we turn into a forest. The trees shift and move, almost alive in the darkness, and the forest swallows our car and spits us out on a dirt road illuminated by the bright moonlight.

After another few minutes, we enter a clearing. It's like we've stumbled upon a hidden fortress surrounded by a tall chain-link fence. I squint through the darkness at a few buildings clustered in the center of the property.

Lily squeezes my hand tighter. "I'm scared."

I meet her gaze. "Me, too."

Dmitri, the tall, black-haired creature who found me, glances in the rearview mirror. "You're safe here."

I meet his eyes. "Nowhere feels safe anymore."

The corners of his eyes crinkle, and I swear they glass over for a second, but they clear so quickly I might have imagined it. He doesn't try to say anything to make me feel better. Instead, he just flicks his eyes back to the road so I don't have to stare at the pity in his reflection.

He drives through the property, maneuvering the car around the tallest building. Small groups of people loiter, and a few try to peer into the window as we pass. I shimmy lower. I'm not in the mood to be the center of attention.

Mason kisses my temple. "Word travels quickly in the compound."

I swallow. "Do they know about me?"

Dmitri stops the car and turns in the seat. "Not about your ability."

I puff out a breath of air. At least it's something. I can hold onto my secrets a little while longer.

Jax hops out from the front seat and opens Lily's door. He hasn't said a word since we left the warehouse. None of us has, really. I don't even know what to say anymore. Talking about trivial things doesn't seem important. It's wasted breath.

Mason props his door open and offers his hand for me to take. My legs wobble when I step out, and I grab the doorframe to steady myself. He tries to slide his arm around me to take some of my weight, but I shrug away. I don't know why I do it. I'm hurting, both my body and spirit, but I want to walk on my own. I want to pretend nothing has happened.

Mason's lips twist downward, and I take his hand instead. He twines his fingers through mine and meanders next to me as I follow the others toward the building. We enter through the back, and I peer around at a simple hallway with wood floors and bright lighting. Dmitri guides us to an elevator, and we silently ride it up to the third floor.

A woman wearing silk pajamas stands in the hallway outside an open door. I recognize her immediately as Mason's mom. Her brown hair frames her oval face, and her hazel eyes sparkle when she sees us. She rushes forward and slides her arms around Mason's shoulders. He stands still without letting go of my hand.

After a few seconds, she pulls away and hugs me, too. I lift my aching arm and pat her back. Her nose crinkles when she takes in my appearance. I smile, wincing as the movement pulls at the sore skin of my scraped chin.

"I'm giving you my apartment tonight. The family cottages are full, and I figured you wouldn't want to be alone in the guest apartments. I just want you all to be comfortable," she says as she glances at Lily behind me.

"Thanks, Mom," Mason says. He leans forward and kisses her cheek. "Would you mind giving them a check up before you leave?"

I clear my throat. "I'm fine, really."

Lily touches my shoulder. "Let them help you, Callie. You were bit by that monster. What if you get an infection?"

Mason's mom steps closer to Lily and offers out her hand. "I'm Dr. Sullivan." She looks between us. "Come in. I've had food delivered from the dining hall. I know it's late, but I'll try to be quick with everything."

Mason nudges me forward, and I remember to move my legs. A cozy tan couch sits in the middle of the spacious apartment. Framed sketches of different people and settings line the walls. I notice one of Mason, his brother, and mom. It's lifelike, and I wonder who the artist was.

Dr. Sullivan points at a heavy, black wood table filled with a small buffet of different foods. My stomach churns, my appetite non-existent at the moment. Lily takes a seat with Jax, and I move across the room to the couch. I sink into the soft cushions, leaning my pounding head on the pillow not even caring that I could be bleeding on the fabric. The pain is all I can think about, and I imagine projecting to escape it, but the pain reminds me I'm alive. It reminds me I'm still human.

MASON

Callie lies next to me on the guest bed. She left Lily in my mom's room because she couldn't sleep. We hold hands without talking, and I'm not sure what to say. I want her to talk to me, to tell me anything, even if it's only that she's okay. I know she's not, though.

She fiddles with an amulet hanging around her neck. My mom cleaned and bandaged her wounds, but she needs a little extra help from elf magic. Thierry, the elf council member, made a healing amulet special for her. It's rare for elves to give away their most difficult to make trinkets without a good price, but Thierry showed up at the door without even asking. I'm sure there will be a lot more gifts to come.

"Can we go for a walk?" Callie asks, breaking the silence.

I nod and roll off the bed to get to my feet. I'll do anything she asks at this point, as long as it gets her to do something other than stare at her chipped nail polish. I waltz around the bed and help her to her feet. Her legs stand steadily, and she doesn't wince with every movement like she did a few hours ago.

We pad out of the room and creep through the living room past Jax asleep on the sofa bed. Callie smiles at me when we enter the dimly lit hallway. Her nose crinkles, and I lean over and kiss her once.

Resting my fingers on her back, I guide her forward to a different elevator than the one we came up on. I push open the front door of the main building, and fresh, tepid air wraps around us. Callie hugs herself, and I slide my arm over her shoulders. A figure sits at the bottom of the steps, just staring into the night. Callie touches Dmitri's shoulder as we pass by, and he nods to us without saying anything, though I feel his stare on our backs.

Callie swerves off the sidewalk, running her bare feet over the bouncy grass. She spins once, the moonlight bathing her in a soft glow, and then she eases to the grass, pulling me down with her, and stares up at the vast, night sky.

Starlight reflects in her blue eyes, and I lean on my elbow to gaze at her. Her soft lips pout for a second, and I run my finger along them before I kiss her. She arches up to kiss me deeper, and I cradle her against me.

She pulls away and stares into my eyes. "I've been thinking a lot."

I don't say anything. Even though she pauses, a thousand thoughts cloud her eyes. Her forehead crinkles as she thinks of what to say next, and I listen to the soft sound of crickets chirping in the distance.

She licks her lips. "I want to do what you do."

I raise my eyebrows. "Even after everything?" I wasn't expecting her to want to put herself in that kind of danger again—I thought it'd be the last thing she wanted to do.

She doesn't look away or blink. "No, *because* of everything. I can't live another day knowing that some other person is experiencing what I did—or worse. If I can help them, I want to."

"What about your family?" I ask.

She sucks in a breath. "I don't know. It's dangerous for them regardless. They might be better off because I feel like—I—how do I live with myself? How do you do it?"

She's referring to the fact that she killed someone. Even though she took the life of the most horrible being in the world, the fact that it lingers with her shows me how beautiful her soul is. I knew it was already, but I can't even grasp her guilt. I touch her cheek. "Like you said. I live with it so others don't have to experience what you went through, and I hate that I failed you. I wish I'd have done things differently, Callie. I should've—"

"Stop." She presses her finger to my lips, waits to make sure I won't say anything, and then kisses me, leaving my heart racing for more when she pulls away. "You did nothing but help me."

I shift onto my back next to her to stare up at the stars, ignoring the pain caused by the cut on my lower back. "I wish I could've done more."

"You still can. I'm ready to fight." The certainty in her smooth voice makes me smile. "The only way this world will ever feel safe to me is if I fight to make it safe, but I need you. I want to fight by your side, because you're the one who makes this world feel right when I know things are so wrong still."

And I'm ready to fight with her.

Callie has shown me what's really been missing in my life. I've been so wrapped up in finding and dealing with the bad guys that I haven't thought much about the innocent. Yeah, I do what I do to protect innocent people and creatures, but it's always been about the evil in the world. About destroying one bad creature at a time. But that's going to change. I'm fighting not to rid the world of the bad guys, but I'm fighting to protect and save those who need it. I'm fighting to help others have a second chance. And I'm fighting for the future we deserve.

CALLIE

Mason curls his arms around me, burying his face into my neck. I train my eyes on the dark sky. Stars sparkle like a thousand pinpricks of light, suspended in nothingness, trying to break free. The vastness of it makes me feel like I'm one of those tiny bright spots, struggling to keep the darkness away.

The tepid air cools the longer we stay outside, clinging to my skin, sending goosebumps up my bare arms. I wasn't sure I'd see the stars in my body again. I wasn't sure I'd even have a body. Certainty didn't exist anymore. I hated that feeling. Looking back at today, I was wrong though. There was one thing I was sure of—I was sure that in the end, I'd have tried my hardest.

And my hardest was enough.

"The evil in the world won't stand a chance against us," Mason says. The moon shines brighter than I've ever seen, and it veils him in silver light.

I haven't known Mason long, but I'd like to know everything about him. I look forward to not having to hide from this side of his life, because it's the side of his life I belong in. I don't know where this new journey will take me, but I know I'm the one carving my path. If I carve it deep enough, I'll go under any bumps that try to force me to swerve. Nothing, not even the weight of the world, can stop me.

I brush my fingers along his temple. "I love the sound of that, but no more trying to protect me, okay?"

He laughs and hugs me closer. "I'll always try to protect you."

A smile crosses my lips. "Unless you're the one who needs it."

I cup his face and kiss him. His warm breath tickles my lips, and I suck his bottom lip between mine. His hands run through my hair as he leans over me. Brushing my hands along his sides, I wrap them around his waist and pull his weight onto me.

Electricity tingles through my essence. I gasp as it trails from my core to my lips. It's the same sensation I felt when I kissed Mason in my ghostly form. He smiles against my mouth, and then kisses me again.

I pull away and gaze into his eyes. "We should head back."

He kisses me once more. "Whatever you want."

I press my forehead against his. "You have no idea how much I love the sound of that."

26

⁓Never Broken⁓

MASON

THE AUDITORIUM IS nearly empty apart from my team, a few enchantresses from the Enchantress Sisterhood, my brother and Nadia, Evie and Alyssa, Cian from The Haven, and Mr. Augustine from Northern Bell High School. Usually meetings like this are open to the entire compound, but today has been deemed a private affair.

Callie sits next to Lily in front of the council. I'd have preferred to have sat on the stage next to them, but this isn't about me and Callie. It's about Callie and Lily and what happens next. What they want to happen.

Jacqueline rests her hands on the table. "You do understand the danger involved in what you're asking, right?"

Callie links her fingers with Lily. "How could we ever forget yesterday? Of course we understand the danger." Her voice rises in annoyance. "But Lily is my best friend, and we talked about it. I'm not letting you alter her memories. She wants to fight, too."

I search around the small crowd. Nadia observes Callie with her head slightly tilted, like she's processing her words. Behind her, I catch Mira and Nate watching me. Mira subtly shakes her head.

I draw my gaze back to the stage.

Lily straightens her shoulders. "I do. I don't care if I don't have some fancy ability to help me out. Anyone can learn combat fighting. Jax has already taught me a few moves." She smiles at Jax. "Not to mention that I've grown fond of being around cr—everyone."

Veronica straightens her shoulders. "I think we can find a place for you. And you're right, not everyone here is gifted with an ability."

Lily's mouth drops open. I bet she was expecting a bit more arguing—I know I was. She nods, her hair bouncing, and then she grins at Callie.

"What about both of your families?" Ana chimes in. She meets the eyes of her sisters from the Enchantress Sisterhood. "How would you like us to proceed with them?"

Callie opens and closes her mouth. She eyes Lily before shifting her gaze to the crowd until she meets my eyes. "Well,

I'm not sure. I plan to graduate high school, so obviously I'm not going to just disappear."

"We can provide an excellent education here," Thierry says.

Callie shifts her gaze to the floor. "I'd like to finish my three remaining months at Northern Bell."

The council members look at each other. Veronica pushes her blond hair behind her ear. "I highly suggest you reconsider."

"No." Callie stands. "It's what I want, and I'm going to do it."

"We can't protect you all hours of the day outside the compound. You'd be putting yourself in jeopardy, especially since you're untrained and unpredictable," Jacqueline says. Her lavender eyes glow against her golden skin.

"Why not?" Callie crosses her arms.

Lily mimics her. "Yeah, it's not like we'll be alone. Mason goes there."

The council shifts their gazes to mine, and I sink lower into my seat. I never told the council about how I got to know Callie, and I'm sure I'll hear about it later. Mr. Augustine raises his bushy eyebrows at me, and I shrug. I guess he assumed everyone knew.

I clear my throat. "I was really bored on my mandatory leave."

Dmitri laughs from his seat next to my mom. It's rare to hear him lose control over his serious demeanor, and I rub a hand over my face to stop from laughing myself.

"Are you willing to continue? You'd be giving up field work for a while," Veronica says.

I drop my gaze to my hands. Could I last going to high school for a few more months without being in the field and doing what I like to do best? I never imagined I'd be going back after being altered, but I guess it won't be that bad. I'd get to remember what it's like to be normal again.

I could use a little normal. It gives me a better perspective and reminds me why I do what I do. I pull my mind from my thoughts. "Yeah, I'd be okay with that."

Callie smiles. "Thank you. You don't know how much this means to me."

Her pale pink soul shines around her, and I find myself smirking. I never expected my life would ever lead up to this moment. I never expected to find someone like Callie, expected to do anything other than my job. She turned my world upside down and scattered all the pieces around, but they fell together exactly how they should be. How I want them to be.

And looking into her endless blue eyes, I know I've done the same for her.

CALLIE

The Creature Council dismisses me and Lily after we all finally agree that we can go home to our families, as long as we allow them to come in and add some safety precautions.

Mason waits for me at the stairs exiting the stage. He wraps his arms around me, and I snuggle my face into his chest, smelling his fresh laundry detergent. He tries to pull back, but I hold onto him tighter, and he laughs.

"You're the best, you know." I tilt my head up to look into his dark eyes. "I couldn't imagine being in your position and having to go back to high school for nothing."

"It's not for nothing," he says. "I know how important it is to you, and you're important to the council...and me."

I suck in my bottom lip. "I feel the same."

"Callie?" I peer over my shoulder to glance at Lily. She leans into Jax. "Dmitri says we can stay another night, or we can go home. The council will send someone to our houses to set things up for us."

I peek at Mason in my peripheral vision. "I'd really like to go home and hug my family."

"That's what I was thinking." She leaves Jax's side and slides her arms around my shoulders. "I can't believe everything that's happening."

"I know. It'll be an adventure."

She rests her chin on my shoulder. "Thanks for choosing to let me come along. I don't ever want to lose you."

Tears leak onto my cheeks. "I'll always worry about you, but I can't imagine not having my best friend with me." I meet Jax's eyes. "Plus, I think the soul sucker has a crush on you."

Lily pulls away and swats my arm. "We have a lot to catch up on."

"I'd like that."

Lily strolls back to Jax, and the two of them head toward the small crowd of people. She shakes a few people's hands while others hug her. She smiles, her face bright enough to light the room, and I can't help thinking that she's better at this than I am. She fits right in.

I hang on the outside of the group with Mason. A girl with

deep blue eyes and black hair breaks from the crowd and heads in our direction. A tall blond boy with green eyes trails behind her before they fall into step together. They link their pinkies and match their footing like they know exactly what the other will do.

Mason bumps my shoulder as they stop in front of us. "You're a little late, Mira."

The girl purses her lips. "Next time you ask for help, I'll drop everything." She steps forward and hugs me. "I'm truly sorry you had to go through that."

Tears line my eyes, and I blink them away. She's the first person to tell me that to my face. All I've heard so far is how lucky or how brave I was. Her concern brings back all the emotions I've been locking away in my mind.

My breathing quickens. "T-Thank you."

She rubs her hand on my back. "I can make you forget, if you want. I know what it's like to be haunted by the terrible things life throws at us."

I swallow. Without her having to give details, I can tell she's been through some terrible things as well. As I look around the room, I think every single one of these people has. It's what has brought us together. It's what has given us the reason to fight.

If she helps me forget, will I still feel the same? Will I still want to fight?

I don't want to find out.

I swipe my hand across my cheek. "That's a tempting offer but no. I need to remember."

She smiles sadly. "The offer will always be here. Same for your friend." She touches my arm. "And if you ever just want to talk, I'm a good listener."

I wrap my arms around her. "Thank you. That means a lot to me."

She turns back to her boyfriend, who I'm assuming is Nate. "Ready?"

Nate studies me for a few seconds. "It was nice meeting you."

They turn away, and I shift back to Mason, Mira's words still swirling through my mind. I couldn't imagine forgetting everything. My soul will forever be scarred from the fear and torment Miss Lana put me through, but no matter what anyone tries, they'll never break my spirit. I can't be broken.

MASON

I stand on Callie's porch and look around. A small, golden thumbtack is pressed into the wood above her door. Creatures use them to keep humans out, but Thierry reversed the spell to keep creatures out.

Mira swung by earlier when everyone was home and compelled Callie's family to wear two different charms—a protection charm and a tracking charm—that'll help the council protect her family without having to monitor them all hours of the day.

Callie's new bracelet jingles on her wrist. "Ready?"

I rub my sweaty palms on my jeans. "Are you really going to make me work on the Dante's Inferno project?"

She laughs. "Yeah, and you're going to like it. This sort of hell is going to be easy."

She steps forward and opens her door. The scent of pasta sauce and garlic wafts through the air. I spot an old man sitting in a recliner in front of the TV, and he sets down his smart phone to smile at Callie.

She races across the room and bends down to hug him. "I feel like I've been gone forever, Pops."

Her grandpa chuckles. "You have, cupcake. I thought you were going to announce you were moving in with Lils." He swings his eyes to me. "But you're not Lily."

I step forward and offer my hand. "I'm Mason. Nice to meet you, sir."

Callie straightens her back. "He's new at school. We're working on an English project together."

"Well, he better help you get an A." Her grandpa picks up his phone and starts messing with it again, and Callie turns away.

She takes my hand and drags me toward the kitchen. A woman, with dark hair the same as Callie's, stands at the stove, stirring a pot of sauce. Perched on a barstool is an elementary school aged kid furiously writing something on a piece of paper.

"Mom, Max, I'm home." Callie ruffles her little brother's hair and kisses her mom on the cheek. "I hope it's okay that I invited someone over. Mason's working on an English project with me."

Callie's mom turns to look at me. "Oh, sure! I always make extras if you want to stay for dinner, Mason."

I nod. "Smells delicious."

I wave at Max, and Callie drags me from the kitchen to a long hallway. She peeks her head in an open door on the right. "Hey, Dad. I'm home."

I stroll up next to her and see a man with dark blond hair reading a book on a desk. He meets my eyes. "You're new."

I nod. "Yeah."

"This is Mason," Callie says.

Her dad's gaze shifts to notice Callie holding my hand, but she doesn't let go. "You staying for dinner?"

"Yes, sir."

He nods. "Good."

Callie pulls me away before her dad starts interrogating us, and she opens the door to her room. She flops on her bed, knocking some purple pillows off, and then she lets out a long breath.

"It feels so good to be home," she says.

I sit on the edge of the bed next to her. "I can get used to coming here."

She flicks my arm. "You better."

Staring around the room, I take in the normalcy of it all. My family hasn't been together in a while, and I almost forgot what it's like. Callie sits up and leans on my shoulder, locking her fingers with mine.

"I hope I never have to give it up," she says, her voice barely over a whisper.

"Me, too."

I'm afraid to tell Callie that she'll eventually have to. She can't expect to join the council's fight while keeping a façade with her family. It's too easy to slip up, or it gets too hard keeping so many secrets from people you love. It puts a wedge in things.

I push my doubt away. I'm not going to worry her now. She deserves to have her life the way she wants it for as long as she can. Who knows? Maybe she'll help wipe out what threatens to destroy her. She's strong enough.

Callie leans over and kisses me. "Ready to embrace your new normal life?"

I laugh. "Nothing about this is normal to me, but yeah. I'm ready for anything with you."

Epilogue

CALLIE

"THIS IS JUST an observation," Mason says. "No interacting with anyone. If anything gets out of hand, I'll handle it. You'll be safe as long as you stay here."

I pull my dark hair into a high ponytail. My pink dress fits the curves of my body, and I fidget with the enchanted necklace Mason had given me as a gift for my first day of training. "Got it."

I peer around The Haven. I haven't been back since Brendan attacked me three weeks ago. I wasn't planning on training until after graduation, but the council asked if I would start early during my free time. I accepted because Mason was anxious to do something other than help me study. He's decided that normalcy is overrated. I don't blame him.

Mason slides closer to me in the booth and wraps his arm around my shoulders. He leans over and brushes his lips to my ear. "What do you see?"

I search over the crowd. I've discovered it's a lot harder than I thought to distinguish creatures from humans. If they don't want to be identified, only someone with a trained eye can tell the difference. No one looks out of the ordinary.

I close my eyes and rack my brain for the list of features that's supposed to stand out to me—sudden subtle changes in appearance, like eye color or uniquely different features like ear shape, skin textures, and even particular habits like excessive blinking or deep breathing—I'm supposed to use my intuition as well. If I concentrate hard enough, I can feel something off.

I point to short boy. His hands sparkle with glitter, which in this world isn't usually makeup. "Pixie," I say.

Mason nods. "What else?"

A few feet away from him is a woman in a short red dress. Her golden hair hangs over her shoulders, and she dances with a man in a suit. Her lips part, and she sucks in a breath, closing her eyes. "A succubus and her partner dance to the right."

"Should we worry about his safety?" Mason asks.

I shake my head. "No, he's wearing a protection charm on his finger which matches her bracelet. He's given consent and knows the risks. They're together." I only know this because Lily told me. She's learned a lot from Jax over the last few weeks about incubi and their female counterparts, succubi, because they've decided to date. I'm so happy for her, and I know Jax isn't the horrible monster a lot of people say he is because of what he is. He's no different than any of us. He's just trying to find his place in the world.

"Good. What el—"

Mason snaps his mouth shut when we watch a woman hop on the back of a man in the middle of the dance floor. The man spins her, causing her to scream the weirdest sound I've ever heard, and she flies across the room. Her arm rips off, landing on the table of a group of people, and my eyes widen. More people scream and yell. Some scatter.

"Oh, my God," I whisper.

Several patrons shout as the woman stumbles to her feet and limps back to the middle of the dance floor. She lunges, and people scramble out of the way, creating mass chaos.

Mason jumps to his feet, sliding his knife from his weaponry belt. "Stay here."

He bolts away without confirming that I'll actually stay, but I'm frozen. I can't take my eyes off the woman who's falling to pieces. Mason pushes through the crowd and hesitates when the woman focuses on him.

The seat creaks next to me. "This is my favorite part."

I jerk my head away from the crowd to meet the bluish-gray eyes of an older woman with silver hair. She raises a manicured hand from her lap and reaches out to touch my cheek.

I cringe away. "Don't touch me."

She smiles. "You're just as I imagined and worth every

penny."

Fear blossoms from my heart, growing and moving through my body. Her words ignite a terror so raw that I can't stop my hands from shaking. I need to get out of here, but I'm afraid to leave. I'm afraid to even breathe.

"Don't worry, dear. I know you're not quite ready yet," she says.

I swallow, wetting my mouth to speak. "Ready for what?" My words drift away with the music.

"To join me."

Before I have a chance to scream, the woman slides from the booth and strolls through the crowd, touching a few people on the back as she heads to the unattended front door. She exits unnoticed, and I sit frozen in my seat.

Tears blur my eyes. I can't believe this is happening. I can't believe that crazy woman thinks I'll join her.

I straighten my shoulders and wait for my heartbeat to slow. The commotion from the dance floor fades, and I focus on staying in my skin. I won't let fear control me. I'm stronger than that. I'm not the same girl I was weeks ago. I don't let fear hinder me. I let it push me forward. It makes me strive for greater, fight harder.

I won't stop fighting until there's nothing left to fight for, which means I'll never stop fighting.

MASON

The decomposing woman thrashes as two shifters hold her down. Her other arm rips off, and rotting goo splats on the floor. Her body's rotting at an accelerated speed, yet she keeps fighting. She screams incoherently, and I slide my knife from its sheath. This isn't some dying woman. She's a reanimated corpse.

The crowd thins out as people charge toward the door. The shifters release the woman when her innards seep through the gaping holes in her stomach. They cover their mouths, abandoning me to face the zombie as she rolls and rises to her feet.

I hold my knife up. "Who sent you?"

Zombies don't just crawl from the grave on their own. They're not infectious either. If they were, everyone in this club would be in trouble. I only know of one creature who can control the dead—a necromancer. But why would a necromancer release a corpse in the club? What purpose does it serve besides sending fear into people's hearts?

"Cal...lie...mus...sst...come." A guttural voice escapes the woman's mouth. She gurgles and black liquid seeps onto her chin. Her milky eyes gaze behind me. "Cal...lie."

I peer over my shoulder. Callie stands at the booth, her hands on her hips, her eyes narrowed. She struts closer, her dark hair whipping in her ponytail as she shakes her head. She stops next to me.

"If you want me, you'll have to come and take me." Her blue eyes shine with a fire I've never seen.

The zombie's mouth gapes open. "B...b...big mis...ss...stake." Her slow words send a chill through me.

I lift my knife and swipe it across the zombie's throat. She drops to the floor as the magic keeping her in her body releases her, setting her dead soul free. Callie steps back before any fluids from the corpse can splash her.

I turn to look at her. "What was that about?"

She inhales a long breath through her nose. "A woman stopped by my table while you were distracted. She claims to have bought me and wants me to join her."

I frown. "A necromancer?"

"You mean the creature you told me about that can reanimate corpses?"

"They can speak to and control the souls of the dead as well," I say.

Her nose crinkles. "But why would she want me? I'm not dead."

Voices sound from the hall. The music cuts off, and I watch as Cian rushes into the room. He stops in his tracks, looking from us to the corpse, and then he tugs out his phone.

I think about Callie's question for a moment. Why would a necromancer want her? The necromancer claims to have bought her, which would mean that the ghoul had already made the deal, but why would she come after her now? The ghoul is dead, and Callie's protected by the council.

Dread sinks into my stomach. "Because she knows about your ability."

Callie blinks. "How?"

I point at the dead body. "Maybe the dead told her."

"I still don't get why she'd want me. Why would she risk even coming here?" She hugs herself.

The thought hits me hard, sending fear through me. I don't even want to think of the possibility, but I have to put the words out there. "Because you're a living ghost, Callie. She controls ghosts, and I bet she wants to control you." I wrap my arms around her. "But don't worry. We'll get her before she tries anything else."

She stiffens in my arms. "This can't be happening. I'm not getting taken again. She can't have me. I won't let her."

She says the words with such certainty that I believe her. There's no doubt in my mind that Callie can take on the world and win. And I'm going to help her.

Together, we'll be unstoppable.

To be continued...

Acknowledgments

THIS BOOK WOULDN'T have been possible if it weren't for my brilliant team, who always puts so much time and effort into my books. Sarah, Jan, and Katie, you are all amazing! Thank you! Another awesome person, who has helped me so much with other book stuff, including a ton of blurbs, is the incredible Nikki. I'd be floundering in pages and pages of uselessness without you.

Lastly, I'd like to thank those who have shown such enthusiasm for the Creature Council world, and especially love for Mason Sullivan. If you're a brand new reader of my books, Mason's character originated in my Destined for Dreams series and continued on through my Finding Nate series. It only seemed fair that he get his own story to suffer—I mean, conquer his own enemies—in.

About Ginna Moran

GINNA MORAN IS a writer from sunny Southern California. She started writing poetry as a teenager in a spiral notebook that she still has tucked away on her desk today. Her love of writing grew after she graduated high school, and she completed her first unpublished manuscript at age eighteen.

When she realized her love of writing was her life's passion, she studied literature at Mira Costa College in Northern San Diego. Besides writing novels, she was senior editor, content manager, and image coordinator for Crescent House Publishing Inc. for four years.

Aside from Ginna's professional life, she enjoys binge watching television shows, playing pretend with her daughter, and cuddling with her dogs. Some of her favorite things include chocolate, anything that glitters, cheesy jokes, and organizing her bookshelf.

Ginna Moran loves to hear from her readers so visit her online at www.GinnaMoran.com. You can also find her on Facebook, Twitter, Instagram, and Snapchat (@Ginna Moran). To stay up-to-date on new releases, sign up to her newsletter. You'll not only get a FREE book, but you'll be able to participate in monthly giveaways!

Ginna Moran is currently hard at work on her next novel.

Other Young Adult Series by Ginna Moran

PARANORMAL
Destined for Dreams Series
Demon Within Series
Finding Nate Series
Going Ghostly Series
Spark of Life Series

CONTEMPORARY
Falling into Fame Series

STANDALONES
Life After Lila